PICK ME

Victoria Schade is a celebrated author of contemporary romance novels and a dog trainer who seamlessly combines her love for animals with her passion for storytelling. When not working on books with tons of sparks and heart, Victoria enjoys dancing, baking, reading, and perfecting her dink shot. She shares her 1850s always-in-need-of-renovations home with Millie the senior smooth Brussels griffon, Boris the chihuahua/pug mix, the occasional foster pup, and her incredibly tolerant husband.

PICK ME

VICTORIA SCHADE

HarperCollins*Publishers* Ltd
1 London Bridge Street,
London SE1 9GF

www.harpercollins.co.uk

HarperCollins*Publishers*
Macken House, 39/40 Mayor Street Upper
Dublin 1, D01 C9W8, Ireland

Published by HarperCollins*Publishers* 2025

1

Copyright © Victoria Schade 2025

Victoria Schade asserts the moral right to be identified as the author of this work
A catalogue record for this book is available from the British Library

ISBN: 978-0-00-878107-1

Pickleball and paddle © Aysha/Stock.Adobe.com

This novel is entirely a work of fiction. The names, characters and incidents
portrayed in it are the work of the author's imagination. Any resemblance to
actual persons, living or dead, events or localities is entirely coincidental.

Printed and bound in the UK using 100% Renewable
Electricity at CPI Group (UK) Ltd

All rights reserved. No part of this publication may be reproduced,
stored in a retrieval system, or transmitted, in any form or by any means,
electronic, mechanical, photocopying, recording or otherwise,
without the prior written permission of the publishers.

Without limiting the author's and publisher's exclusive rights, any unauthorised
use of this publication to train generative artificial intelligence (AI) technologies is
expressly prohibited. HarperCollins also exercise their rights under Article 4(3) of
the Digital Single Market Directive 2019/790 and expressly reserve this publication
from the text and data mining exception.

This book contains FSC™ certified paper and other controlled
sources to ensure responsible forest management.

For more information visit: www.harpercollins.co.uk/green

Dedicated to everyone with repressed middle school gym class trauma.

PICK ME

Chapter One

"Underwear or panties?"

My roommate, Meredith, paused with her hand hovering over her gym bag. "You mean to wear?"

"No." I shook my head and pointed at the mostly blank page on my laptop. "The words. 'Underwear' sounds clinical, but 'panties' is sort of infantilizing. I struggle with what to use every time. It's not like I can write, 'Austin fisted her *undergarment* and ripped it clean off.' That doesn't sound sexy."

"Um," Meredith considered it. "Knickers, maybe?"

"Too old-timey."

"Foundationwear?"

"My heroine is a cook on a ranch in Montana; I doubt she wears Spanx." I sighed and fell back against the lumpy futon in our living room.

"What's this one called again?" she asked as she resumed packing. "*The Rancher's Sassy Fake Bride and the Doorstep Baby*?"

"Close." I sighed. "It's *The Montana Cowboy and His Fake Fiancée's Baby Surprise*."

Meredith zipped her bag and slung it over her shoulder. "And how many words have you written?"

I squinted at the screen. "Let's see . . . As of this moment, one hundred seventy-five words."

She let out a low whistle. "Okay, and when's it due?"

"Two months. I have sixty days to write sixty-five thousand words."

Admitting it out loud sent my stomach into a seasick dip. I had never, *ever* let a deadline get away from me like this. But then again, I'd also never tried to write a steamy happily ever after while nursing a thoroughly fractured heart.

Meredith walked over to my makeshift office and perched on the edge of the chair opposite me, so as not to disturb the notebooks piled there. Our brick-walled apartment was long on charm but short on space, which meant that the shared areas did triple duty. Meredith could've easily tapped the Bank of Mom and Dad and moved out on her own ages ago, but she was determined to scrimp and save her way to opening a Pilates studio all on her own. Which meant living like we were still in college even though we were six years past graduation. It worked for me since there was no way I could afford solo rent with my by-the-job lifestyle.

"Okay, that's easy," Meredith said. "A thousand or so words a day. You've got this."

Her can-do, problem-solving approach to life was one of the many things I loved about her, but not in this moment.

I shoved my laptop to the side with a groan. "Sure, it *sounds* totally doable, but I just . . ." I flailed my hands around to try to convey my current helpless state.

The corners of her mouth turned down. "I know, and I'm sorry. What can I do to make it better?"

I frowned back at her. "Find my muse?"

Not being able to write was painful for me on a bunch of different levels, the primary one being the credit card bills shoved in the notebooks behind Meredith. But it was more than just the terrifying financial implications of writer's block. I felt like I'd been *born* with a pencil in my hand. I had diaries that dated back to when I was ten years old, detailing hot gossip like the weather and how I did on my spelling tests. Writing was a way of making sense of my life and the world around me. I felt lucky to consider it my career, even when my bills forced me to do the less glamorous stuff like write a press release for a new energy drink called Heart Attack in a Can or edit an ebook about corporate HR policies.

My primary writing gig was ghostwriting cowboy romances for Liaison Publishing as Dakota Sinclair, which I'd hoped would eventually transition into me finding the confidence to write under my own name. The drenched-in-family-drama book club read I'd written, *Truth and Beauty*, had been good enough to score my agent, Celeste, but it had failed to sell, which basically crushed my spirit. In the meantime, I needed to keep churning out books about lovestruck cowboys and their feisty fillies, both equine and human, without her support, since I worked directly with Liaison. The books barely charted on Amazon, but Dakota was huge in Germany.

Meredith tipped her head. "Hold on a sec . . . You're talking about ripping panties off, and you're not even two hundred words in. Does this one start with a sex scene?"

She looked a little scandalized at the thought. Meredith was Grace Kelly with biceps and undoubtedly the most prim and proper bartender-slash-Pilates instructor in all Manhattan. The woman wore a *slip* if she thought a skirt was too sheer, and she'd perfected her "I'm so disappointed in you" look to deal with the pushy drunks who hit on her at closing time.

"While I would *love* to open one of my books with hayloft cunnilingus," I said for maximum shock value, "it doesn't work in the genre."

Meredith pretended to be scandalized even though she'd been subjected to plenty of spicy content as my beta reader.

"I was trying to jump-start myself by writing a sex scene," I continued. "I thought it might help to at least get the first one on the page since that part of the story is mechanics, you know? I can fill in the emotional beats later. His mouth goes here, her hand goes there, sighs, flutters, penetration, orgasm, and *scene*." I paused to consider my readership. "Or even sighs, flutters, fingers, mouth, orgasm, THEN penetration. But I can't write a thing. Have I even *had* sex? Because so far what I've got sounds like an Amish wedding night instruction manual."

"Brooke," she began gently. "It might help if you stopped being borderline agoraphobic and left the apartment, you know? Maybe you can come to class with me a couple of times a week? It might get the blood flowing back to your brain."

"I'm sorry but that's *never* going to happen," I replied quickly. "I know you'd make a huge deal out of me being there, and all your regulars would watch me the whole time. Like, 'Oh, I bet she's super advanced because her roommate is an instructor. They probably do the hundred every day before breakfast.'"

"And that's why you're a writer," she mused with a smile. "You make up stories for every scenario."

"Thank you for the offer, but I don't own anything cute enough to wear to one of your classes," I replied. "The answer will always be no."

"Maybe that's the issue here?" Meredith said as she stood up. "You lead with no. Maybe you should try saying yes for a change?"

I opened my mouth to bicker with her, then snapped it shut. The woman knew how to drop a zinger.

"Is that really how I come across?" I asked tentatively.

"Not always, but ever since Leo . . ."

She didn't have to finish the sentence.

It wasn't like Leo and I had been together long, and we'd never even come close to admitting how we felt about each other in the four months we'd hung out. But the man had outright *wooed* me like he'd studied romance novels. Not just the obvious stuff, like flowers and nice dinners. He was creative, like the time he bought me the book about a French seamstress I'd mentioned in passing and tucked in a vintage postcard from Paris as the bookmark. I'd used Google to translate the flowy script message on it and discovered that it was a love note from 1957, addressed to *ma moitié*, "my other half."

Four months wasn't long enough to admit out loud that I was falling in love with him, but the words had been taking root in my heart.

Until he ghosted me.

I thought I was going crazy at first, or he'd died and everyone knew but me. I was still mortified by how stalkerish I'd gotten as I tried to put the pieces of his disappearance together. Finally, a photo on his Insta feed featuring a close-up shot of his hand entwined with delicate, ballet slipper pink–nailed fingers solved the mystery for me.

He was alive and well, and I'd been replaced without an explanation. And now, weeks later, I was still questioning if anything I'd experienced with him was real. Not exactly a great foundation for creating heartwarming HEAs.

"Mere, I don't have the *time* to say yes to anything right now," I protested weakly. "My deadline . . ."

"Yeah, but I've seen what happens when you're inspired," she replied. "You plop down on that futon, go into the drone zone, and the next thing you know you've finished a couple billion words. You can do this, Brooke." Her eyes went soft as she watched me. "You just need to find some sunshine, literal *and* metaphorical, and then your muse will find you."

I hated the prickly sensation in my nose at her gentle coaching. Lately, my baseline reaction to anything emotional, from reels with rescue dogs to feedback from my editor, was tears. I blamed Leo for leaving me feeling like the top layer of my skin had been scrubbed off. *Everything* chafed.

But each day I rotted on my couch was another one lost to him. Leo was out there living his best life with a beautiful girl I'd learned was named Isodora, and I was watching it unfold online while wearing a mayonnaise-stained T-shirt.

"Yeah, you're right," I finally admitted, wiping my nose with the back of my hand. "Maybe I'll take a break and go for a walk?"

"*There* she is," Meredith cheered. "How about right now, with me?"

She knew me—that my good intentions would probably flame out into me staring at my laptop screen and stressing about each passing, unproductive minute.

"Okay." I slapped it closed. "Look at me; I'm saying yes."

I think we were equally shocked when I stood up.

"Where are you headed?" I asked, finally noticing her pink tank top and short, pleated skort. It was workout wear—no surprise there—but not her usual leggings and sports bra for class.

"Colton convinced me to go to his little pickleball club in Chelsea," she explained. "Which I guess isn't so little because the guest fee is sixty bucks."

Meredith's boyfriend, Colton, was a certified quilted-vest-and-navy-slacks finance bro who jumped on trends, like moving his dealmaking from the golf course to the pickleball court.

"He finally wore you down?" I asked as I stretched my arms over my head and rolled my neck like I was getting ready for a marathon and not a stroll down the block.

"Yeah, because we made a bet. If I win, he has to come to my 7 a.m. rise and shine class, and if he wins, I have to play again."

Despite her never having stepped on a court, my money was on Meredith. She was one of those people who could master anything physical, from pole dancing to paddleboarding.

I changed out of my pajamas and into shorts and a stain-free T-shirt, and even shoved my hair into a semi-presentable micro-ponytail.

Leaving my bubble made me feel twitchy before I even crossed the threshold. I had to convince myself that all I'd miss in the thirty minutes I'd be outside was beating myself up for not being productive. And maybe I'd luck into some inspiration?

We stepped outside, and the first few seconds of summer heat on my skin felt like a hug after being in air-conditioning for way too long. Summer in New York was brutal, which meant that little moments of joy like this one needed to be celebrated.

"You were right," I said, bumping my shoulder against hers as we set off. "Thank you."

She smiled at me. "Happy to light a fire under my favorite author. You're going to fly through those words once you get back."

A car drove by blaring an ancient dance song.

"Of *course*," I exclaimed as I listened to the words. "She's wearing a thong!"

Meredith frowned at me. "Huh?"

"Abby, the heroine in my book, is wearing a thong, not underwear or panties. How did I forget about thongs?" I muttered to myself.

"See? Inspo is all around you," Meredith said triumphantly.

"You're right. I'm so mad at myself for staying cooped up. Sometimes all it takes is a single word to trigger—"

"*Watch out*," a voice shouted from behind us. "Don't walk there!"

Meredith squealed and jumped to the side right as I planted my sneaker in a fresh pile of dog poop.

So much for celebrating the moment.

Someone ran up to us while I hunched over and tried to figure out what bit of street trash I could use to clean the mess that stretched from toe to heel.

"I am *so* sorry. I was about to pick it up, but Brutus got scared by the loud car and darted," the deep voice was saying. "I have paper towels—hold on."

I finally glanced up from my ruined shoe to find a Rottweiler, yellow Lab, and Yorkie being held back by a guy wearing a T-shirt that said "Call Me the Houndmaster" across the chest.

He smiled at me as he shifted the three leashes from one hand to the other and slid off his backpack. "Don't worry. I have a spray bottle with water too," he said as he dropped to his knee and dug through the bag. "I'll get you all cleaned up."

He had the cheerful air of someone who was lucky enough to make a living hanging out with dogs all day and tanned treetrunk legs that showed off how hard he worked. He was decent looking in that "leading man's best friend" way. I'm sure moms adored him.

I glanced at Meredith and she gave me an encouraging look.

He wasn't the type I'd normally go for, but there was something very meet-cute about the Prince Charming glass slipper vibes of the scenario.

Minus the poop, of course.

"By the way, these are my clients Brutus, Star, and Bella. Brutus is very sorry for what happened to your shoe." He smiled up at me and nodded toward the remarkably well-mannered dogs. "And I'm Adam, Houndmaster and shoe fixer. Please hand it over."

Yup, he was flirting with me. I kicked off my sneaker and hoped that he didn't have a foot fetish.

Meredith spoke up before I could. "This is Brooke, and I don't matter because I have to go meet my boyfriend. *Bye!*"

She jogged backward and, once she was fully behind him, mouthed, "Say yes," to me.

I considered it while Adam the Houndmaster got to work on my sneaker. Cute, good with animals, Boy Scout level of preparedness . . . Sure, why not?

I was desperate for inspiration of *any* sort, so saying yes was about to become a way of life.

Chapter Two

So far, my "say yes" campaign was turning up mixed results. The Houndmaster had indeed asked to hang out after our meet-poop, and right as I was starting to think that we were clicking over coffee, he'd mentioned his yearlong, on-again, off-again "situationship." He'd actually looked surprised when I excused myself, before I was even halfway through my latte.

But there were highlights to saying yes as well, like a front row seat at an experimental theater performance with a group of writer friends (the show was terrible, but we laughed our butts off) and going to a top secret purse sample sale with a woman who literally "psst"-ed me as I was walking by and told me that I could be her plus-one to get in. I'd walked out with a coin purse in the shape of cherries, a little treat that I couldn't afford.

The inspiration itself so far wasn't great, but I'd been managing about two hundred not-so-solid words per day since I'd started saying yes to random stuff. My muse hadn't returned, but at least I'd have *something* to show once my due date rolled around, even if it was bound to get savaged.

In this moment, I was second-guessing my willingness to be open to new experiences. I headed to Meredith's room feeling like a fraud in borrowed workout gear after having said yes to what now felt like the worst idea ever.

"Oh my gosh, you look *so good*," Meredith exclaimed when I walked in. "Daniel's going to love you!"

I squinted at her, then down at the white sleeveless shirt and black skort she'd loaned me. "I feel like I'm impersonating you."

As if anyone could confuse me for the willowy goddess. The skirt that looked cheeky on her was downright Catholic school uniform on me, and not in a sexy Halloween costume way. In an "I was elected hall monitor; I need to see your bathroom pass" kind of way.

It didn't help that I was still in a growing-out-a-breakup-haircut phase. Hacking off six inches of my chestnut hair had felt like the right move in the moment, but now I was stuck with a lob that was too short for a real ponytail. When I actually put forth a little effort, I could make it look semi-cute, but lately nothing had felt worthy, which meant I was about to subject the world to a ponytail the size of a cocktail weenie.

"Stop, you're totally owning it! And that's half the battle," Meredith said. "Look like you know what you're doing, and everything else will follow."

"But I *don't* know what I'm doing," I protested gently, plucking at the skort. "I'm not exactly athletic."

"Trust me, pickleball is super easy."

"Says the woman who's basically ready to go pro after a week of playing."

As predicted, Meredith had dominated the court and fallen in love with the game, so when Colton had suggested a round of mixed doubles with his buddy Daniel from work, she used my "say yes" campaign to trap me into playing with them.

"Honestly, this is less about pickleball and more about you meeting Daniel," she assured me. "Colton swears he's great."

She'd shown me his photo and he was decent-looking, so I wasn't totally dreading that part of the pickleball equation. Sandy hair, a square jaw, and a smile that made him look like he'd just told a joke and was waiting for people to laugh. In any other scenario, I would've passed, but Meredith had giddily reminded me that I didn't have much of a choice.

Which was why I found myself on the hallowed grounds of the Chelsea Pickleball Academy, a *way* fancier place than I'd anticipated. The vibes there felt more upscale coworking space than gym, with a clean black-and-white aesthetic and windows overlooking the skyline. My initial understanding of people who played pickleball was that they skewed boomer and wore visors, Skechers, and "It's Five O'Clock Somewhere" T-shirts. The people on the courts around us all looked like part-time models, especially Colton and Meredith, with their matching, blinding blondness.

Daniel was cuter in real life than his photos, a surprise plus. After we were introduced, I'd caught his reflection in a window as he pointed at me, then did a victory fist pump, making Colton laugh and me feel better about my outfit. I knew right away that I wasn't going to be into him, but maybe I'd still enjoy our forced fun?

If I wasn't so sports averse, I might've admitted that a date on the pickleball court was a decent first hang. Rather than dealing with awkward small talk, we'd gotten right to the rules, with all three of them trying to dumb them down for me but making it twice as confusing.

Dinking in the kitchen zone, mandatory double bounce—it was a lot to take in for someone who'd stopped playing organized sports in middle school. What made it worse was that the court we'd been assigned backed up to the club's juice bar, which meant everyone camped out for a postgame smoothie could watch my carnage.

"Let's get out there," Colton had finally suggested after going over the rules twice. "We'll just have some fun."

"You've got this," Meredith said to me as she moved into position across the court from me.

"Hey, don't fraternize with the enemy." Daniel laughed but sounded a *little* serious at the same time. He looked at me. "Remember, pickleball is easy to learn but tough to master."

I gulped as I nodded at him because even the learning part had been hard for me so far. I glanced around as they all got into position and assumed serious, spread-legged stances.

"Yo, keep that paddle up, Brooke," Daniel coached over his shoulder at me. "If you *stay* ready, you don't have to *get* ready."

I refrained from rolling my eyes at him. There was a fine line between helping and mansplaining.

"Zero, zero, start," Colton announced as he got into position for the underhand serve that kicked off the torture.

Of course, the ball came directly to me.

I wasn't about to fail right out of the gate, so I rushed toward it, swinging the paddle back and forth around my body like it was a flyswatter.

"Brooke, watch the *kitchen*," Daniel scolded as my paddle connected with the ball. "Come on!"

I was thrilled that I managed to hit the ball but mortified when it popped straight up and went flying onto the next court over, which was occupied by two very intense players.

I grimaced and hunched my shoulders to my ears when they both froze and turned to glare at me. "Sorry! Sorry!"

The guy closer to me scooped the ball and then served it back in my direction, and when I reached up to try to receive it, the ball ricocheted off my paddle and back to his side. He opted to jog it over to me.

"First time?" he asked, smiling as he handed over the ball.

I tried to answer him and couldn't find any words, because the slightly sweaty guy grinning at me was jaw-droppingly good-looking. Between the messy hair, black-brown eyes, bright smile, and adorable little mole next to his mouth, I was an instant goner.

"Yup, total virgin here," I finally managed. I did a stupid little wave with my paddle, making my response that much more mortifying.

He graced me with a half smile. "Hopefully they'll be gentle with you, then. Good luck out there."

He dashed back to his court before I could say anything else, and I stood there watching his calves for what felt like a solid five minutes.

"Brooke?" Meredith called. "You okay?"

I snapped back to life. "Yup, all good. What happens now?"

Daniel stalked over to me, and I pretended to pay attention while he explained everything I'd just done wrong, as well as what I needed to do to fix it. I nodded along, but all I kept thinking was *WHO IS THE PICKLEBALL GOD ON THE NEXT COURT?*

It was an involuntary full-body reaction that left me incapable of doing anything but sneaking glances at the court beside us. It felt like that tender part of my heart had been cauterized ever since Leo, like the only way for me to continue existing was to cut off the blood supply to a faulty organ. So what was this hopeful sweaty palms feeling?

And more importantly, did my muse just flit back into my life?

Daniel seemed to figure out that playing doubles with me was the equivalent of being on his own, plus I stopped trying after realizing that he kept reaching in front of me any time the ball bounced near my zone. Meredith mouthed, "Sorry," across the net to me after twenty minutes of trying to stay out of his way.

We wound up losing, no surprise, and the moment the game was over, I focused all my attention on the court beside us, hoping that my new obsession might glance my way. He didn't, but his opponent, a bigger, burly guy in a black bucket hat that looked completely off-brand for the club, couldn't stop glancing my way.

Daniel walked over to me, forcing me to tone down my gawking. "Losers buy the winners smoothies. I can put it all on my house account if you don't have your credit card with you."

"Oh, uh, I, um," I stuttered, momentarily stunned that he was implying that I, as the biggest loser of our team, deserved to foot the bill. "It's in the locker room. I can go get it or . . ."

"It's fine." He waved his hand at me peevishly. "Let's go."

Daniel walked away to join Meredith and Colton in line at the bar, smacking his paddle against his leg with each step. I didn't know him, but it was clear he was *not* happy being paired with me, my cuteness notwithstanding.

And we still had two more games to go.

"It's your grip," a voice echoed from behind me.

I turned to find the bucket hat player from the next court over holding his paddle in the air in front of him, his eyes burning holes into me.

He looked like he was dressed to clean a garage, in a white

Chelsea Pickleball Academy–branded T-shirt and oversized red basketball shorts. I half expected to see Nike slides and gym socks instead of sneakers when I looked down at his feet.

"What do you mean?" I asked.

He stalked closer. "The reason your ball kept flying up was because your grip was off. Instead of doing this"—he mimicked the awkward way I hadn't realized I'd been holding the paddle—"try this."

He held the paddle up vertically, placed his right palm on the hitty part, and then slid his hand down to the handle to grip it.

"Like a handshake," he explained. "It should feel really natural. Try it."

He nodded to the paddle in my hand and I mimicked his movements.

"There you go." He nodded approvingly. "Your next game should go a little smoother now. If your partner will actually let you take a shot."

I spotted the hot guy he'd been playing against heading toward us, freshly showered and in his street clothes. It was summer, so he wasn't in the Midtown dude uniform of navy slacks and a gray vest, but I could tell he probably worked in finance by the light blue button-down and the massive silver linked watch on his wrist.

My heart sped up as he walked closer to us.

"Oh, my doubles partner?" I replied in an overloud voice, sneaking a glance to see how far away the hot guy was and timing what I was about to say next so he'd be able to hear it. "Just met him today. I barely know him."

The hot guy paused right next to us as I finished. Perfect. He glanced at me, then at Bucket Hat.

"Good time, bro," he said, offering Bucket Hat a fist bump. "Thanks."

"You know it."

I smiled prettily at my obsession. "Hey, thanks for saving my ball."

He looked at me like I'd just entered his field of vision. "Oh yeah. No problem. Hope losing your virginity wasn't too painful."

I laughed way harder than was necessary as he walked away, until I glanced at Bucket Hat and saw his sour expression.

He was actually sort of cute, in a disheveled way. If he cut the scraggly mullet poking out from beneath the back of the hat and shaved his five-o'clock shadow, I'd even call him handsome, but the guy seemed committed to looking like a janitor.

"Kai," he yelled after my fake boyfriend.

Of *course* his name was Kai. It was a quintessential hot guy name, which was why I'd used it for cowboys in three of my books.

"Yeah?"

"You gotta fortify that volley," Bucket Hat shouted to him. "Drill it, okay?"

It was another language that I was suddenly more interested in mastering.

"Done," Kai said as he backed away. "See you Thursday."

And now I knew his schedule. Perfect.

Bucket Hat glanced back at me. "Anyway, good luck. If you keep that grip, I promise you'll do better on your next game. Don't be afraid to take your shot, even if your partner gets in your way."

"He's not officially my partner," I reminded him, *just* in case.

"Right," Bucket Hat replied with a nod. "You can't be a real partner until you learn how to play."

I was about to pretend to be insulted by his implication, but he turned and walked away before I could say anything.

Meredith joined me, holding out a pale yellow smoothie. "Recharge." She glanced over her shoulder to where Colton and Daniel were practicing various swings. "That was . . . not great. Sorry. Do you hate it?"

"No, not at all," I lied. "Because I think I just met my future husband."

Chapter Three

I didn't consider watching the soccer match on my iPad while I "wrote" at Hell's Coffee true procrastination since it involved family and would dominate the afternoon's group text. I wasn't really paying attention since the only player I cared about hadn't been on the pitch yet. I half listened as Barnham City got wrecked yet again, pretending that I was working when all I could think about was how miserable my brother was probably feeling. He was edging past his prime years playing for a team that was under a perpetual black cloud.

My older brother, Wes, was a nepo hire in the worst possible way—the son of Albert Nelson, a beloved goalkeeper who'd helped take the Chelsea Football Club to victory in the late eighties, then retired to the States, married my mom, had Wesley, and died unexpectedly way too young. The long shadow cast by his late father meant that Wes rarely had a chance to shine in his own right, especially because he'd opted to play for an English team.

I jumped when someone tapped me on my shoulder and tried not to frown as I lifted one of my headphones to see what the stranger wanted.

The old me was fine with occasional interruptions when I

was working in public, because so many rom-coms started with coffee shop serendipity. *Can I share that outlet with you? Do you like the book you're reading? Does the French roast taste burnt to you?* And then the next thing you know, you're shutting the place down hours later, thanking your lucky stars that Mr. Blue Eyes had the balls to shoot his shot. After all, it was how Leo and I had met. A crowded café (not this one, of course), with just one open chair left at my little table in the corner. Cue the banter, prolonged eye contact, and butterflies.

Now I knew better. It didn't matter how cute the meet; it would always end in disaster. Sure, I was still saying yes, thanks to my pact with Meredith, but it didn't matter because a misanthrope had evicted my tenderhearted romantic soul, which was why I was staring at a blank page on my laptop.

But . . . *Kai*. Every time I thought about the run-in with him on the courts, I felt that dormant flutter of possibility. That inexplicable spark of attraction had to mean *something*, and I was willing to bet my next book to find out.

I narrowed my eyes at the tattooed stranger who was *not* Kai.

"Come on, you gunners!" The guy pointed at the screen, where Coventry was celebrating yet another goal. "Am I right?"

Technically, he *wasn't* right because it was Arsenal's chant and they weren't playing, but I didn't want to get into it.

I bobbed my head, keeping my expression neutral. "Yup."

He leaned closer to squint at my tablet. "Are you for Barnham City or Coventry?"

"Barnham."

"Oof, sorry about that." He flinched dramatically. "Why?"

I wasn't about to mention Wes, because I didn't want to get

into the inevitable questions about how it was possible that we were related given our different skin tones. After twenty-eight years as siblings, the "half" part didn't even register to us. We had the same eyes, sense of humor, and love of stupid memes.

"I like their logo," I replied with a shrug.

I did have more than my fair share of merch featuring the Barnham City owl mascot.

"Good thing it's an exhibition match," the guy said. "They still have a chance to get it together before the season starts."

I glanced back at the screen just as the camera panned to Wes as he got ready to sub in. The family group text lit up right on cue.

"Sorry, I need to respond to this." I held up my phone and shrugged as it pinged with messages composed of emojis and exclamation points.

"Just when it's about to get good," the stranger said, nodding toward my brother's pensive face filling the screen. "Wesley Nelson is amazing."

The man had a point. I put my headphones back on and refocused on the messages piling up. My parents, aunts and uncles, cousins, and Wesley's father's family in England were all on it, offering their take on every aspect of the game. If positive vibrations and manifesting were a thing, the spirit in the group text should've been enough to guarantee a Barnham win.

My mom took advantage of the fact that I was active on it to message me solo.

> You okay, sweetheart?

I'd basically gone dark over the past few weeks, chalking it up to my deadline and downplaying the whole broken-heart thing. But she knew better.

> Yup, all good. Working

A pause as the group text swelled with pride when Wes appeared on camera again.

> So handsome!

> Looking fierce and ready!

> Choke on it, Coventry!

> Here we go, here we go, here we go 🎵🎶

How's the book coming? my mom texted me. Better I hope?

I scrolled over to my email account before writing back to her, hoping that there was a miracle in the form of a deadline extension waiting for me. The only message from my editor, Piper, was the one from a few days ago that I'd ignored, asking if I was on track for my first ten-thousand-word review. I flipped back to my draft and felt a familiar dread claw at my throat.

I'd written 1,152 words. Crappy ones at that. Hollow, simplistic, high-schooler-trying-to-hit-the-book-report-word-count words that suggested I'd never felt a real human emotion.

Getting there, I texted back to her.

When it came to my mom, less information was always the best course of action. She was a worrier by nature, taking on the stress of her loved ones like she was volunteering as tribute.

I knew she was already maxed out helping my dad rehab from his latest training-induced injury, which had the potential to keep him from running in the Philadelphia Marathon with her in the fall.

> How's Dad?

We paused to briefly celebrate a pass to Wes.

> Better! He hates the reduced workout schedule, but he knows it's the only strategy for his knee. I have to train when he's not around, otherwise he tries to join me!

Running was the foundation of my parents' relationship. They'd met when my mom took it up after she lost Albert as a way to channel her grief into something tangible and manageable. She'd told me that every ache she endured as she ran was a reminder that she was still among the living, even though her broken heart made her wonder why she bothered. But she had two-year-old Wes and the hope that maybe the endorphins she got from the Montgomery County Striders Club would be enough to get her out of bed each day.

Then she met my dad during a 6 a.m. fun run (a total oxymoron), which proved that it was possible to have *two* soulmates.

> Ha. Dad's addicted to exercise. I need to get back to work now. I'm nowhere near my daily word count goal.

> Do you want me to read what you've got?

My mom had been my beta reader for *Truth and Beauty*, but there was no way I wanted her reading about my strapping, horny ranchers and the women who preferred riding cowboys over horses. There wasn't a single romance on her bookshelf lined with literary bestsellers, which was more than enough reason to keep my work from her, plus the fact that my last book, *Saddled Up with the Sheriff's Daughter*, had the word "clit" mentioned nine times.

I knew that my ghostwritten books weren't great works of fiction, but they did have something going for them: guaranteed happily ever afters plus scorching open-door sex scenes. I made sure that there wasn't one magical penis among my heroes, just hardworking men who put in overtime between the sheets.

> I'm okay, thanks, love you!

> Hootie hoot, fight blue fight. Hootie hoot!!!!!

She replied with the nonsensical Barnham stadium song.

I glanced back at my tablet as the camera zoomed in on Wes running down the field. He was so damn *graceful*, like clearing the length of it at top speed took no effort at all.

The athletic genes that defined the rest of my family had hopscotched right over me. I'd made my peace with my two left feet, but now the whole Kai situation made me wish for at least a little hand-eye coordination.

But maybe I could fake it? Meredith was already good enough to teach me the basics, and she'd be thrilled to broker a meet-cuter with Kai. And then once he figured out that I wasn't just goofing around on the courts, that I was *serious* about the sport with the silly name, then maybe sparks would fly?

And once that happened, I could almost guarantee my muse would be back for good.

Chapter Four

On Thursdays we wore Lululemon.

Or at least on *this* Thursday, I was decked out in borrowed athleisure once again, crossing my fingers that Kai was consistent and would show up at the Chelsea Pickleball Academy at approximately the same time as the week prior.

Yeah, total stalker vibes, but I was on a mission.

No surprise, Meredith had jumped at the chance to be my wingwoman. Unlike me, her belief in romantic serendipity was unscathed, and she was convinced that we were starting chapter one of a great love story.

I hoped that she was right for so many reasons.

When we walked into the place, the rhythmic pops of gameplay were an instant reminder of what I was attempting. I was *not good* at sports. Any of them, from softball to bowling, so what made me think that my nonexistent skills could woo someone who obviously took the game seriously?

But that could be yet another in with my inspo. I was a newbie looking for an expert to show me the ropes, and that was a total turn-on. Hell, I'd used the concept in my book *The Rancher's Romantic Rival*, where true love bloomed between a shy nanny and her cowboy employer when he taught her how to ride a horse. The lessons had allowed Molly to discover the tenderness hidden beneath Dirk's gruff exterior, and Dirk had loved being the subject matter expert and showing off his skills.

Of course, I still had some complications to work through, like Kai actually showing up and then me angling to look just the right amount of clueless. A little helpless but still competent.

It was going to require a *lot* of acting, because once I had a paddle in my hand all bets were off. Ball going straight over the net? Unlikely. Ball zipping over to smack a bystander in the gut? Almost guaranteed.

Meredith and I stood at the counter while the front desk woman chatted with someone in an office behind it. Meredith cleared her throat to signal that we were waiting and then rolled her eyes at me.

"This would never fly at Harmony Pilates," she whispered out of the corner of her mouth. "Client check-in sets the tone for the rest of the experience."

I was too busy scanning the courts for a certain dark-haired expert to notice that we were being ignored. There were plenty of beautiful people smacking balls around but no Kai.

I suddenly wanted to abort our mission, but it was too late. The gum-smacking front desk person finally made her way over to us.

"Sorry, I was busy watching our mascot being adorable," she explained, not sounding sorry at all.

"Hi, I'm a member but my friend has a day pass," Meredith explained, nodding toward me.

I smiled and held my phone out to her with the QR code I'd discovered online enlarged, so all she had to do was scan it.

The woman's expression went confused. "Day pass? I've been here six months, and I've never heard of that. Lemme see."

She yanked my phone from my hand and zoomed out on the screen.

"There's no expiration date," I explained helpfully as she studied my phone. "I checked everywhere."

"Hold on," she said with a sigh, then walked back to the office with my phone. "Hey, Grip, do you know anything about a day pass thingy?"

I couldn't make out what the deep voice said in response, but the woman came back after a few minutes, looking resigned.

"It's your lucky day; he said he remembers seeing you." She flipped her hand to point up at the camera mounted in the corner. "We normally wouldn't allow it because this is from when we first opened, but you're good this time." She scanned the code, then tapped on the computer keyboard like she was making reservations for an international flight. "Court thirteen."

I followed Meredith to the swanky locker room, trying not to be too obvious about the fact that I was scanning every face we passed. She pulled the paddles out of her bag and handed a gray-and-red one that she'd borrowed from Colton to me.

"Don't be nervous," she scolded me gently, accurately translating my expression. "This is supposed to be fun. It's an adventure!"

"It's a quest," I corrected. "I need a hit of serotonin or else I'll be lucky to write fifty words today."

"Then let's get out there," she said with a wink. "I have a good feeling."

Court thirteen had to be the worst offering in the place for the other players, but I loved the fact that it bordered a wall. That meant only one court would be stuck fielding my crappy shots.

"I'm ready if you are," I said, taking another glance around the space. No Kai yet, but maybe he'd show up as we were finishing up, so I'd be glowy from exertion and he wouldn't have a chance to see my lack of skills.

"We're just goofing around right now, getting a feel for it," Meredith reminded me. "But first, stretching."

"Seriously?" I gaped at her. "This is just a bigger version of Ping-Pong; why do I have to warm up?"

She slid her left leg out in front of her and bent over at the waist, bracing her hands on the opposite thigh. "Because I'm going to make you *run*, girlie. Happy endorphins, coming right up."

She led me through light Pilates for a few minutes, which I had to admit felt sort of good, then walked to her side of the court. "No pressure to be perfect. We're just going to have some fun."

"Trust me, perfection won't be a problem over here." I laughed as I got into position and mimicked her stance.

I looked down at my hand and realized that I was doing the same choke-hold grip as the last time I'd attempted to play. I let go and adjusted it the way Bucket Hat had shown me and hoped it would help.

"I'm a big fan of learning by doing," Meredith explained. "I'm sure if you were taking a real lesson, you'd be going over all sorts of foundation stuff. But today, no score, no rules. Just vibes to start. Ready?"

I looked around the space again and was disappointed he hadn't arrived but relieved to see that no one was watching. "Yup."

Meredith dropped the ball and smacked it out of the air and toward me.

With no Daniel jumping in front to claim the ball, all I could do was freeze and stare as the thing whizzed by.

"That's fine," Meredith called to me. "But next time maybe try a little?"

I nodded and hunkered down like I was serious about hitting the ball. She swatted it toward me again and "try a little" echoed in my head as I got ready.

Amazingly, my paddle connected with the ball with a thwack, and it careened over the net and headed for the far corner of the court. The luckiest shot ever! I grinned as I watched Meredith dash after it.

But then she let out a high-pitched yip and tumbled to the ground.

"You okay?" I laughed, but Meredith didn't pop up like I expected. "Mere?"

She was still on the ground, clutching her ankle, when I reached her, her face pinched with pain.

"It really hurts." She looked up at me as her eyes filled with tears. "*Bad*."

I dropped to my knees beside her. "Oh my god, I'm so sorry! Do you want me to get someone?"

She shook her head. "I don't know. Give me a sec." She pursed her lips and blew out a shuddery breath.

I gently moved her hand away from her ankle. "Mere, it's already swelling."

"Fuck."

I looked around the space for help and spotted Bucket Hat heading our way.

"Hey!" I waved my hand. "Excuse me?"

I glanced between him and Meredith as he walked closer. Despite the concern on his face, there was an ease to the way he moved, like he was at home in the space. He sped up to a jog.

"Oh shit, what happened? Are you okay?"

"She tripped," I offered. "It's my fault."

"Stop, I'm the dummy who ran for it. Great shot, by the way."

Meredith tried to smile, but it crumpled into a grimace of pain almost immediately. I could tell she was trying to play it cool as her ankle blew up.

He knelt down beside us, frowning. "Can I take a peek?"

Meredith nodded and sniffled again, trying to keep from crying.

Bucket Hat gently placed his hand on top of her sneaker as he surveyed the damage. "Wow. Shit. Okay, that's not good. Do you think you can stand up?"

"Yeah, I'll try," Meredith said, shifting her weight so that she was on her hip, then onto her knees.

"Go slow," he coached. "We're not in a rush."

Meredith moved her leg out so she was on one knee, took a deep breath, and started to rise.

"Grab on," Bucket Hat said.

She gripped his offered hand, got halfway up, then crumpled to the ground again, letting out a little cry of frustration and pain. "I can't. It hurts too much."

"Okay, wait here," Bucket Hat said. "Be right back."

He gave me a nod like we were members of the same rescue squad, and I bobbed my head to confirm it before he jogged away.

"Am I delirious or is that guy *super*cute?" Meredith whispered to me, still trying to play off the pain like it wasn't a big deal.

"Stop," I chastised her. "The only thing I'm thinking about right now is you."

A few minutes later, Bucket Hat was back, pushing a rolling

office chair in front of him. "Your Uber, miss? And I brought you ice."

He held up a small white pillow-shaped pack, then crushed it in his palm until it made a popping sound.

"Start icing it," he said as he handed it to Meredith. "And take this." He pulled a packet of aspirin from his pocket and handed it to her along with a mini water bottle.

"Wow, you're very prepared. Does this sort of thing happen a lot?" Meredith asked as she tried to hide a grimace.

Bucket Hat nodded. "Injuries happen way more often than people realize. Now, let's get you in the chair."

He managed to divide his attention between Meredith and me as we moved her, guiding me how to best grab onto her while checking in with her to make sure we weren't accidentally causing more discomfort.

"You good?" he asked once she was settled.

She bit her lip and nodded. "I'm okay, thank you."

I could tell she was lying. Meredith didn't like being a bother.

"I can take it from here," I said. "Thanks for this." I nodded toward the chair.

"Absolutely not," he said with authority, stepping in front of me. "I'm driving."

He set off, pushing the chair through the courts, and our little parade attracted quite a bit of attention. We reached the reception area, bickering about our next steps. Meredith wanted to catch a cab home while I insisted that she needed to go to a walk-in clinic.

Or in this case, a hobble-in clinic.

"Sorry, but I really think you need to have that looked at," Bucket Hat interrupted us. "It's more than a sprain."

I pointed at him triumphantly while I glared at Meredith. "See? You're outnumbered!"

Meredith opened her mouth to argue, but a loud voice echoed from behind us.

"Yo, Gripper. What's going on?"

I turned around, but my gut already knew who it was.

There was Kai. Grinning right at me.

Chapter Five

I spun around to refocus on Meredith, because I could feel my eyes bugging out of my head in a very not-cute way.

My already spiking anxiety from Meredith's injury leveled up even more seeing Kai right *there*, in the flesh and not my fantasies. After a week of obsessing about this person I'd only interacted with once, seeing him again was like running into a celebrity. I felt like I knew him, thanks to my overactive imagination—in my mind, he'd already wooed me in a dozen creative ways—and I was about to greet him by name when I realized how absolutely weird that would be.

I scanned him quickly and was a little distressed to discover that my memory of his looks didn't do him justice. Was he actually a model? Because the jawline that was essentially a hard right angle belonged up on a billboard.

"I tripped," Meredith answered him. "My friend Brooke here hit a kill shot."

Typical Meredith, hyping me up despite her softball-sized ankle. My ride-or-die wingwoman.

"Well, that sucks," Kai replied. "Sorry to hear it."

He glanced at me with a sad smile.

"And I'm just calling for an Uber for these two, because they're headed to Urgent Care," Bucket Hat added.

I turned to him, happy that I had a reason to look away from Kai. "Oh, that's super generous, but you don't have to."

"Nope," he replied as he pulled his phone out of his pocket and started typing. "No worries, I've got you."

There was something calming about the way he took control of the situation. He wasn't bossy or know-it-all. It was more like he could read the room and sensed that Meredith was going to put up a fight unless he stepped in to handle it.

"It'll be here in four minutes," he continued. "Black Escalade, so there's room to elevate that ankle. You need to keep the ice on it!"

Meredith nodded and shifted the pack back in place. The three of us stood in silence, watching her press it to her ankle.

"Hey, uh, not to be a dick or anything, but is my lesson still on or . . . ?" Kai asked. "I can reschedule if that's easier."

Meredith and I exchanged a quick look, as he'd just revealed important new intel. Kai was taking lessons and Bucket Hat was his instructor. No wonder Mr. Hat seemed above the law when it came to the club dress code. Today he was in a slightly less faded CPA logo T-shirt and shiny black basketball shorts.

And the hat, of course, which on close inspection I could see was Nike, with an orange band around the middle part.

"No, we're still good. I don't have anyone after you," he answered. "Go get changed, and I'll meet you on court eleven."

"Done." Kai nodded. He raised his chin toward Meredith. "Hey, good luck at Urgent Care. Hope it's not too bad."

She gave him a tight smile, no doubt because she was processing both her discomfort *and* the meet-ugliness of what was currently going on.

"Thanks," I squeaked out, the first word I'd managed to say to him.

He finally locked onto me. "Oh, right, you're the virgin. Good to see you again!"

Tension flooded my body, because I needed to respond with something witty. He'd set me up with a perfect opener, and all I had to do was volley back with a cute quip about . . . how virginity was a social construct? That I was now in my ho phase? The fact that I'd been daydreaming about him taking me even further from virginity for the past seven days?

Instead, all I came up with was: "You too!"

And I *waved* at him after he'd already turned his back and walked away from us.

"Uber's here," Bucket Hat said, frowning a little. "I'm going to help you get settled."

"It's really not necessary," Meredith said. "I'm fine."

But of course, he didn't listen and wound up hoisting her into what I realized was an UberX. He shut the car door and turned to where I was waiting on the crowded sidewalk.

"Can you let me know what they say about her ankle? I like to stay on top of what goes on here, injury-wise."

A car waiting behind the Uber honked, and he flashed a friendly "one second" finger at it.

"Uh, sure," I answered. "I'll call the main number—"

"No, let me give you my cell."

I pulled out my phone, and he recited it to me. My finger hovered over the screen since I couldn't enter it under "Bucket Hat" with him staring me down. "What's your name?"

He chuckled. "Yeah, that's right; we didn't even have a chance to introduce ourselves." He held out his hand to me. "I'm Owen Miller."

"Brooke Murphy," I said as I slid my palm against his. "And that's Meredith Waxman on injured reserve."

"Hey, go easy on her the next time you play." He smiled at me, and it reached all the way up to his dark eyes. "Sounds like you're already lethal out there."

I laughed at the thought of it. "Not even close. Lucky shot, that's all. And now my instructor's injured. I'm actually hopeless."

The car honked again, and Owen started backing away toward the building, still smiling at me. "I could help you change that. It's sort of what I do."

"Maybe," I replied quickly, because there was no way it was going to happen. "Anyway, thanks for everything."

Owen raised an eyebrow as he pointed at me. "Text me about her diagnosis, okay? Good luck."

"I will. Thanks again for your help," I said. "We'll figure out how to pay you back for the ride."

"Stop, there's no need."

He stood on the sidewalk and watched the car like a worried dad as I got in.

Meredith had her head back with her eyes pinched shut when I slid next to her. She opened one to peek at me.

"I ruined everything. I'm so sorry."

I reached out to put my hand on top of hers. "Oh, stop. It was an accident. And hey, we managed to make contact with Kai again. That's worth a couple of hundred words at least." I tapped my temple. "I recommitted his face to memory so now I can write Austin's character description."

She closed her eyes again. "I do *not* need this injury. I'm so mad at myself."

"You'll be back on your feet in no time. I'm sure it's just a sprain."

I gave her hand a squeeze and looked out the window at the

world passing by. Spending a couple of hours at Urgent Care wasn't on my bingo card either, but I had my notebook tucked in my bag, so I could jot down my thoughts while we waited. Because yay, I actually *had* thoughts. The tiniest little embers of ideas were glowing within me.

Just a few minutes of Kai exposure was all it took.

A text buzzed in from my brother in our usual no-context-photo shorthand. It was a picture of an entire cooked fish, eyes and all, on a plate in front of many glasses of wine, with his hand giving a thumbs-up beside it. I texted back a close-up of Meredith's purpling ankle. Whoever broke first and asked for an explanation lost.

> Damn. Are you okay?

> It's Mere. We were playing pickleball and she tripped.

> Hold up. YOU? Pickleball?

> IKR? I suck tho

> I've been playing. Love it.

> What's with the fish?

> Fancy team dinner. Gotta go. Bye xo

"*Brooke*, oh my god, now I can't teach you how to play!" Meredith wailed, interrupting my moment of sibling bonding. "If I'm injured, how am I going to be your wingwoman?"

There was no way I wanted to pile on while she was in pain. "We'll figure it out."

"Maybe Colton can help you instead?" she offered.

I shook my head and tried to hide my disappointment from her. "No, the vibe is different with him, plus Kai might think we're together. Anyway, you're going to be fine. I feel it in my bones. A couple of days of rest and you'll be good as new."

She leaned over to move the ice pack. Her swollen ankle now resembled a water balloon.

"Or not," I said, watching my dreams of us playing adorably but powerfully in flippy skirts go up in flames. "Does it hurt as bad as it looks?"

She squinted and nodded at me. "Yeah. I'm sort of in agony, but I'm trying to mind over matter it."

I leaned and looked out the window again. "We're almost there. I'm sure they'll give you some good meds."

Thanks to the traffic stacking up in front of us, we *weren't* almost there. Normally, we'd get out and walk the rest of the way, but it clearly wasn't an option in our scenario.

"You know, that cute instructor guy could teach you," Meredith offered softly.

I snorted at the thought.

"No, it's actually *perfect*," she said as she warmed to the idea. "He has direct access to your man. You could totally feel him out to get the intel on Kai and then get him to set up a match with him." She paused. "Once you learn to really play, of course."

"Mere, I'm sure lessons are way beyond my budget. But we'll figure it out; don't worry about me right now. Let's get you healed up."

Taking lessons with Owen wasn't the worst idea. If I really

wanted to figure out the game and, by association, gain access to my inspo, then I probably needed to learn from an expert and not just goof around with Meredith. And the instructor formerly known as Bucket Hat obviously knew his stuff if he was a trainer at such a fancy club.

He didn't look like the rest of the polished people at CPA, but Meredith was right, he was cute in a "big brother home from college" kind of way. He probably gave excellent hugs and made up silly nicknames for his friends.

The Escalade rolled to a stop again and I sighed. I needed to embrace the wait, because there was no doubt we'd be doing quite a bit of it for the next couple of hours. Meredith had her eyes squeezed shut, so I pulled out my notebook and started dreaming up all the ways a charming cowboy could delight his fake fiancée.

Writing happily ever afters required me to go into a flow state that was only possible when my head was in the right place. The breakup with Leo had all but guaranteed that I'd never find my way back to that cotton-candy, dreamy, true-love-wins way of looking at the world in time to finish this book. I'd tried channeling my pain into the third act breakup scene, a space where it was okay to let bleakness take the wheel for a couple thousand words. When I'd reread what I'd written the following day, the level of bitterness and venom in the scene felt all wrong. Yeah, things were supposed to go upside down during the breakup, but what I'd written was downright cruel. I could already see Piper's "yikes" edits in the margins.

Now, though, I had a new direction, plus a little spark of inspiration. Was it ridiculous to pin my output on a silly crush?

Of course, and probably dangerous as well, since for all I knew the guy could be a gaslighting asshole.

But in this moment Kai was a delicious unknown who'd given me something I'd been missing since Leo crushed my heart.

Hope.

Chapter Six

"I *hate* being still." Meredith smacked the futon in frustration. "This is torture."

I glanced up at her from my workspace at the tiny kitchen table, where I was camped out just in case she needed help during day one post-injury. "You're being forced to rest today for a very good reason. Lean into it. Maybe this is the time to try a new hobby, like crochet?"

"The day I start a sit-down hobby is the day when—"

"I take up a sport," I finished for her, wearing a prim smile. "Stranger things have happened."

She made a noncommittal noise and tossed her phone on the coffee table. "I hear you tapping away. Writing going okay today?"

"Sort of, yeah," I said. "I'm not in the zone, but I'm managing some decent output."

Meredith adjusted the pillow behind her head and kicked her newly acquired orthopedic boot up on the back of the futon.

"How's your pain level?" I asked her.

"It's aching."

Meredith's "sprain" was actually a hairline talus fracture, a bone in the ankle that I didn't know existed. Even the doctor couldn't quite figure out how she'd managed it, but the good news was that it wasn't severe enough for surgery. Still, she was going to be in a boot for at least six weeks, and I could only imagine the lengths she was going to go to in order to exercise. If it were me, I'd happily take up residence on the couch and shoot for *eight* weeks of inactivity.

For the healing, of course.

"I can probably still teach class," she said, half to herself. "I can sit in a rolling chair and harass everyone that way."

"Mere, stop." I sighed. "Just try to be still. It hasn't even been twenty-four hours."

"There's just so much I'm supposed to be doing right now." Her voice pitched up. "Work is scrambling to cover my shifts, and the studio is calling in subs who are super dicey. Colton and I were supposed to play doubles with a couple of people from his building so he can get invited to this huge Hamptons Fourth of July party. And now I can't help with your Kai quest . . ."

I frowned at my laptop screen, because even though it felt small to admit it, I was bummed about it too.

"I still think you should try that instructor," she added.

"Oh crap." I grabbed my phone. "He wanted to know about your diagnosis. Maybe for insurance reasons?"

Meredith laughed at me. "Did you read the waiver we signed before we could even walk past the front desk? I could get electrocuted in the locker room and they'd be blameless. I guess that's one of the benefits of them having founders in legal and finance."

I typed a quick update message to Owen, and he responded almost immediately.

> Can you talk?

"What did he say?" Meredith asked.

"Okay, that's weird," I said. "He wants to *talk*."

"Live?"

My phone rang and I held it up to show her it was him. I stood up and dashed the two steps over to the window, as if it afforded me any privacy.

"Hi, what's up?"

I wondered if it was protocol to get a full witness statement after an on-site injury, because why else would we need to chat on the phone?

"Hey, just wanted to say that I'm sorry to hear about Meredith's fracture and see how she's feeling."

The sincerity in his voice suggested no ulterior motive except genuine care.

"Oh, that's nice of you. Yeah, she's definitely feeling it today."

"That sucks. Is she on pain medication?"

"Yup, she is." I traced patterns in the air-conditioning condensation on the window. "Thanks again for your help when it happened."

"Oh, no problem. Listen, I was thinking," he said. "You mentioned that she was helping teach you, and since that's off the table, I wanted to offer my services. I'm usually booked up, but I have a couple of open slots on my calendar, if you could handle mornings."

Did Kai ever show up in the morning?

"Oh, that's really nice of you, but I don't think lessons are, uh, feasible for me right now. And I'm not a member or anything."

Meredith slapped the futon to get my attention and mouthed, "Say yes," at me, over and over. I frowned at her and turned away.

"You don't have to be a member," he replied. "Lessons give

you access for the session and thirty minutes on the courts afterward."

"Huh," I said as I ran depressing calculations in my head. "How much is a lesson?"

"Private lessons come in four-packs, for six hundred."

"*Dollars*?" I squeaked out before I could stop myself.

Owen chuckled, and it sounded almost like he was embarrassed. "Yeah, sorry. I don't set the price."

"That's a little out of reach for me," I admitted. "But thanks anyway. I really appreciate the offer."

"What if I give you the injured-friend discount? Ten percent off."

He sounded so hopeful that I wanted to say yes, and not just because of his Kai proximity.

"That's kind of you, but I just can't swing it right now," I said. "I wish I could."

"Got it, no problem," he replied affably. "But my offer stands if anything changes on your end."

"I appreciate it. Thanks again for everything."

"Yeah, thanks from me as well," Meredith shouted from the couch.

Owen chuckled. "I heard that. No problem, tell her I said heal fast. And you take care, Brooke."

He hung up before I could say anything else.

"Well, that was super nice of him to check in personally, but I don't think it was all for me," Meredith said with a teasing lilt in her voice.

"It *was* nice." I ignored her subtext as I settled back in front of my laptop.

"So how much are lessons?" she asked.

"Way too much."

"Private lessons with me at Harmony are one twenty-five per hour," she offered.

"It's more," I said as I tried to refocus on the last paragraph I'd written about a visit from Austin's veterinarian ex-girlfriend.

"Hmm," Meredith said as she reached for her phone. "I mean, private instruction of *any* kind in Manhattan is pricey. Wanna learn how to roll sushi? Teach your kid violin? Arrange flowers? Pay up."

"Remind me again why I live here?" I grumbled as I cupped my chin in my hand and stared at my blinking cursor.

"Because you love everything about this city."

It was true; I did. Even the relentlessness of summer, which perfumed the air with hot garbage.

A few seconds later, a text pinged through, which reminded me that I needed to silence my phone. I reached over and tipped it with one finger so I could see who it was from, because picking it up fully would lure me into scrolling.

I turned around and asked Meredith, "Why are you texting me when I'm right here?"

"Read it."

I clicked on the link in the message. "*What?* You bought me the lessons? I can't accept this!"

She Cheshire cat grinned at me. "I said yes for you."

"Meredith . . ."

"I knew you were going to be mad, so here's the deal: I did it partly because I'm going to need to lean on you over the next few weeks, literally in some scenarios. Colton is in the middle of his busiest quarter at work, which means that he's not going to be around as much, so consider the lessons a little thank-you in advance for helping me."

"For fuck's sake, that's not an equal exchange for me running to get you glasses of water now and then. And it's not like you're incapacitated; it's a *boot*. You'll be thumping around in no time."

She held up her hand to silence me. "You didn't let me finish—there's more. Now, I *know* you have another Brooke Murphy book inside of you, so once you finally shift your focus back to writing for yourself and sell a book under your own name, then you can pay me back. But *only* then. Deal?"

Meredith had always been sneaky generous, from sharing pizzas with toppings that I preferred to staying up after a long shift at the Hickory Bar to read through my latest manuscript before I submitted it. I did my part by always washing the pots she left piled in the sink without complaining and letting Colton crash at our place.

"Mere, there's no way I can—"

"The lessons are nonrefundable," she cut me off. "So you better use them."

I bottled up my mixed emotions and jumped out of my chair to run over and hug her.

"Watch the leg, watch the leg." She laughed as I knelt down next to the futon and wrapped my arms around her.

"You're the best. I owe you." I moved back on my heels and smiled at her.

"All you owe me is a book and some good horny stories from when you and Kai hook up."

"Yes! Speak it into existence." I traced an arc in the air above my head.

I wasn't exactly thrilled that I was going to be exposing my lack of skills to Mr. Hat, but after feeling hollowed out after the breakup, he was my express ticket to word count.

Chapter Seven

I was a morning person when it came to everything but sports.

Getting up early for sexy times, eating, writing, shopping, or travel? No problem. But getting up to do anything that required coordination beyond making my pour-over coffee was out of the question. Unfortunately, the seven o'clock slot was all Owen could offer me. I was free to pick any day of the week but only at that heartless time.

I'd obviously opted for Thursday, since I was now two-for-two on Thursday Kai sightings. I knew it was unlikely I'd run into him at the crack of dawn, and when Owen met me at the front door to unlock it for me, I realized that it was downright impossible. My first lesson would be Kai-free, but maybe I could bring my laptop to the next one and then spend the rest of the day using the fancy coworking space in the hopes of running into him again?

Yeah, it was weird, but I was on a mission.

"Good morning," Owen said as he stepped out of the way to let me in. "Welcome to the first day of your new obsession."

For now, I was fine with letting him think that my true obsession was the game and not the player.

"Good morning," I answered as brightly as I could, given

my grogginess and nerves. I looked around at the empty space. "Are we the first ones here or . . . ?"

"Yup," he answered as he locked the door behind me. "We're not open yet, so it'll be just us for a bit."

Owen was wide-awake, bucket hatted, and completely focused on me. He was in green basketball shorts, and he'd branched out in the T-shirt department, this time in a black Wimbledon 2014 option, which, judging by the holes scattered at the seams, had clearly seen lots of action. I still couldn't understand how such an integral member of the Chelsea Pickleball Academy team could write his own dress code. The other employees I'd encountered the two times I'd visited, from the people running food to the front desk staff, all looked ready for an Insta feature. I assumed that he was a good enough coach that he could sweet-talk his way into doing what he wanted.

Walking into the space without the sound of paddles thwacking balls and only half of the lights on made it feel eerie. I shot a glance at Owen, hoping that he wasn't a pickleball-playing serial killer.

I shook my head. Impossible. The meanest thing about him was probably his serve.

"I see you're ready to go." He nodded at my borrowed outfit, a different pleated white skort that was actually pretty cute on me. Wasted, though, because Kai wouldn't see me in it. "Do you want to drop your stuff in the locker room?"

I held up my small black duffel bag, which only contained my wallet, keys, and water bottle. "I'm good. Ready to start when you are."

Because the clock was ticking. I had a check-in call scheduled with Piper later today and I needed to crank out some words beforehand, so I could report semi-honestly about my progress. When it came to Austin and Abby, I was still running on fumes.

"Okay, let's get you set up with a paddle," he said. "Or do you already have one?"

I showed him my empty hands. "I have nothing, not even coordination."

"Stop," he chastised gently, smiling at me. "You're going to do great."

I knew better.

A few minutes later, I was following him with a paddle in hand to the only courts with the overhead lights on above them. I cursed Meredith for forcing me into a scenario where an expert was going to be watching every move I made and then *critiquing* it all. I was self-conscious enough about my lack of grace without focused concentration looking for areas that needed improvement.

"Tell me about your background," Owen said, fixing his gaze on me and spinning his paddle in his hand. "What type of sports have you played?"

I grimaced. "None?"

He laughed good-naturedly, like I was joking. In a few minutes, he'd see the reason why for himself.

"What about workouts? What's your preference?"

"Also none."

Admitting it out loud made me feel soft and not in a moisturized way. In an I-have-no-idea-what-kettlebells-are-for way.

"Wow, okay." He nodded. "Absolute beginner status, got it. So what drew you to pickleball?"

He watched me with a look that suggested what I said next would direct everything we did together. I hadn't been smart enough to come up with a cover story, and admitting that I was chasing a crush on a stranger in order to find my muse would make me look certifiable.

"Uh . . . the social aspect?"

"Got it. You're in the right place; pickleball is a great way to meet new people."

I breathed a sigh of relief. First hurdle crossed.

"This sport is all about community," he continued. "I don't offer group classes, but after we finish up, you might want to take some with Brandon. He's basically the social director around here."

I wasn't about to admit right off the bat that the lessons were nothing more than a four-week fast track to Kai.

"Good to know," I replied.

Owen moved a little closer to me. "Okay, first we're going to talk grip. I noticed that's what was tripping you up a couple of weeks ago, and it's a foundational aspect that I obsess about. I'm a firm believer in focusing on the basics. The worst thing you can do is start your pickleball journey with bad habits and then try to unlearn them." The corner of his mouth turned up. "That's why I love newbies like you. Clean slate."

I felt heat rush to my cheeks at being appreciated for my beginner status, possibly for the first time ever.

"They call me the Big Gripper around here for a reason," he continued. "Connecting your hand to your tool the right way is the first piece of the puzzle. Show me what you've got." He nodded to my paddle.

It felt like a pop quiz, and I wanted to prove that I was a good student. I mimicked what he'd shown me the first time I came and gripped the paddle so tightly my forearm tensed.

"Nice, that's a perfect Continental grip. You're halfway there."

He nodded. "But are you trying to murder that paddle? Loosen up that hypergrip. Gimme some Satan fingers."

Owen held out his paddle and released his pinkie and pointer fingers, which made him look like he was a metalhead at a concert. "Rock and roll." He gently closed his fingers around the paddle again.

If I couldn't get something as simple as how to grip right, I was in trouble. I felt like I was *already* fucking up. Typical. I loosened my choke hold and mimicked him.

"Yes, there it is." He nodded. "Let's put it to work. Swing time. Now, if you had a tennis background—"

"Which I definitely don't," I interrupted.

"Right," Owen continued. "But if you did, we'd have to work on getting rid of your backswing, because a lot of the action in pickleball is out here." He swirled the air in front of him. "To start off, all we're going to do is . . . *push* the ball." He swept his paddle in a graceful arc. "Try it. *Push*."

His voice softened as he said the word, like gentling his tone translated to the swing of his paddle.

I started off by accidentally strangling my paddle again, then corrected myself, and tried to look graceful as I moved it through the air. I watched him carefully as he observed me, preemptively flinching, because even though he was trying to hide it, I could tell by his expression that I was doing it wrong.

As usual.

"Not bad," Owen lied. "But *where's* the action?"

Another quiz, and I was ready. "Here." I circled the air like he just demonstrated.

"Yes! The stuff back here?" He stuck his hand out to the side, then moved it backward, like he was winding up to hit a little yellow ball into the next dimension. "At this point, it's unnecessary. We just need to connect with the ball and . . . *push*. Easy. Now you."

Owen nodded to me and I commenced with pretending to hit a fake ball and feeling dorky.

"So close." He frowned a little, and I felt a familiar dread creep through me at my inability to copycat. "One more, with *all* of your action up front."

How could I be failing already? I tried again.

"Yes, you're almost there," Owen cheered like I was a baby trying to feed myself a strand of spaghetti. "Hold on a sec."

He jogged the few steps over and came to a stop about a foot behind me, close enough that I could almost *feel* him there. "Now swing."

I turned abruptly. Pickleball wasn't a contact sport, but he was close enough to me that if I brought my paddle back, I'd . . . And the genius of his little lesson dawned on me.

"Okay, now I get it." I chuckled. I walked forward a few steps.

"Nope." He moved with me, like my shadow. "I'm going to haunt you right here until I see it. I'm risking bodily harm to help you get your swing right."

In a way, it was easier to pantomime playing without him staring me down, although he was close enough for me to catch the scent of soap on his skin.

I fought against every instinct to draw my paddle back, because if I did, I'd smack him in the dick, and pushed it forward instead.

"Yes! *There* it is. Again," he shouted, ridiculously close to my ear.

I felt a little swell of pride as I repeated the motion.

"Nice! Now let's try it with a ball."

Owen jogged to the ball basket next to the court and then got into position opposite me beyond the net.

"Just a little push," he coached as he dropped the ball and hit it so it landed right in front of me.

How the ball ended up whizzing past Owen once my paddle connected with it was a mystery, because I'd even chanted "just a push, just a push" in my head as I reached for it.

"Well, you've got some power going for you, but you don't need it yet." He chuckled. "Let's try it again, but this time, *push*. Everything is happening right in front of you; no need to crank it back."

And so we continued for another ten minutes, with both sides of the court getting increasingly frustrated. I either missed the ball completely or got too excited when I sensed that I was actually going to hit it and bombed it past him.

No surprise, I was hopeless.

"All good." Owen stalked over to me, his easygoing expression now a smidge tighter. "We're gonna downshift for a bit. Grab a ball."

I picked up one of the many littering my side of the court.

"I think we jumped in a little too quickly. Our focus now is going to be basic paddle and ball handling. Try this."

In any other scenario, I would've taken advantage of the low-hanging fruit of him saying "ball handling," but I was too in my head to joke around.

Owen held his paddle horizontally in front of him, dropped the ball onto it, and bounced it rhythmically, keeping his body still except for the hand holding the paddle. He made it look easy, like the ball was connected with a short elastic string, so that it smacked the exact same spot on the paddle over and over. It was the sort of drill he'd probably use for kids just figuring out their hand-eye coordination.

Still, I went along with it and managed three bounces before the ball ricocheted away from me. Clearly *I* was the kid still figuring it out.

"Again," Owen said in a tight voice. "Keep at it."

I sighed, grabbed another ball, and attempted to not flail. I was having even less fun than I'd imagined.

"What's that pointer finger doing?" Owen chastised as I awkwardly attempted to keep control of the ball. "This isn't Ping-Pong."

I realized my finger had migrated off the handle to the paddle part, and the shift back to the proper position caused the ball to fly away again.

Owen was decidedly less teddy bear now. He watched me, wearing a frown that suggested he was regretting finding a spot on his calendar for me.

"You're very tight," he said as he gestured up and down my body with his paddle. "Your forearm is flexed, which means you're death-gripping the paddle again, and that's why you can't keep control of the ball. When we play, we need to be loose . . . easy . . . soft. But it's okay. We'll work this foundation stuff until you master it. We've got *plenty* of time."

My frustration at myself boiled over when the ball flew from my paddle for the billionth time.

"But I *don't* have time," I complained. "I need to be out there, playing like I know what I'm doing, ASAP!"

My voice echoed around the empty space.

Owen regarded me in silence for a moment as the last bits of cheerful, encouraging coaching drained away. "Okay. Explain. Why are you really here?"

Chapter Eight

His suspicious expression made me regret my blurt.

Suddenly, the club felt airless, and the hum of the overhead lights had the same annoying, barely audible whine as bug zappers.

I stood motionless with my paddle hanging limply at my side, trying to come up with a reason why I needed to fast-track my lessons. Making up stories was what I did for a living, so why couldn't I spin a convincing juke that would keep Owen from thinking I was an obsessed stalker?

But he was also my conduit. If I was honest with Owen, maybe he'd figure out a way to broker a game with Kai?

My desperation must've telegraphed across my face, because he softened as he studied me. "Is it a work thing? You need to brush up on your skills so you can play with clients or something?"

I bit the inside of my cheek as I considered how much to tell him. He looked worried, like he was as invested in my quest to master the sport as I was, no matter the reason. In the past hour, I'd experienced a couple different versions of Owen: a supportive, you-can-do-it coach and a hard-driving taskmaster. I liked this new side of him, the one reassuring me that we're a team and we've *got* this.

"I'm a writer," I began slowly. "I've been writing romances for a few years now. Cowboy romances."

Owen bobbed his head. "Very cool. I'm a big reader. Where can I check out your work?"

My heart melted a little at his question. Most guys made jokes about "mommy porn" when I mentioned what I did for a living. Even Leo had asked to read "just the dirty parts" of my books. I'd quickly schooled him about the clean/dirty debate in the romance world, making sure that he understood that "spicy" was a much better descriptor, since sex wasn't inherently dirty.

Although sometimes it was, in the best possible way.

"Online mostly. They're ebooks," I explained, without mentioning that I wrote under a pen name. "Anyway, I've been in a rut lately. I had a bad breakup, and getting into the right headspace to create happily ever afters has basically been impossible for me."

The corners of his mouth turned down. "Oh, wow. Sorry to hear that."

"Thanks. I have a deadline coming up fast, so I'm sort of desperate to find some inspiration."

Owen eyed me suspiciously. "And *pickleball* is going to inspire your writing? Kind of a stretch, but okay. I'm down to help you get where you need to be."

Part of me didn't want to admit that I was only into the game for the vibes and not the love of the sport. It seemed shallow, and as much as I never wanted to be *that* girl, it felt very pick me. I was pretending to be into pickleball to attract a guy's attention. Still . . . desperate times. A deadline. Bills. I forced myself to keep going.

"You know that guy you teach on Thursdays? Kai?"

Owen took off his hat and smoothed his hair back. I tried not to stare, because it was the first time I'd seen him without his ubiquitous hat, and I was shocked by how good he looked naked headed. The mullet-esque section that looked a little scrubby peeking out the back was actually luxurious in its full glory. Thick, wavy chestnut hair that was so healthy I wanted to ask what kind of shampoo he used.

"Kai Dorset? What about him?" Owen asked warily as he pulled the hat back on.

His last name—another piece of the puzzle.

I cleared my throat. "It turns out he's sort of like . . ." I steeled myself to admit it out loud. "My muse. Or he's going to help me *find* my muse. Or a combination of both. I hope."

It came out sounding even weirder than I'd imagined.

Owen shook his head like he couldn't process what I was saying. "*How?* Do you even know him?"

"I don't actually, and that's where all of this comes in." I gestured around us with my paddle. "I figured if I could get good at pickleball, it would be an easy in with him. A meet-cute. And once we're hanging out, hello inspiration."

A beat while Owen furrowed deeper and considered what I'd just revealed to him.

"So you're only learning how to play pickleball to meet a guy you have a crush on? A stranger. And that's going to fix your writer's block?"

Yeah, it definitely sounded worse spoken out loud. My face went hot at getting called out by him.

"It's hard to explain," I said slowly, gathering the nerve to reveal myself. "Have you ever met someone, and you feel this immediate *bam* reaction to that person? It's a connection you can't explain, like everything around you is fuzzy and they're the only thing in focus. It doesn't make sense, but all you want to do is stare at them. Be close to them. You're intoxicated with the very *idea* of that person. In book world, it's called insta-love."

Owen's expression went even more skeptical.

"Hold on—you're in *love* with Kai?"

"Oh no, not at all." I laughed, hoping to dial down the strangeness of the conversation. "In this scenario, it's more like insta-attraction, not love. Trust me, I'm not ready for anything heavier than that. Ever since my breakup, I've felt like my heart is in hibernation."

Owen's jaw flexed as he stared down at the paddle in his hand. "Got it."

As awkward as it felt revealing myself to him, I pushed on to finish, hoping that I might be able to tidy up the mess I was making on court thirteen.

"When I ran into Kai, it was this, like, full-body-sparks kind of sensation. This indescribable pull to get to know him. Totally weird, I know." I paused. "Has that ever happened to you?"

Owen flipped his paddle around a couple of times, still not looking at me. "Yeah. I'm familiar with the sensation."

"Okay, then you get it," I exclaimed, relieved that he understood the free-falling feeling. "It doesn't make sense when you try to put it into words, but when it comes to the heart, what does?"

"Have you had an actual conversation with Kai?" He shuffled in place as he seemed to digest my strangeness.

I wrinkled my nose, feeling very called out. Somehow, Owen managed to zero in on fault lines in my fantasy.

"Sort of? You were there for the extent of both of them."

"Do you want me to just introduce you to him? Might be

easier that way, since you don't seem to be enjoying the lesson," Owen said gruffly.

My face went hot, because I didn't want him to feel bad about his instruction. Sure, I could tell that Owen was a little frustrated with me since I wasn't the easiest student, but he'd kept finding ways to switch things up, to make the best of what little I had to offer skills-wise. He was a great teacher; it was the student side of the equation that was the problem.

"Oh my gosh, I hope I didn't come across that way!" I replied quickly. "It's not you; it's me. I'm a mess when it comes to sports, as you're well aware of by now."

"No, I disagree." Owen narrowed his eyes at me for a moment, and I felt even more exposed, because the guy seemed to notice everything. "You're overthinking everything—*that's* your problem. It's not an abilities issue. Your head game is off."

He was being way too kind.

"Oh, come on, it's more than that." I chuckled.

"So do you want me to just introduce you to Kai or not?"

Owen sounded peevish, like he now thought that I was wasting his time with my dating drama. Maybe I didn't make it clear enough to him that my career was hinging on my heart status?

"I mean . . . yeah, that would be great. If we can do it in a way that's not too obvious. Could we arrange a game this week? Like, you and me on one team and him and someone else on the other team?"

Owen threw back his head and let out a throaty laugh that didn't sound at all joyful. "Yeah, *no*. Kai takes his game very seriously; he only plays with people who have a skill rating over 4.0."

The number meant nothing to me so I pushed on.

"Okay, how about a casual, accidental hang here, then? Like, I could swing by when you have a lesson with him, and we could all grab smoothies afterward."

"Sure, I could try to arrange that," Owen said. "But he did tell me that he's got no time for dating right now. His work is intense, plus he's training for a tournament out west in the fall. He's pretty focused on that."

"So you're telling me it's hopeless." I felt my shoulders sag.

"Not necessarily," Owen replied flatly. "You're right; the best way in is definitely through pickleball. If you commit to practicing, I can help you get to a point where you could hold your own, and then I could engineer a game with him."

"In four weeks?" I asked. "What are you, a miracle worker?"

He spun his paddle like he was a Wild West gunslinger. "Sort of. But you'd have to come twice a week at least."

"But I'm not a member, and I'm maxed out with these four lessons," I reminded him.

He glanced around the space, then back at me. "If you can be here before we open, Tuesdays and Thursdays are yours for the next four weeks."

"You mean three weeks, since my first lesson is already over."

He waved his hand through the air dismissively. "It's fine. I can do four. I guess the question is, can *you*?"

I straightened my back. "Whatever it takes."

Owen frowned at me. "You're really into Kai, huh?"

"As of now, I'm into the *idea* of him," I replied quickly. "I'm assuming he'll live up to my hype. You'd know that better than me at this point. Is he a good guy?"

"He's fine, I guess," Owen said with a shrug. "Great player. Always on time. Obviously very good-looking."

A shrill bark echoed around us, and Owen glanced over his shoulder to the offices.

"That's Marti. She needs to take a walk. Gimme a sec and we'll head out with you."

"You're dog friendly here?" I asked as he jogged away.

He turned around and jogged backward, something he'd told me during the lesson was a pickleball no-no. "Not really, but Martina doesn't care about the rules."

I tried to envision what sort of dog Owen could have and settled on something big and goofy, like a Rottie or pit bull. The scruffy little purse dog that skittered across the courts to check me out was the last breed I expected to meet.

"Well, hello, you!" I dropped to my knees to try to pet the pup as she barked and spun in circles. "She's so cute! What's her mix?"

Owen watched her proudly. "A chihuahua-terrier combo, rescued from a hoarder. Best dog in the world."

Marti was chihuahua-sized, with brown-and-white wiry fur and the most impressive muttonchops and mustache combo I'd ever seen. She had the sort of crazed expression that suggested she had a lot of opinions about everything and needed to express them all, right this minute.

The little dog finally stopped barking and spinning and allowed me to rub her shoulders. She panted up at me, leaning against my hand.

"If you don't stop petting her, she's never going to let you leave," Owen cautioned. "Hey, Marti, suit up. Let's walk."

Owen pulled a leash from the pocket in his shorts and clicked the clasp a couple of times, which woke Marti from her trance. She ran over to him and danced on her back legs. He scooped her up, clipped the leash onto her navy harness, and gave her a quick kiss on top of the head before setting her on the ground again.

They were adorable together. Tall, solid Owen and sassy, little Marti, who walked in front of him like she was a protection dog and not actually appetizer-sized.

"Ready?" Owen asked me. "I want you to take a paddle and a couple of balls home with you. Work on those forehand and backhand drills."

"Pickleball *homework*?" I laughed as I put the paddle I'd been using in my bag. "I thought this was supposed to be fun."

Owen either didn't hear me or he pretended that he didn't. I joined them on the way to the lobby, where the morning shift employees were just filing in.

"Morning, Grip; hey, Marti." A couple of them saluted the pair with their coffee cups as they passed by.

Owen turned to me once we were out on the sidewalk, pausing to let Marti sniff the base of an overfull garbage can.

"If you're serious about getting good, I can help you," he said, fixing me with a stare that felt sharper than the way he'd been watching me during the rest of our lesson. "But you need to commit. And you need to stop going on and on about how you're not athletic."

I snorted lightly. "But it's the *truth*. I'm a realist."

"Nope." Owen fixed his dark eyes on me. "What we tell ourselves forms our reality. You keep saying you're clumsy and hopeless, and you *will* be—I promise you that. From now on, your new mantra is 'I'm a work in progress.'"

I smiled at his accidental symmetry. "I'm a WIP, huh? That's what writers call our unfinished books. I like it."

He ignored my attempt at levity. Now that he knew I had a goal and a deadline, his entire persona seemed to have shifted to all business. "I know it's short notice, but can you meet this Sunday morning?"

"Is that going to count as one of my four actual lessons or . . . ?"

Owen frowned at me. "I told you not to worry about it. If you can be flexible, I'll slot you in wherever." He paused. "As long as you're enjoying the lessons. The second it's not fun, you need to rethink this whole plan."

I didn't let on that our first lesson hadn't exactly been a party. But there'd been moments when Owen had praised me for managing to get the ball over the net that made me feel a little glowy inside. I'd been frustrated enough to contemplate giving up a couple of times, only to get an obscure Owen compliment for something like my foot placement or ball focus, and it was enough to keep me going.

"I'm in it to win it," I replied. "We're going to have a blast."

Owen watched me for a beat longer like he was a police interrogator waiting for me to crack. I nodded hard, smiling so wide that my cheeks hurt.

It was my most harebrained scheme yet, and he'd been roped in as my unwilling accomplice. He finally nodded back at me.

I was on my way.

Chapter Nine

Piper's unsmiling face on the Zoom call made me jittery, because I wasn't great at lying. I felt like she could see my duplicity as I faked enthusiasm for Austin and Abby's story.

I did love them—I loved *all* the characters in my books—but I still couldn't connect with them, which meant our sexy little threesome was stuck on the front porch.

Luckily, I was alone in the apartment, so Meredith couldn't critique my on-screen performance. She was back at Harmony, teaching despite the giant, clunky boot.

"So when do you think you'll be able to get some pages to me?" Piper asked. She took her black-rimmed glasses off to wipe the lenses, which made her face look like an unfinished painting. The Superman/Clark Kent phenomenon was real, because I could only see Piper as my editor when she had her glasses on. With them off, she looked as kindly as a kindergarten teacher, all swoopy bun and pink cheeks. But once the glasses went back on, *business*.

"I'm getting there." I clumsily sidestepped the question.

I'd never missed a deadline or questioned an edit in all my years of working with Liaison, which made me assume that I had a bank of goodwill I could withdraw from when necessary. Piper's expression suggested otherwise.

"Brooke, I need a firm date," she said, her clipped accent making it sound like an order. "We can give you a little wiggle room on the first 10K but only if it doesn't alter your final due date."

Liaison ran on efficiency. The category romance world was simultaneously ravenous and oversaturated, so in order to capitalize on their readership, Liaison needed to churn out books at a breakneck speed. Missing a writing deadline could push a book's release date back, and a lapse meant that our readers might wander off to find a horseback HEA from a different publisher and leave us in the dust.

Not only that, but my output directly impacted the rest of the team. Beta readers, line edits, the cover design, foreign translations, social media content—all of it was mapped out nearly to the hour on Pro Depot, our project management platform. I was used to seeing green next to my name, not an angry bloodred.

"I can get something to you by the tenth," I replied before I could second-guess if it was the truth.

I padded in what I hoped was enough extra time past my actual deadline, banking on the fact that I could muster up a thousand words a day. My eyes landed on the paddle and ball sitting on the edge of the coffee table, where I left them after my lesson.

Piper sighed and leaned slightly off-screen to write something down. "Okay, I suppose we have to make that work."

"I'm so sorry; I feel terrible about the delay," I said in a rush. I decided that the best course of action was honesty after never venturing much past the "How was your weekend?" version of small talk. "I've just been in a bad place, uh, mentally lately. Writing has been really hard for me."

We were colleagues a couple of time zones apart, not friends, so exposing myself felt awkward. I braced for her no-nonsense "keep calm and carry on" response.

"Oh, Brooke. I'm very sorry to hear that. Why didn't you *tell* me?"

I paused to process, because Piper's expression had transformed from taskmaster to maternal concern.

"I thought I could power through." I shrugged. "I've never dealt with writer's block before, and I just assumed that I'd get back to normal once . . ."

Once my heart healed.

"Once I rediscovered my muse," I finished. "I'm getting there; it's just been bumpy."

"I'm sorry to hear that you've been struggling. In any other scenario, we'd make adjustments to account for you needing time," Piper explained. "But this book is already well underway and to make major changes now will have a cascading effect on the rest of the timeline."

"Of course," I said quickly. "I totally understand."

"Related, there's something else I wanted to address on this call in addition to your current timetable."

I swallowed hard and tried to keep my face expressionless as I waited for what had to be a bombshell. My hands went clammy.

"I recognize the timing isn't ideal considering you're having a rough go right now, but we're wondering if it would be possible for you to write books two and three in this series at the same time, once you finish this one?" Piper asked. "We're looking to release them back-to-back."

My mouth dropped open. Here I was, staring into an endless white space that was my current output, and the thought of trying to write *two more* books in my state of mind felt like diving headfirst into that vast unknown.

"There's no pressure to give me an answer now," she continued. "And if it's not possible for you, we can assign one or both to Janet Li. She's looking to transition out of mafia romance."

I snapped my mouth shut. I knew that I wasn't the only Dakota Sinclair—the pen name had been churning out books for close to ten years—but for the past couple, I'd been the only contracted version of her. I still needed to find my way as Brooke Murphy, writer, but for now I felt comfortable living in Dakota's skin.

I wasn't sure I wanted to share her with another writer, but I also didn't know if I had the inspo to churn out *three* back-to-back, no-breathing-room cowboy romances given my current output.

Plus, if I was being totally honest with myself . . . I was sort of tired of writing side plots about sick cows, irrigation issues, and land disputes. I felt myself yearning for a world where the stakes were different. Bigger and less tied to scary real-world shit like climate change and predatory rancher billionaires.

But Dakota was my port in the very unpredictable storm that was the publishing industry. I wanted to write, I *needed* to write, and doing it as Dakota was the only way my work got out there. And without Liaison pushing me, well, I worried that I'd stop writing fiction altogether.

"Wow, that's quite a shift in production. If it's okay with you, I'd like to give that some thought?" I asked.

"Of course," Piper said. "We're roughing out the calendar now, so just keep an eye on Depot as we firm up the dates." She paused. "We plan to release them in quick succession no matter what, so please don't feel pressure if it's not going to work for you. We'd love to have you write them, but we understand if it's too much."

I'm sure she didn't mean for it to sound like a threat. She probably thought that the fact that they had a plan B would take the pressure off me, but all I heard was *You're replaceable*.

"Okay," I said in my cheeriest voice. "I'll get back to you either way soon. And I promise you'll get some Austin and Abby vibes from me in a week. I have a good feeling."

My gaze landed on the pickleball paddle again.

"Lovely," Piper replied. "Looking forward to it. Talk soon, *ta*."

Instead of stewing about the Liaison drama, I felt drawn to grab the paddle and ball. A couple of meditative bounces would be a good energy shift from the tension of the call to the stress of the blank page.

Of course, I managed two bounces before the ball fell off my paddle and rolled away. I dropped to my knees to retrieve it from under the futon. A text sounded out from my back pocket when I was contorted with my arm stretched out and my ass in the air.

It was Owen, like he could sense my sorry attempt at coordination.

> Hey. Good session this morning.
> Don't forget to practice.

I held up the paddle, snapped a pic of it with my bookshelf fuzzy in the background, and sent it to him.

> Nice. And a color-coded bookshelf? Scared of you. I looked up your name and couldn't find any of your books. Where are they available?

I usually didn't tell people about Dakota, seeing as I was contractually bound to keep it a secret, but Owen didn't strike me as the type to out me on a Goodreads forum.

> I write as Dakota Sinclair. Shh, don't tell!

> A pen name, got it. Which one should I read first?

I frowned at my phone. He was serious about reading one of my books?

> Definitely The Hart Ranch Brothers Book One; Rogue Cowboy.

I blushed when I remembered the extended sixty-nine scene after Trent and Eliza's midnight skinny-dip. How was I going to look him in the eye once he knew I'd written the phrase "come on my tongue, you sweet girl"?

> Done. See you Sunday.

I put my phone down and picked up the paddle, deciding that I'd keep practicing until I was able to do ten bounces in a row.

Twenty minutes later, I was a WIP that made it to twelve.

Chapter Ten

A broken lock and lax building management meant that Meredith and I had secret rooftop access. We could tell that a few other tenants in the building were aware of it as well, based on the cigarette butts that occasionally appeared (and we cleaned up), but we'd never run into anyone else, so we considered it our private oasis.

It was a generous descriptor since the space wasn't cute or even all that comfortable, especially in the summer. The heat forced us to sit in the shadows of an ancient wood water tower, near the peaked skylight over the staircase and a big metal humming box. Still, we made the most of it, stringing up some star-shaped, solar-powered lights Meredith had found at IKEA and stashing our beach chairs behind the box.

Thanks to a break in the weather, it was the perfect night to picnic with our dinner takeout, courtesy of Colton. I'd been worried about his ability to step up when Meredith got hurt, seeing as he was a quintessential handsome good-time guy, but he'd gone all out since her accident. I was a happy beneficiary of the bouquets and takeout meals dotting our apartment.

"Mere told me you had your first lesson with the Big Gripper," Colton said. He was forced to sit on a blanket since we only had two roof chairs. "How was it?"

I held up a finger as I chewed my massive bite of falafel sandwich. I'd been trying to figure out how I felt about the lesson, because Owen had made me question a long-held truth about myself; maybe I *wasn't* hopeless when it came to sports? Of course, my performance at lesson number one was downright embarrassing, but it was his insistence about the mental side of the game that made me wonder if maybe I could mind over matter my way to passable skills?

"I thought he was just this big, friendly dude, but he's sort of a taskmaster," I answered.

Colton nodded as he threw back a Modelo. "Yeah, I've heard he has a split personality. Nicest guy in the real world but a killer on the court, both as a player and instructor. He played tennis at Princeton and he was *really* good, so I guess you can't get away from that kind of drive."

"Oh, one hundred percent," Meredith said as she shifted and propped her boot up on the wall next to her. "For me, the hardest part of moving from dance auditions to teaching Pilates was letting go of feeling like I had to 'win' every class. I still get a little bit of that competitive feeling even now when I'm in a room of other instructors. Striving to be the best becomes a part of your DNA."

I was tangentially aware of that drive, thanks to Wes and my parents, but I'd never come close to experiencing it for myself. We'd all figured out that my role in the family was sidelines cheerleader. I even refused to do anything ball-centric in the yard with Wes and my dad growing up, because every casual game somehow turned into real competitions, and all I had to offer was comic relief.

"Did you have fun?" Colton asked.

I tipped my head as I considered it. "Um, not exactly? But I'm on a mission, so . . ."

"Right." Colton nodded. "Meredith told me. That Kai guy. Talk about a killer on the courts."

"Don't say that," I griped as I fell back against my chair. "I need to feel like I have a chance to play with him."

"Hey, if anyone can get you there, it's Grip. Just do everything he says and you should be golden."

I'd actually been putting in the work in preparation for our second lesson in just twelve hours. My forehand paddle skills had improved to me doing twenty ball juggles in a row, but my backhand was still dicey. My perfectionist tendencies meant that any time I had a writing lull I found myself reaching for the paddle to practice, which I discovered was sort of the equivalent of squashing a stress ball.

"How much did you write today?" Meredith asked. "Is breathing the same air as your crush at CPA helping?"

The corner of my mouth turned up. "Yeah, I guess it sort of is. I managed to plow through a healthy thousand words that I don't hate."

"Any spice?" Colton waggled his eyebrows at me.

I shook my head. "Sadly, no. Austin is currently dealing with a fence line dispute with the ranch next door."

"And how's the brainstorming going for your next Brooke book, hmm?" Meredith asked as she polished off her shawarma.

Colton swiveled to look at me. "You're going to write a book under your own name?"

"Yes, she is," Meredith answered for me. "Brooke has an outstanding balance at the Bank of Waxman, and the only accepted payment is in the form of a book deal advance."

I reached for a second beer, which was a bad idea considering how early I needed to be up. "I might have a rough concept."

"Wait, *what*?" Meredith slammed her hands on her beach chair armrests and screeched at me, causing the pigeons congregating above us to fly away. "You do? Tell me everything!"

The idea had come to me in the shower, which happened frequently enough to make me consider buying a waterproof whiteboard. The concepts didn't stop; it was my willingness to plot them out that was the issue. The moment I tried to flesh out my stories, the self-doubt from the *Truth and Beauty* failure hijacked my creative impulses.

"I don't *know* everything yet; it's just a thunderstorm of thoughts at the moment," I answered. "But it feels very different for me. A new genre." I cocked an eyebrow to build suspense.

"Well?" Meredith rolled her hand in the air to urge me to spill it.

"Romantasy."

"*Ooh*," Meredith and Colton said in unison.

"That's big money," Colton said. "I read an article about some woman who started off self-publishing romantasy stuff, and now she's got, like, an empire. They're making a movie based on her series. Maybe it'll work out the same for you?"

I gave him the same indulgent smile I used on my parents' friends when they asked when someone was going to turn one of my ghostwritten books into a movie. "Sadly, that's the exception, not the rule. If Margo Delgato still hasn't had one of her books adapted, the likelihood for little old me is nil. Her fantasy and romantasy books have been on the bestseller list for *years*. And give me a chance to start writing the darn thing before we start dreaming up getting optioned."

I wasn't convinced that the idea would grow beyond the seedling stage.

"This is perfect," Meredith said. "You're going to finish up *The Rancher's Black Market Baby*, then get to work on this other book."

"Why not both?" I asked, ignoring her purposeful title mangling.

The idea of writing two Liaison books at the same time felt impossible, but somehow my new concept kept edging me closer to attempting a twofer, or if I agreed to write the rest of the cowboy series, a fourfer. The pull to sketch out a few basic plot points had me scribbling ideas in the back of my notebook during sanctioned Austin and Abby time.

"Okay, make it happen, then," Meredith replied, as pushy as ever.

After a dozen false starts with other books, she probably didn't believe that I'd see this one through.

Colton's phone chimed and he paused to read the text. "Here we go. Invitation to the official party of the summer is *secured*."

"Oh, yay, the Hamptons over the Fourth of July holiday." Meredith frowned. "We better leave now if we want to make it on time."

When we'd moved to the city together after college, Meredith and I had done the Hamptons pilgrimage on a few weekends and decided that the overcrowded shared house situation and long lines at the bars weren't for us.

Colton pointed at me. "You're coming too, right?"

Meredith did prayer hands under her chin. "You can be my boot buddy when I want to leave the party early."

"Whose party is it?" I asked.

"A guy from another firm in our building. I don't know him well, but I tapped a few mutual friends to put in the good word for me and now we're in. My boss said we can stay at his place in Sag Harbor for two nights since he's still in France."

"How many other people will be staying there?" I asked. I was too old to subject myself to fighting for sleeping space. "Because I aged out of sharing rooms a million years ago."

"Agreed," Meredith said.

"Aged out? Please, you're not even thirty yet. Anyway, it's just us," he answered. "My boss said he'd kill me if we invited extra people over. Check it out."

Colton scrolled on his phone, then held it out to me. The gray-shingled home in the photos was stunning and plenty big, plus it had a pool.

But I still wasn't in a party frame of mind.

"Honestly, I think I want to just chill over the holiday . . ."

"I believe that someone is still contractually required to say yes," Meredith reminded me. "Plus, I guarantee you'll get tons of inspo during the trip."

I frowned at her. "Please tell me how a ritzy beach town and a Montana ranch are related."

Although we both knew that she was right. Getting me out of the apartment and into new scenarios always turned up something usable, even if it was only an unimportant side plot. But hey, word count was word count.

"Um, hold on you two." Colton looked up from his phone and at me. "I have an update that might change your mind, Brooke."

Meredith and I stared at him.

"The hosts of the party both work for Atria Capital. And you know who else does?"

He held his phone out to me, and there on the screen was a LinkedIn bio for none other than a stupidly handsome Mr. Kai Dorset.

"Okay. I'm in."

Chapter Eleven

"Yes," Owen yelled as the ball bounced next to him. "*Good* serve. Now let's see it five more times in a row with no pauses. Just like that. Go."

He pointed his paddle at me, and I felt like I was in front of a one-man firing squad.

The idea of five repeat performances froze me in place. "Oh, that was a lucky shot. I don't know if I can do it again."

We were working on serving, which felt like an impossible mix of power, pushing, and precision. All I had to do was drop the ball, then hit it across the net to where Owen was standing. So far, my serves had either been landing in the net or on the wrong side of the court. The fact that I'd been able to marry my paddle skills with enough oomph to send the ball over the net and into the correct zone was the exception, not the rule.

Owen frowned at me. "Why can't you say, 'I'll try'? You're a WIP, remember? Your first response is always negging yourself. How about a little positivity?"

I wanted to ask him the same question, because he'd been a drill sergeant since I walked in the door. Sure, Owen praised me—*lightly*—when I managed to do something right, but it was as ephemeral as a soap bubble. A quick "nice" or "good," and then he went back to demanding more.

"I'm a realist," I replied quickly. "I know my limitations."

"Is that a fact?" Owen straightened up out of ready position and dropped his hands to his sides. "Then we might as well quit now."

"*Excuse* me?"

We stood in a silent stalemate in the half-lit space, staring at each other across the net.

"You always say something negative before I can weigh in. Even when you do something amazing, it's like you need to reassure yourself that you'll be back to sucking in no time. Why is that?"

"I'm not good at this sort of stuff; I *told* you that."

My voice echoed around the space. He'd touched a nerve.

Owen walked to the net, studying me like he knew more than he was letting on.

"This isn't about your skills, Brooke. I'm here to help with that part. I mean how you talk about yourself."

I looked down at the paddle in my hand. "Just calling it like I see it. I'm not athletic."

Normally, admitting my athletic shortcomings turned into a punch line, but Owen wasn't about to let me get away with it. And honestly, with two lessons under my belt, it sort of felt like an indictment of *him* as well.

"And how do you define athleticism?" Owen asked.

Visions of my parents with silver thermal blankets wrapped around their shoulders postrace and Wes sprinting down the field with a ball dancing between his feet crowded my thoughts.

"Coordination. Endurance," I answered. "Grit. None of which I have."

And all gifts I'd seen Owen exhibit as we smacked the ball

around, even though he probably handicapped himself to kindergarten level to play with me.

He pulled a ball out of his pocket and lobbed it at me, and through some miracle, I managed to spring into ready position and swat it back in his general vicinity.

"And what was that?" he asked, pointing his paddle at me.

"Luck?"

He threw his head back, let out a frustrated groan, and marched in a circle. *"Seriously?"*

I stomped a few steps closer to where he was having his little fit. "You're supposed to be teaching me how to be a better player, not lecturing me."

"And you're supposed to maintain a positive attitude so you can actually try to accomplish the things I'm showing you."

"Well, I'm not feeling very positive." I could barely hide my frustration.

Owen finally fixed his gaze on me. "Then that's going to be an issue. You might as well kiss Kai goodbye right now."

It was a record scratch during our tense conversation. Owen clearly knew how to drop a name for dramatic effect.

"Are you saying I should give up?"

"Only if you want to." Owen's eyes searched my face. "I'm not about to force you to try to play if your heart isn't in it."

My heart was at the center of the whole ridiculous scenario, but I wasn't about to remind him of the fact.

We both went silent until I snorted out a realization. "Are we really having such a serious conversation about *pickleball*?"

He held my gaze before answering. "It goes deeper than that and I think you know it."

I floundered because I was feeling observed and dissected by someone who was gifted at both. "I don't have coordination."

Owen tossed another ball my way without even looking in my direction—a fake out—and I slapped it back so efficiently that I shocked myself.

"Liar."

My cheeks went hot at the way he was studying me.

"It's like you have a *block* . . ." Owen said, half to himself as he rounded the net and stalked to my side of the court. "Your body is absolutely capable, despite what you keep saying."

I blushed a little harder at the thought of Owen watching my body, which today was in yet another very cute and very tight Meredith hand-me-down skort and tank combo.

"Is your family anti-sports?" he demanded. "You're all too bookish to bother with sweaty stuff?"

I laughed in his face. "Oh my god, no. My parents are big-time runners, and my brother plays professional soccer in England."

"Seriously? Which team?"

"Barnham."

A nod of recognition. "Did they compare you and your brother? Make you feel like you didn't measure up?"

"Absolutely not." I shook my head. "Never."

"So your entire family is athletic, which means you've got to have *some* innate genetic ability. I mean, I've definitely seen glimmers of it, but then it's like your brain shuts you down. Like you're almost afraid to let go and try hard."

I shrugged. Pickleball lessons were somehow morphing into a therapy session that I hadn't signed up for.

"Did you *ever* enjoy sporty stuff? Like at recess or in gym class when you were a kid?" Owen asked in a far gentler voice.

I snorted. "Well, sure. Who doesn't like zombie tag and scooter boards?"

He was unmoved by my attempt at levity.

"What changed? Was it the competition aspect maybe?"

"No." I frowned as I thought back to elementary school gym class. "I kicked ass at the Presidential Fitness Test. No one could beat my flexed arm hang time."

An uncomfortable feeling stirred inside of me. I'd never really considered my anti-sports origin story, but thoughts of my echoey middle school gym came trickling back.

And Mr. Albertson.

It was one of those buried-but-not-forgotten memories, a "yeah, that happened" scenario that I'd let go of once life moved on. But now, given what Owen was dissecting, I let the feelings resurface.

"I think it started when my sixth-grade middle school teacher made fun of the way I ran in front of the entire class."

His face clouded over. *"What?"*

Owen's reaction added some heft to a memory I'd written off.

"Yeah." I nodded, staring across the empty room as the pieces of what had happened swam back into focus. "We were doing some dumb indoor sprinting thing, and right after I had my turn, Mr. Albertson told the class that I looked like a drunk penguin when I ran. And everyone laughed at me."

"A *teacher* said that?" Owen asked with shock in his voice. "Why?"

I huffed out a laugh. "I was a lot back then. Sort of a ringleader. Loud and silly. Probably annoying. Maybe he wanted to—I don't know—take me down a peg? Shut me up? Let me tell you, it worked. Every time he made a crack about me, like calling me 'Little Miss Cement Sneakers,' I wilted. Some of the boys would imitate me in this really obnoxious way. Eventually, I stopped trying."

"That fucker crushed your spirit."

It was an angle I'd never considered.

"I started manufacturing a lot of headaches and stomachaches so I could sit out gym class," I continued. "When I got a little older, I added cramps. And when I was forced to participate, I tried to change the way I ran."

"Is *that* why you do that little skipping thing when I tell you to run toward the net? I thought you were just being cute."

He thought it was *cute*?

"I guess that's my work-around?" I let out a shuddery sigh as all the old self-conscious feelings flooded through me.

"Well, it stops now," Owen said as he pulled his phone out of his shorts. He fiddled with it, and a few seconds later, obnoxious EDM music filled the club. He reached out and grabbed my hand. "C'mon. Let's run."

"What?" I sputtered as he pulled me along. I leaned back and resisted, tripping behind him.

"We're running together," he yelled over the music. "Exposure therapy."

"But . . ."

His hand was gripped around mine, warm and tight. My choices were either to let him drag me along like an unruly puppy on a leash or to kick my pace into overdrive to keep up.

I dropped the nine-dollar pink-and-yellow Amazon paddle I'd bought, which Owen had told me was an insult to the game, and tried to avoid tripping over my own feet.

I felt myself reverting to my usual baby steps, but Owen's tempo was unforgiving. He was flat-out sprinting, so fast that his hat wobbled around on his head. He reached up to fling it off mid-stride, and when he looked back at me over his shoulder, my heart triple-timed.

Up until this moment, I'd never seen him *really* laugh. A few grins, sure, but the way his face transformed into a crinkly, eye-squinting guffaw was so joyful that it was impossible not to laugh with him, despite the way my calves were already shrieking. We probably looked as silly as it felt, dashing around the place like two dorks running from the rain.

The noise must've woken Marti up from her bed in the office, because suddenly she was right there jogging beside us, her barky commentary adding to the insanity of the scene.

The music was loud enough that I could almost feel it in my chest, and I found myself adjusting my pace to the beat with Owen.

"Open up that stride," he coached over the music. "Try to match mine."

As if it was actually possible given the height difference.

There were too many competing sensations to focus on any one, so the fact that we were *holding hands* was buried beneath my need to just keep up. We both could've let go—the closeness was a little overpowering considering we barely knew each other—but for some reason, the sensation of Owen's hand gripping mine was perfect in the moment.

"There she is." Owen chuckled as I started to pull ahead.

Marti cheered me on as well, spinning and barking right next to my feet.

It actually felt shockingly *good* to let go and run without worrying what I looked like. My mom had always told me that our similar builds—ectomorph on the shorter side—meant that I'd be a good marathoner, which had turned into a family joke. *Brooke*, running?

We completed a lap and a half around the entire place, laughing and tripping along, and I finally had to squeeze Owen's hand and slow down to signal I couldn't take much more. The moment he let go, it felt like my tank dropped to empty. I might've been built to run, but I certainly wasn't conditioned for it. I bent over at the waist and braced my hands on my knees, panting.

"Was that okay?" Owen asked. He pulled out his phone and turned off the music.

I glanced up at him and his hopeful, earnest expression made something tangle in my chest. Without the hat, he was a handsome stranger, someone I was meeting for the first time. His dark eyes were full of concern for me, which was a nice break from what I'd been experiencing with him on the court.

"Yeah," I breathed out, still clutching my knees. "But let's not make it a habit, okay?"

"No need at this point, but once you really start honing your basic skills, you'll have to work on conditioning. Believe it or not, pickleball requires endurance."

I straightened up and laughed at the thought of it. "You're really giving me a lot of credit."

Owen shrugged. "You told me you have a goal; I'm going to help you achieve it. It's what I do."

His brow knitted, a microexpression I wouldn't have noticed if he was bucket hatted. I wasn't sure if it was because of the impossibility of helping me get good at pickleball or the reason why I wanted to in the first place.

I hoped he'd forget that his hat was still in a sad mound on the other side of the building from us. I felt privileged seeing all of his face, like he was sharing a secret side of himself with me. I sort of deserved it since I'd just confessed buried childhood trauma to him. The least he could do in return is allow me to take in the full range of his expressions.

Like now. His gaze rested on me with a softness that told me he understood how momentous the lesson had been for me.

"Let's get to it," he said, nodding toward the court. "Time's wasting. I'll put Marti back in the office, otherwise she'll steal the balls."

He scooped up the little dog and kissed the top of her head so quickly that I almost missed it.

I didn't consider spending time with the kinder, gentler Owen Miller wasted time. Now that I knew he existed, I hoped he'd stick around.

We headed back to what was becoming "our" court. Owen detoured to grab his hat, and I was half tempted to tell him to leave it off.

"I started your book last night," he said as he bent over to retrieve my paddle. "I'm *really* enjoying it."

I had my usual seasick reaction to hearing that a new acquaintance was reading one of my horny, feel-good stories.

"Oh, thanks," I replied as my cheeks went warm. "I'm glad."

I wondered if he'd gotten to Trent and Eliza's first kiss. I liked writing slow burns, but once that imaginary boundary between my couples was breached, watch out. *Someone* was getting off.

"I know you're looking to Kai to be your muse, but I have some thoughts that might help you."

He handed over my paddle, then walked away to grab his, leaving me to wonder what editorial insights my pickleball instructor was about to offer me.

Chapter Twelve

"Well, damn, that's the first time you've stopped typing in an hour," my writer friend Nia Bishop said to me over her laptop.

I winked at her as I gulped some water. "Gotta love a sprint."

Which thankfully had been happening quite a bit during our little writing jaunt to Bryant Park. Normally, I wasn't one for writerly dates, but my "say yes" campaign had me agreeing to meet Nia in the park despite the fact that we were surrounded by Ping-Pong, shuffleboard, a knitting club, and a juggling class. If I wanted to be distracted, there were plenty of people-watching opportunities all around me. But the words were flowing for a change, and to my great delight, I'd already knocked out a couple hundred.

For the wrong book.

"How's it going for you?" I asked.

Nia glanced around, then leaned closer to me. "I'm currently researching if a body encased in cement stays intact or if it degrades," she said in a low voice. "Turns out it slows down decomp, but it won't preserve the body indefinitely."

"Well, okay then." I nodded. "I'll file that away for future use."

Nia and I had met on an online "submission commiseration"

group. Our debuts went out to publishing houses at the same time, and while *Truth and Beauty* had died a long, slow death, Nia's debut, a horror novel called *Formido*, scored her a three-book deal at auction. She'd gone on to win a bunch of awards and now had a die-hard fan base that clamored for anything she put out. But her backstory included six unpublished books prior to *Formido*'s success, so I considered her proof that perseverance eventually paid off.

"I need to stop researching and get back to work." She pulled her mirrored sunglasses off and rubbed her eyes. Her dark pixie cut was standing straight up, probably due to the fact that she fussed with it when she was feeling stressed. "I can't believe pantsing works for you. I've plotted an outline for every single beat of this book, and I'm still having a tough time."

"I'm loving the freedom of it," I replied. "I know who my characters are and what they want, so now we're all going on an adventure together as they bicker and fall in love."

Nia propped her chin in her palm and frowned at me. "Maybe I should add some romance to mine?"

"Oh, totally. You've got all the elements of a great love story—stalking, murder, and corpse desecration. A feel-good Hallmark hit for sure."

She pretended to be insulted. "Hey, now hold on a minute. She doesn't consider it desecration; those body parts are *mementos*."

We both chuckled and refocused on our laptops.

I felt the pull to pick up where I'd left off, a welcome but foreign sensation lately. My cowboy books were always a delight, but they weren't truly *my* stories. I was executing someone else's vision, which meant that I didn't always agree with the choices. I'd even gotten in a few email wars with Piper when I tried to push back on unrealistic plot points.

"Do you have a title?" Nia asked, right as my fingers were poised above the keyboard.

I nodded. "I have two in mind: *The Bowstringer's Son* or *The Archer's Paradox*."

"Ooh." Nia's dark eyes widened. "The son one is a little commentary on all of those books with daughter, wife, or girl in the title. Let's go, feminism."

I laughed. Nia's books all featured complicated women doing awful things that her readers loved. Her soon-to-be-published sophomore novel, *Speak Softly*, was about a group of self-proclaimed witches who, depending on your belief system, used either magic or pharmaceuticals to chemically castrate abusive men.

"I'm leaning toward the second," I said. "Since they're both master archers."

Or my hero *would* be, after he completed his training with my heroine. I'd left off with my reclusive, angry lead named Einar meeting his teacher-to-be, Zandria, when she accidentally strayed onto his property while pursuing a parasitic creature called a diogondii.

"So you're cruising on your romantasy, but what's happening with your ghostwriting stuff?" Nia asked me, not realizing that she'd stepped into a minefield.

The vise that lived at the base of my neck cranked a little tighter. "It's, uh, sort of in stasis right now."

I didn't want to spill the whole a-stranger-is-my-muse aspect.

"What's the company again?"

"Liaison Publishing."

Just speaking the name made me feel a little nauseous. I was basically cheating on one of my primary sources of income to work on a book that had no guarantee of going anywhere.

Nia frowned. "Huh. I think I read some stuff on a forum about a dark romance writer not getting paid by them."

"Recently?"

"Not sure," she replied. "I didn't check the date on the post."

Liaison had always been okay about paying me. It took them over thirty days, sometimes closer to forty-five, but the money ended up in my account eventually.

"Maybe other divisions are having problems?"

I hoped so, for the sake of my bills.

Nia let out a long, dramatic sigh. "I'm feeling very uninspired," she said, staring beyond me at the group of older men tossing metal balls in the gravel. "Let's go play pétanque. Or get coffee. Anything but writing, because this is torture."

"I've been living in that very headspace for too long, but I'm actually in a good place right now," I said. "Sorry, not trying to brag."

"Consider me jealous." She pouted. "I'll shut up and do a deep dive on how fast lye dissolves a human body."

"A literal burning question for me as well; please share what you find."

I refocused on the not-blank page on my laptop, settling into the joy of two characters trying to ignore their blistering attraction to each other while jockeying for dominance. My plan had been to write for an hour and then shift to poor, ignored

Austin and Abby, but I couldn't pull myself away from the tension of Einar and Zandria's first contact.

My cowboy would have to wait.

A text came through as I was absolutely cruising through a tense moment of eye fucking. I peeked at it and discovered it was Owen.

We'd been forced to end our Sunday morning session in a rush when the CPA front desk attendant called out sick and Owen had to step in until backup could arrive.

> Just finished Rogue Cowboy. SO good.

I smiled to myself. I loved an unexpected rave. Plus he'd finished insanely fast.

> Thanks! But you said you had thoughts, which I'm sort of terrified to hear. FYI, the book is published so I can't go back and change anything.

> Of course. It's no biggie. I figured since you've got writer's block my idea might help with your WIP.

Adorable that he remembered the acronym.

> Hell yes, I'm listening!

> We can talk about it at our next session. It's sort of out there.

I squinted at my phone. What could he be thinking?

> Very intrigued. Can't wait to hear.

> See you soon. Remember your POSITIVE ATTITUDE.

I laughed softly.
"What?" Nia asked.
"Long story," I answered with a shake of my head.
A long story that was becoming a page-turner.

Chapter Thirteen

"Dinking at the kitchen line," I repeated back to Owen as we walked to our court. "Make it make sense."

He chuckled. "I blame myself for taking so long to get to this part of the game because it's a foundational skill. But then again, our lessons have been unorthodox so far."

Yeah, the therapy session and forced jogging at the last one were definitely not what I'd expected when Meredith signed me up.

The first time I'd visited the Chelsea Pickleball Academy, I'd felt like everyone could tell I didn't belong, as if my lack of skills hovered around me like a cartoon cloud. But being there off-hours, with just Owen and Marti, drained the friction from the place. I didn't have to worry about witnesses; all I had to do was get better. Of course, that presented a different sort of stress, but after the last session, I was feeling slightly more hopeful.

Unfortunately, the hat was back, which meant I'd have to really stare at him to try to decipher how he was feeling. It was almost like the hat was an invisibility cloak to make him look less attractive.

Now that I'd seen him without it, I knew the truth.

"Not only is dinking a critical part of the game, it's also Kai's specialty," Owen said. "If you want to impress him, you need to master this aspect."

As if I didn't already have enough pressure. Owen bringing up Kai refocused me on my mission. Life at the ranch was idling while the clock wound down, meanwhile I couldn't stop returning to Einar and Zandria.

"How's your head?" he asked.

I forced myself not to say "no complaints so far," and in the few seconds that I struggled to come up with a socially acceptable response that didn't reference oral sex, Owen must've assumed I didn't know what he meant.

"Are you feeling open and optimistic?" he asked.

I couldn't admit to him that he'd burrowed into my brain and uncovered a repressed memory as efficiently as a therapist. I found myself revisiting my middle school memories on nights I couldn't fall asleep and then dreaming about crowds of people laughing at me.

"I'm going to do my best," I replied. "Don't forget I'm trying to rewrite some old scripts." I tapped my temple.

He nodded as he rolled the ball from one side of his paddle to the other like it was magnetized to the thing. "Yup, that's exactly what you're doing. But you're aware of the 'why' now."

"Thanks to you."

Owen paused with the ball cemented to the center of his paddle and fixed his eyes on me. "I appreciate you saying that. After our last lesson, I had a coaching hangover, like I'd pushed you too hard."

"Listen, I put my art out into the world, and people do *not* hold back in their reviews. I'm resilient and open to feedback," I replied.

He bounced the ball up and snatched it out of the air. "Good to hear."

"Speaking of my art . . ."

I was both eager and not to get his thoughts on *Rogue Cowboy*.

"Nope, let's wait till the end. We'll get derailed and we have too much to accomplish today." He pointed to the opposite side of the court. "Get into ready position over there."

I nodded and jogged over without doing any of the exaggerated bouncy stuff I normally did.

"Right up here." Owen pointed to the white line along the strangely named "kitchen" portion of the court that bordered the net on either side.

I moved closer to it.

"*Knees*," he reminded me, all business.

The words "on your" flitted through my mind, and I wondered if Owen was bossy in all aspects of his life.

I dutifully bent my knees so I could be quicker to react and released the tension in my grip before he could correct that as well.

"Dinking is all about control and finesse. Strategy too, but we'll get to that later," Owen explained. "Remember how we focused on that push at our first lesson? We're back at it today. I also want you to think about your wrist. No floppy stuff." He demonstrated by doing figure eights in the air with his paddle. "You'll send the ball everywhere but where it needs to go if your wrist isn't solid."

I nodded and tried not to hypergrip my paddle.

"I want you to swing from your shoulder, not flick your wrist." He elegantly mimed the move, making it look simple enough for me to do as well. "Light taps so the ball clears the net and bounces low. Make sense?"

It did in theory but I wasn't sure how my body would translate it all. "Yup!"

"Aim for a compact swing, just like we were practicing at our first lesson. Like this."

Owen dropped a ball and lobbed it over the net with an easy little shot. I wasn't sure if I was supposed to return it or not, so I watched it bounce right next to me.

"Let's go."

I nodded and moved into ready position, trying to ignore the nerves buzzing inside of me.

Owen straightened up, frowning at me. "Hey, we're having fun, remember?"

"What do you mean?"

"You look *so* tense," he said gently as he took a few steps closer to the net. "It's okay, Brooke. We had a breakthrough last time; now you've got your head on right and you're going to be great."

I nodded and shook my hands off to try to drain some of the tension. "I'm feeling the pressure."

"Don't overthink. Just dink."

"The terminology is *really* goofy—you have to admit it." I laughed.

He narrowed his eyes and pointed his paddle at me, trying to hide a smile. "Don't blaspheme my sport, got it?"

I saluted him. "Yes, Coach!"

We both dropped into position at the same time, Owen dinked, and the next thing I knew my paddle connected with the ball and sent it right back to him.

"Yay," I cheered.

"Stay focused; let's keep this volley going," he said as he tapped the ball back to me.

I was ready the second it landed. I tried to remember all the various body parts that I needed to move in tandem and sent it back to Owen.

"Nice."

I lapped up his praise.

We continued the back-and-forth for way longer than I thought was possible. I felt a little more confident with each successful shot.

"There she is," Owen cheered as I managed to switch from forehand to backhand. "Kai's going to be so impressed."

It was the second time he'd mentioned Kai, like he was trying to remind himself why he was wasting his time with me. *Kai* was the goal we were working toward.

The rest of the session passed in a happy blur of me doing solidly okay to decent, with a couple moments of darn good.

"Thanks for going a little long today," I said, nodding across the courts to where the staff was shuffling in. I grabbed my water and took a drink.

"You were having fun." Owen grinned at me. "I wasn't about to interrupt that."

"I hope I wasn't the only one enjoying it."

"Oh, I absolutely was." He nodded. "I love seeing a player blossom."

He thought that I was *blossoming*?

We paused at the edge of the courts, before we got to the front desk area where staff was congregating.

"I think you're going to make fast progress from this point on. Maybe we should arrange a Kai run-in when he's here for a lesson with me? I mean, there's a book on the line, and you need your inspo. Or your muse or whatever he is to your writing."

Third mention.

He pulled his hat off to wipe his brow, and I had to process the fact that I'd actually made Owen sweat during our session.

"That's right—I still need your feedback on *Rogue*!" I slapped my paddle on my thigh. "I've been dying to hear what you have to say." I paused and shot him a suspicious look. "I think."

He laughed, complete with crinkly eyes. "Right, okay. It's not bad, I promise. So I really loved the book. The tension between Trent and Eliza was palpable in those early scenes."

My heart sank preemptively. "I'm waiting for the 'but' . . ."

He shook his head. "There's no 'but.' I told you, I have a weird idea that might help you. I'm no Kai clearly"—he gestured down his body—"but I think it could provide inspiration."

Fourth mention.

Owen paused and seemed to gather himself before continuing.

"Horses are a big part of what you write, correct?"

I tilted my head. "Well, if the outline calls for it, yeah. I've written a couple where horses were barely mentioned."

"How about the one you're currently working on?"

I grimaced. "If I could actually write it, yes, there will be horses."

He bobbed his head. "Perfect. One thing I noticed was that there's a beautiful missed opportunity with the husbandry aspect of owning a horse. The *Rogue* cowboys throw on the saddle, hop on, and off they go. But that's not how it works, if they truly care about the animal."

"Oh, they *definitely* care," I said quickly, as if I was talking about real people.

"Of course they do. Which means they need to take their time with grooming before they ride. It's an important step because it allows the rider to assess the horse's health, plus it helps with bonding. And from a story perspective, well, if you've got a city girl who don't know nuthin' 'bout horses"—he slipped into a drawl—"it's a great opportunity for your cowboy and his lady to bond as well. He can show her how to do it and explain all the cool nuances of it."

I loved that he read my book closely enough to identify a theme and offer a way to make it even better.

"That's a perfect idea, thank you." I smiled at him. "I wasn't a horse girl growing up, so I'm missing that DNA strand. There's obviously a lot I don't know about horses, but I can do research online—"

Owen shook his head. "No, I have a better idea. Why don't we go on a field trip and I can *show* you how it's done?"

The offer didn't compute at first so I just stared at him.

"I spent some time working on a horse farm," he explained quickly. "I know my way around a barn. It's in Jersey, about an hour and a half away."

"Seriously?"

"Yeah." He sighed sheepishly. "Long story involving one of those horse girls."

"No, I mean you'd seriously do that for me?"

Owen looked like he didn't understand my question. "Well . . . yeah. Why wouldn't I?"

Because it was above and beyond what he was contracted to do. Because it meant investing at least four hours with me, alone. Because it required leaving the city.

"It's just so *nice* of you."

He chuckled and glanced at me out of the corner of his eye. "Is that out of character? Me being nice?"

"No, not at all!" I sputtered. "I mean it's, like, generous with your time. You're busy." I gestured to where members were filing in. "It's a half-day commitment at least. Do you even have a car?"

"I have a car," he replied. "And you're busy too, but I think it would be worth it. It gives me an excuse to go back and visit old friends, and hopefully you'd get a ton of ideas. I know I'm not at official muse status, but maybe I could be a lesser one? Kai is your Kalliope and I can be your . . . I don't know, Melete, maybe?"

"Hold on, you know the *muses*?"

He looked a little sheepish. "I'm a big fantasy reader, so yeah."

"Calliope is the muse of . . ." I paused because I wasn't sure what exactly he thought Kai represented to me.

"Epic poetry, so books basically," Owen replied. "And Melete represents . . . take a guess."

"Epic fails on the pickleball court?"

He smirked. "Would you stop? No, Melete is the muse of *practice*."

I loved that Owen granted himself muse status.

"Totally works." I nodded. "Yeah, you're definitely my Melete."

We stared at each other for a beat, a little sweaty, tired, and content.

"And I would *love* to go on a field trip to meet some horses. Thanks for suggesting it."

Owen started backing away from me. "Okay, I'll reach out to the barn rats for some possible dates and times and then text you. More to come."

I watched him walk away, then pause and turn back to me. "You did great today. Really impressive improvement."

I beamed at him. "Thanks, Coach."

I walked out of the Chelsea Pickleball Academy feeling way luckier than usual.

Chapter Fourteen

I'd gotten used to Meredith's stomp-step-stomp noises around the apartment, but based on the note taped to our door, our neighbors downstairs still had a problem with it. I walked in, holding it up in the air.

"They called you a Clydesdale this time." I laughed.

She looked up from where she was meal prepping in the kitchen. "Ouch. I think I like 'roller derby reject' better."

"Should we respond?"

"Sure. I'll make it look like I have a black eye, grab a crutch, then go down and knock on their door to apologize for being noisy using an Elizabethan orphan voice. Guarantee they'll stop giving me crap."

"Please. Have you ever been confrontational in your life?"

"No," she admitted as she expertly trimmed a handful of green beans. "But maybe it's time to start?"

"You know I'm a fan of the strategy." I dropped my laptop bag on the futon and plopped down next to it.

"How was writing?" she asked.

"My first 7,562 words are now sitting in Piper's inbox." I pumped my fist half-heartedly.

Meredith frowned at me. "But I thought you needed to turn in—"

"I *know*, I know, but now I can bill them," I interrupted her. "I did the best I could. She said as long as I hit my real deadline, we'll be fine."

"And how likely is that?"

She stopped chopping to stare at me.

"We both know what needs to fall in line in order for me to get my mojo back," I said. "But I'm inching closer. Owen said I'm 'exponentially better' at every lesson."

We'd had another since my second breakthrough session, and I finally felt it as well. My court confidence was getting stronger with every dink and volley.

"Don't forget that Kai might be at the Hamptons party," Meredith added. "So there's a chance you could run into him there, make him fall in love with you, which, *duh*, and then all of the pickleball stuff will be unnecessary. You have enough knowledge now that you can talk about it like you really play. Perfect icebreaker."

I stared at the ceiling, imagining how it would go down if I did manage to corner Kai in the Hamptons. How cheesy would it be to call him a "big dill" as my opener?

"Have you been getting intel about him from Bucket Hat?" Meredith asked.

"Owen," I corrected. "Yeah, no, I haven't. He keeps me working the whole session, and since we finish right as the club opens, it's not like we have time to hang out and chat."

Plus it would feel awkward pumping him for information about another client. When he mentioned Kai, it was always in passing, and to pause and ask something like, "Yeah, about Kai . . . Do you happen to know if he maintains positive relationships with his exes?" or "How does Kai treat the support staff here at the club? And does he have a good sense of humor?" would be awkward. We were busy enough during my lessons using every second trying to get me to the next level.

Or *a* level, since I'd started in the basement.

"You still enjoying it?" Meredith asked, eyeing me with the tip of the knife planted in the cutting board.

"You think I'm going to say no, don't you?"

She placed the trimmed beans in a glass storage container. "I mean, based on your *history* . . ."

"Okay, okay." I laughed. "Point taken. It might go against everything you know about me, but I'm really liking it. Once we figured out my weirdness, it was like everything changed. I'm nowhere near as naturally athletic as you and my family, but I'm not as bad as I assumed I'd be. At least not anymore."

"He's a really good coach if he was able to help you work through that," Meredith said as she moved on to peeling boiled eggs. "Intuitive and observant. It's what I try to do with my students. Find their blocks and help them move past them."

"I didn't even know I *had* a block."

"And that's my point. Sometimes you need an outsider to help you see what's right in front of your face."

The fart odor of the eggs wafted over to me and I wrinkled my nose.

"Sorry," she apologized. "I tried to make them when you weren't home."

"Do you have any other workout hand-me-downs I can borrow?" I asked. "I think Owen's getting tired of seeing me in the same two skorts."

Meredith raised an eyebrow at me. "Worrying about how we look on the court, are we?"

"No, not at all," I said quickly. "I just figured since you're not using them, at least not for . . . How much longer are you in that thing?"

"Three more weeks until Frankenboot comes off!" she cheered. "Early!"

"Overachiever," I fake-grumbled at her.

"Sounds like I'm not the only one," she shot back. "Someone's becoming the teacher's pet."

I grinned at the thought of it. "And now we're going on a field trip."

"When is that?"

"Next week. It's perfect timing because a big part of *Archer* involves alicorns, and it'll be cool to weave in some of my new horse knowledge."

"And an alicorn is . . . ?" Meredith asked.

"A Pegasus and unicorn hybrid. Everyone in Verdantia thinks they're extinct, and only Einar knows there's a herd of them living in the woods. Which is great because Zandria needs them for the resistance army."

Meredith stacked her prep containers and turned to load them into the fridge. "And this new horse knowledge will also translate into the cowboy book that you're actually getting paid to write, yes?"

I frowned at the thought of poor Austin and Abby, who were both signing up to work the pie booth at the county fair when I left off. It should've been a layup chapter to write, but instead of focusing on their simmering sexual tension over cooked fruit, I'd opted to research the ten most popular country fair pie flavors for an hour.

Apple was number one, obviously.

"Yes, of *course*!" I answered quickly. "It's the main reason I'm doing it."

She stomp-stepped over to join me on the futon and perched her boot up on the coffee table. "Is it going to be weird hanging out with him off the courts?"

I was caught off guard by the question. "I hadn't even thought about the possibility of it being weird, so I guess that means no?"

"From what I've heard, he's a good guy. Colton loves him. And little Martina? Come on, they're adorable together."

"Yeah, I feel pretty lucky getting coached by a pro."

"Speaking of, haven't you run out of lessons?" Meredith cocked an eyebrow at me.

I shook my head. "Since I can get there early, he's letting me do some extras."

"And why is that?" She leaned toward me, now in full therapist mode.

"Beeeecaaause . . ." I elongated the word as I tried to figure it out for myself. "He appreciates the writer's struggle, and he wants to make sure this muse thing happens for me?"

"Right, of course." Meredith nodded and pursed her lips. "That's such a normal thing to do for someone who's basically a stranger. And then take said stranger on a date to a horse farm. Got it."

"Oh my god, it's *not* a date!" I insisted. "Mere, he knows I'm into Kai. Owen brings him up all the time, actually."

Five times, to be specific.

"Okay, okay." She put her hands up in surrender. "Point taken. It's just very . . . *generous* of him to do all of that."

My phone rang right as I opened my mouth to give her shit for suggesting an ulterior motive. "My mom," I said when I glanced at the screen. "Weird that she's calling." I answered. "Hey, iseverythingokay?"

It was my typical shorthand any time she called without texting first.

"Hi, sweetheart—yes, everything is great! Has your brother reached out to you yet?"

"Not in a week or so. Why?"

"He's sneaking home for a quick visit before the season starts! It turns out your father and I are signed up for a race the Saturday he's here, so we were thinking he could come into the city and hang out with you that day. Maybe spend the night?"

I glanced at Meredith and she was already nodding. She pointed to her ear. "I can hear her and it's fine," she whispered.

I refrained from reminding my mom about my punishing writing schedule because I wasn't about to miss time with Wes.

"Yeah, that would be great," I said. "What are the dates?"

As we mapped out his visit, I tried to ignore the echoes of a lonely cowboy, wishing I would finally let him fall in love.

Chapter Fifteen

I stood outside my apartment on the sidewalk, scanning the morning rush as I waited for Owen to pick me up for horse school. I had no idea what kind of car he drove so every passing vehicle was fair game. Was it going to be a sensible Honda? An electric car? Something that belonged outside the city, like a pickup truck?

I moved under the meager shade of a tree that had seen far too much canine marking to actually flourish. Owen told me to wear jeans and sneakers or boots, none of which were ideal for the late June heat. Thankfully we were meeting at eight so I wasn't sweating too much yet.

A delivery truck in a no-parking zone right in front of me pulled away and a black Wagoneer took its place. Owen waved at me through the windshield.

I didn't realize that he was hat-free until I was sitting next to him in the blessedly cool car. My heart did an unexpected jig when he smiled at me.

"Good morning," he said. "Ready to meet some new friends?"

"So ready! Honestly, I don't think I've even touched a horse since I was like ten. Which I guess was obvious since you picked up on it in *Rogue*."

Owen slid into traffic. "Now, hold on, I never said that. I said you could enhance the story with more details. I loved the dynamic you created between Trent and his horse Wildfire. It felt very real to me. You're *good*."

He glanced at me out of the corner of his eye, and I wondered if the heat in my cheeks was obvious.

"Well, thank you. That was just from watching a bunch of YouTube videos."

"Impressive. I can only imagine what you're going to do with hands-on knowledge. And then once we make the Kai thing happen? You're going to be unstoppable."

We. Owen and I were a team in the forthcoming Kai connection. Kai-nection?

I'd assumed Owen's sloppy sartorial choices were a lifestyle, but there wasn't a single crumb or balled-up receipt inside the car. And not only was he hatless, but he was also dressed like he actually cared how he looked, in jeans and a navy golf shirt/button-down hybrid that made my black tank top, washed-out jeans, and sneakers feel junky in comparison.

"I've been thinking about your next steps on the court, and we need to start group play," Owen said as he zipped through a yellow light. "Private lessons are great for building your foundational skills, but pickleball is a team sport."

It was a leveling up that I didn't feel quite ready for yet. I *liked* practicing in the deserted club, with just the two of us and the occasional Marti cameo.

"Yes?" he asked. "Do you agree?"

"I mean, yeah? But with who? CPA members are great players, so who's going to want to dumb down their game for me? Meredith is obviously out. I could probably get Colton for a mercy round or two, but we need a fourth."

"Fair point. You're not ready to ask Kai quite yet. I'm sure I could rope someone in, but what if you try a public court too?"

I looked over at him with wide eyes. "You mean play with *three complete strangers?*"

Owen took his eyes fully off the road to glance over and laugh at me. "Well, yeah. That's a big part of the game. Unless you come to the sport with friends, it's how you build your community."

"But . . . but . . ." I sputtered. "I still don't understand all of the rules!"

"That's the beauty of a public court; I can guarantee that someone else will. Just tell them you're a novice. You'll be fine."

I stared out the window and imagined showing up to one of the courts dotting the city. Thanks to Owen, I was learning the unwritten rules of playing at CPA, but I assumed that public courts had their own ecosystem and bylaws that were different from the fancy club vibes. Not understanding them *plus* my sketchy knowledge of scorekeeping spelled disaster.

"If you want, I'll go with you the first time."

My heart warmed at yet another unexpected kindness from him. I glanced over to take in his profile as he navigated the traffic.

"Owen, that's too much. You're already doing a ton to help me; you don't have to."

"It's no big deal," he pshawed, still staring ahead. "Plus, it might be good for me to get out with regular players for a change. CPA is sort of a heightened reality. The members are all high-level players in a rarified setting. It's not a typical pickleball experience."

"So you're saying that a public court will probably have more seniors and crappy players?" I paused to consider it. "I could probably take down a seventy-year-old."

"Look at you, trash-talking." He chuckled. "You'd be surprised; you think they're at a disadvantage because of their age, but what you're forgetting is they have the time to focus on *strategy*. So you might have speed and agility going for you, but they're playing chess. They're gonna stand at the kitchen line and swat down every ball you try to hammer home."

"Like I need to be humbled more," I complained.

"It's all part of the process. Losing helps you grow as a player, trust me."

The landscape transformed from a thousand lanes of traffic to six, then four, then two, until we ended up on twisty, narrow back roads lined with lush green trees.

"How did you wind up in horse world?" I asked him, a little mortified that I hadn't used the drive to uncover Owen's backstory.

His jaw flexed and he gripped the wheel a little tighter. "I spent a couple of years chasing down all of the weird stuff I'd always been curious about. Trying on different lifestyles. So I spent time training to be a rafting guide out in Colorado, and I learned how to make cheese in Switzerland. I got my pilot's license. Learned how to tango in Spain. And I'd always loved horses so I spent time working at Evergreen Stables."

It was a Pandora's box of information that didn't compute. Was it all an effort to find a career path? Because pickleball coach and cheesemonger were at opposite ends of the work spectrum, if they even existed on the same chart at all. And what was the tango thing about?

"Rafting?" I sputtered. "And you can fly a plane? What kind of cheese did you make?"

"All kinds." He laughed. "But the specialty was obviously Swiss cheese."

I tried picturing him in the various roles. Rafting guide? Sure, that made total sense. I'd feel safe with Owen fitting a life vest on me and then helping me navigate rapids. Pilot? Totally on brand, because he had an eye for detail that meant the souls on his flights would always reach their destination. But the cheese, dance, and horse stuff were all beyond me.

"Okay, I guess my biggest question is *why*?" I asked. "Is there some sort of through line that I'm missing?"

A shrug. "I was lucky enough to spend time letting my curiosity lead me."

I chewed on the inside of my cheek as I tried to come up with a polite way to ask about the intersection of curiosity and finances.

"But, like . . . how?" I managed.

"Easy," he replied with a tiny shrug. "You do your research, book a ticket, and go."

I had a feeling that he knew exactly what I was asking, and the gentle brush-off was his way of telling me that it was none of my business. I had plenty of time to unravel the mysteries of Owen Miller, so I opted for a side step rather than pushing.

"How did you wind up at this barn?"

The verdant green around us opened up to long stretches of fields dotted with horses and cows alike. We were definitely getting closer to the farm.

A quick frown, then his profile settled into his usual neutral expression. "I've always thought the cowboy lifestyle was cool, so I looked into farms that were sort of close to the city to try riding. I picked Evergreen because they had the best website, not realizing that they're an English riding barn, not Western."

"Ooh, ooh, I actually know the difference between them!" I waved my hand as I interrupted. "English is formal and Western is more relaxed."

"Exactly." He nodded. "I probably should've switched to a different barn when I realized that Western was a better fit for me, but . . ."

Owen trailed off, and I stared at him while he seemed to collect his thoughts.

"The horse girl?" I asked softly, convinced that I was *really* overstepping.

"The horse girl," Owen agreed. "She boarded at Evergreen. And Ivy, the owner, had lost a couple of employees and needed help, so I wound up working there for a while."

I couldn't resist pushing a little more, since he hadn't shut me out quite yet. "I'm guessing you and the horse girl didn't ride off into the sunset together?"

"Nope, not even close." Owen huffed out a hollow laugh.

"When did it all happen?"

"We finally stopped talking a year ago," he replied.

His use of the word "finally" suggested that it was a long, messy breakup. I wanted to know all the details about the woman who'd clearly picked the wrong man. Everyone agreed that Owen was amazing, so why couldn't she see it too?

"Have you been back since . . . everything?"

He shook his head. "This is my first trip."

My heart pinched at the realization that he was making the journey for me. But then again, maybe he had an ulterior motive? Was I just his conduit for some ex sleuthing? Not that I blamed him. I'd done my time spying on Leo online, and once, in a moment of desperation, I'd staked out the coffee shop I'd seen him post about.

"Is there a chance she might . . . ?" I trailed off when I saw his jaw clench.

Owen cleared his throat. "No, Sophie only goes to the barn on the weekends. But we might have a Josh sighting. He's an instructor so he's there plenty."

"Josh?" I stared at his profile, waiting for him to continue, and he finally glanced over at me.

"She had the two of us fighting over her for a long time, and then she made her choice. It obviously wasn't me."

"*Ouch*," I said in a low voice. "A love triangle is one of the least liked tropes in Romancelandia. I'm sorry you had to go through that."

"Lesson learned," he replied. "Anyway, today isn't about me. This is about helping . . . What's your cowboy's name in this book?"

"Austin."

He bobbed his head. "Once we get done with this, Austin will be able to teach his lady the finer points of grooming and tacking up. It's not romantic per se, but I'm sure you can make it all bated breath and fluttery feelings. Maybe he'll put his hand on top of hers to show her how to use the currycomb?"

I watched Owen's eyes flick to my hand, and for a second, I thought he was going to demonstrate.

Which wouldn't have been the worst thing. I knew how comforting it felt to have his warm hand wrapped around mine.

"Anyway, I hope it'll be worth it," he added.

"It's going to be *fantastic*. I know our focus is on husbandry stuff, but . . . will I be able to ride a horse?" I squeaked out.

"Hell, yeah, of course you will." He laughed. "I made sure that a lesson pony would be available while we're there."

Owen slowed down and turned onto a long dirt driveway.

"Let's find you some inspiration," he said.

The horses watching us roll by all but promised that it was going to happen.

Chapter Sixteen

"I barely recognize you all cleaned up," the woman said when she finally pulled away from hugging Owen.

"Hey, hand me a shovel and I'll be back in business," Owen said, giving her an extra squeeze before turning to me. "Brooke, this is Ivy, my old boss."

Ivy was one of those people who seemed to be in motion even when standing still. Her white hair was pulled back in a low ponytail, and the dusty, sleeveless T-shirt showed off tan, well-defined arms that proved she wasn't just a figurehead on the farm.

She'd met us in the parking area near a brown building that didn't look anything like the old-timey red barns I wrote about. The cicadas were screaming in the morning heat, and the sun felt even more intense than in the city. A white-faced horse poked his head out to scrutinize us, and I had to keep from cooing over it, because horses weren't a big deal to people who worked with them every day.

To me, they were a mystery I'd spent too long pretending to understand.

"Nice to meet you." She shook my hand with an unsurprisingly hard grip. "Owen tells me you're a writer?"

"On good days I am," I replied. "But I have a feeling I'm going to find all sorts of inspiration here. Thanks for letting me nose around."

"Anything for this guy." Ivy hitched her thumb at Owen. "You sure you won't come back to work for me?"

"Maybe someday." He grinned at her. "Now, who have you got for us today?"

Ivy glanced at me. "I think Cedar is a good fit. Right?"

Owen gave me a quick once-over, as if he'd never seen me before. "Perfect choice. Are we good to go?"

"Do your thing." Ivy swept her hand toward the barn just beyond us. "Holler if you need me. Oh, your buddy Josh is here. I know you guys used to pal around. I'm sure he'll be glad to see you."

My stomach dropped. I turned to study Owen, expecting to see a glower, but his expression was as neutral as ever.

"Fantastic," he said convincingly. "That's great."

Owen gave Ivy a nod, then started for the barn. I had to jog to catch up to him.

"Should we leave?" I whispered out of the corner of my mouth even though no one was around. "It's fine if you want to go, I swear."

"It's a big barn," he said, staring straight ahead. "We won't run into him if we don't want to."

"Yeah, but what if Ivy tells him you're here, and he comes to find you." I envisioned how it would play out and reflexively smacked him in the stomach, getting a shocked "wunf" out of him. "What if he wants to *gloat*?"

Owen just kept stomping through the barn like he hadn't heard me.

"You know what? I have an idea." I kept talking to fill the silence. "I write about it in my books; now we're going to do it in real life."

Heat rushed to my face. Owen had just finished one of my books with plenty of "doing it" in a barn, but that wasn't what I meant.

"Fake dating," I blurted out. "If Josh comes anywhere near us, I'm morphing into your devoted girlfriend. I hope you can handle some PDA, because I'm going to grab your hand and squeeze it until your fingers turn blue. I'm going to hang on you like we're magnetized. Just *wait* until you see my fluttery eyelashes."

Owen allowed the faintest hint of a grin at my threats. "He won't come find me. Sophie convinced him that I was just her friend, but I still got the feeling that he was threatened by me."

"As he should be." I nodded vigorously.

Owen came to a stop by an open stall. "Wait here. I'll go get Cedar."

I sighed, feeling responsible for whatever drama was coming for us. As much as I didn't want a confrontation, I was totally game to show off my acting skills.

And holding Owen's hand wasn't the worst thing.

I finally remembered why we were at the barn and grabbed my notebook, because every single thing around me could be helpful in a moment when I couldn't manufacture emotion but I still needed word count. I took a few photos while I waited, then threw on a riding helmet that was hanging on the wall and took a photo wearing a goofy expression to send to Wes.

> Motorcycle or horse?

> Horse. Book research.

> Go you

A photo followed of a cup filled with brown sludge that looked like something you'd find in a diaper, but I knew it was one of his disgusting smoothie concoctions.

> No thank you, xo.

The barn was busy with other riders, a couple of chickens, and a very friendly orange barn cat. I was surrounded by a world that I'd pretended to know all about for my last dozen books, and now that I was in the middle of it, I could see how much of the vibe I'd missed. Sure, we weren't on a Montana ranch, but a horse farm in New Jersey could still provide tons of insights.

I had my head down taking a few notes about the flooring, so I didn't see Owen leading Cedar until he was a few feet away. When I finally looked up, he was striding in my direction with his eyes locked on me, embodying the smoldery cowboy thing I'd written about but never witnessed in real life.

My heart did a reflexive backflip, because this was yet another side of Owen.

He was wearing a little side smile, like he was proud and excited and couldn't wait to introduce me to the chestnut beast walking next to him. I tried not to make it obvious that I was memorizing everything about the way he was stalking toward me. How his hand gripped the lead casually, like he was holding onto Marti's leash and not guiding a beast that probably weighed several hundred pounds. The confidence in his gait, even when Cedar veered to the side and threw his head in the air. The way he spoke softly to Cedar after he fell back in line.

I finally needed to fully admit it to myself; Owen looked *good*. Seeing him all competent and cowboy-adjacent forced me to acknowledge what I'd been ignoring.

No, he looked better than "good."

Owen was fucking hot.

There was something undeniably sexy about a person in their element, especially when it was an unexpected one. To me, Owen read "city," but his ease around the barn suggested there was more to the Big Gripper than I realized.

"Wow," I breathed as the pair came to a stop in front of me.

"I know. He's a stunner, huh?" Owen ran his hand down the side of the horse's smooth neck.

I cleared my throat and nodded.

"Let me get him by you," Owen said, nodding to the open area behind me.

I realized that I was mutely staring at the pair. I jumped out of the way.

"He's so *big*," I said as Owen got the horse rigged up with the strapping system that would hold Cedar in place in the stall.

"Cedar? Nah, he's Welsh pony and quarter horse cross on the small side. Now c'mere."

I took a baby step toward Owen. Cedar was eyeballing me like he knew I was a novice.

"Ready?"

Owen asked it as if he could sense my hesitation. I wasn't scared. I just wanted Cedar to like me, and equally important,

I wanted Owen to be impressed with how quickly I took to horse chores.

"So ready."

"Okay, the first step is the currycomb." Owen held up a pink, oval plastic brush with hard little bristles that slipped over his hand and rested on his palm. He moved beside Cedar and started making rapid circles on the horse's side. "This loosens up any dirt or stray hairs."

I stood off to the side taking notes. "And that's important why?"

"Well, first it's a good way to take a physical inventory of your horse. You'll see any bites or bumps that need attention. Plus brushing away buildup prevents sores from debris under the saddle." He slid the comb off his hand and held it out to me. "Your turn."

I glanced between Cedar and Owen. "Just like that? No safety talk?"

"Good point. Remember when you walk behind him, stay close and keep one hand on him. No loud noises or abrupt movements. Other than that, Cedar's pretty bombproof."

"Can he tell if I'm . . . tentative?" I asked.

"Oh yeah." Owen smiled at me as he nodded. "They're very perceptive, down to your body language and facial expressions."

Sort of like Owen himself. Fantastic.

I forced a grin to hopefully convince Cedar that I was unfazed by his mysterious horse-ness. Owen held the comb out to me again.

"Don't be stressed; he's used to children and newbies," he encouraged me.

I placed my notebook on the ground and slipped the comb on. Cedar might've been a not-so-big horse who was gentle with kids, but to me he was a gigantic unknown creature with a profiler's skills. I placed the comb against the horse's smooth side and started making circles.

"Nice, there you go," Owen said, sounding just like he did when I managed to serve to the right side of the court.

I half expected Cedar to jump away from me, but the horse stood patiently while I worked my way around his body. He was solid, like cement coated in velvet. Owen went on to present me with two additional brushes, all the while dropping little insights as I prepped Cedar that made me want to grab my notebook.

"One last step before we get to tack," Owen said. He placed the soft brush I'd just used into the plastic storage tub. "The hoof pick. Now *this* gets addictive."

He walked to Cedar and stood shoulder to shoulder so that he was facing the horse's tail, then ran his hand down Cedar's leg, gently lifted it, and turned the horse's foot over in his hand. He pulled a black plastic tool out of his back pocket that had a small silver dagger at a right angle on the end of it.

"You really need to get in there to get the packed crap and rocks out," he said as he scraped the pick against Cedar's hoof. "All along the frog, right here." He dug in next to the triangular part of Cedar's hoof and pulled out satisfying clumps of dirt. "And along the wall." He flipped the tool to the brush section. "Then sweep off any excess."

Watching him work while tossing out yet more terminology I'd never heard made me a little swoony.

He stood up and wordlessly handed the tool to me.

"Now you."

I widened my eyes at him. "By myself?"

"You've got this, B," he said in the same warm voice he used to coax a soft dink out of me. "Rear leg. Go."

He patted my back, and it felt like heat zipped through my entire body, then pooled where his hand had rested on me.

"Like this?" I lined up by Cedar's hip facing his tail, then bent over and looked over my shoulder at Owen.

And caught him checking out my ass.

"Yeah," he said quickly, averting his eyes. "Run your hand down his leg and up you go."

I tried to mind meld with Cedar, seeing as horses probably possessed the gift of telepathy in addition to strong observational skills, to beg him to go easy on me, then slid my palm down his leg. The clairvoyance must've worked, because the next thing I knew I was holding a big old horse hoof upside down in my hand.

"I did it!"

"Of course you did," Owen said. "Never doubted you for a second. Now get in there and pick."

I started off gently tracing the pick along Cedar's hoof and it was enough to loosen some dirt.

"Harder," Owen insisted, and once again I needed to refrain from a "that's what she said" joke.

With a little more muscle, the packed dirt started falling from his hoof.

"So remind me how this is sexy?" I asked, quickly glancing up as I pried out more crap.

Owen snorted out a laugh. "*You're* the writer. I'm sure you can come up with something." He paused. "Maybe not about this specific part of the process. Speaking of, you can move on to the next one."

I remembered his advice about keeping a hand on Cedar as I walked behind him, then got to work on the hoof, which Cedar offered to me without hesitation.

"What's the relationship between your characters?" Owen asked.

I picked out a little rock that was packed in with the dirt. "He's a grumpy cowboy who's trying to transform his family's busted-down ranch into a viable tourist destination, and she's a chef who lost a bet and now has to spend the season working in his kitchen. They hate each other. He's too closed off and she's too headstrong. He falls first, but he burned too many bridges with her so he has to woo her to win her. Oh yeah, and they have a drunken one-night stand, and she winds up pregnant."

"Wow, okay then. Next hoof," Owen instructed. "So wait . . . she doesn't like him?"

I was picking like a pro now. "Not at first."

When I glanced at Owen, he was frowning. "Yeah, that's a tricky scenario. Pursuing a woman who isn't interested only leads to heartbreak. Take it from me."

I wasn't sure how to respond. Clearly the barn ghosts were doing their thing, unearthing Owen's old hurts.

"Well, he was a dick to her at first, so he brought it upon himself," I clarified.

"What if this grooming process is a moment of change between them?" Owen mused. "She thinks he's an asshole, but then she sees how caring he is with his horse, and it shows a totally new side of him?"

"Ooh, what if he adopted a horse that was abused, and Abby watches him gentle his way closer? Like, this grooming stuff is a bridge to a new relationship?"

"For the horse *and* the human," Owen added. "He catches

Abby watching him, and he invites her to help since the horse isn't afraid of women." He glanced closer at the hoof I was working on. "You're done."

I stood up and rubbed Cedar's neck. "I think we're onto something. You keep it up and I might owe you a cowriter credit. It's an unpaid gig, of course."

He chuckled. "You can keep your paycheck—don't worry. I'll be right back. I need to grab the saddle."

I watched him walk away and discovered that he'd been hiding a darn good butt in his saggy court shorts.

"How am I doing so far?" I whispered to Cedar.

He flicked his ears around, and I realized that I knew nothing about horse body language.

"Are you happy or sad?" I asked him. "Am I standing too close to you?"

I stroked his nose, and he flicked his head away, making the cross ties jingle.

"That's a 'no,' huh?"

"You telling Cedar your secrets?" Owen's voice echoed from behind me.

"Just trying to figure him out," I answered. "This is *such* a different world for me."

He placed the saddle on a rail behind him.

"Well, get ready for yet another new horizon, because it's time to ride."

Chapter Seventeen

I immediately knew the guy sauntering across the dirt ring toward us was Josh, and even though Owen hadn't agreed to my fake-dating scheme, I was going to force the issue.

Owen was focused on lining Cedar up at the mounting block so he wasn't prepared for my sudden shift to girlfriend mode. He froze when I slipped my arm around his waist.

I went up on my tiptoes to whisper in his ear. "Incoming."

A constellation of expressions flashed across his face, and I half expected him to step away from me. Instead, he met my eyes with a softness that was real enough to make me question if my acting skills could compare.

"Okay," he murmured to me. "I guess we're doing this."

As much as I wanted to assess Josh as he walked closer, I couldn't tear my eyes from Owen's. My arm around his waist felt familiar, normal even, despite the fact that we'd only touched once before. When I wrote about fake dating, I always highlighted the awkwardness of the initial stages, the fumbling of two people forced to fast-track intimacy. Based on the way it felt with Owen, I seriously needed to recalibrate my approach to the trope.

He tucked a strand of hair behind my ear and I melted a little. *Damn*, he was good.

"Well, hey, man," Josh said. "Been a while."

Cedar jostled as Josh came to a stop in front of us, hard enough to pull Owen away from me.

"Hey, yourself," Owen answered, reaching his hand out to Josh. "Good to see you. This is, uh, my girlfriend, Brooke."

I was on. I smiled prettily at Josh and nestled close against Owen, like I couldn't bear to not be touching him. He draped his arm around my shoulder. "Hi. I'm sorry, what's your name?"

"Josh McLain. I'm an instructor here." He puffed up his chest like he was insulted I didn't know who he was.

There was no question that Josh was conventionally handsome. Tall, fair-haired, with a regal carriage that was probably due to years of horseback posture scrutiny. But to me, he looked plastic. His eyebrows were unsettlingly light, making his face look like it was halfway through a drag makeover.

"Ivy just told me you're doing something with *pickleball* now?" Josh asked, sounding incredulous. He crossed his arms and eyed Owen. "Always jumping on the next trend, huh? Good for you."

I felt Owen stiffen. "Yeah, I wouldn't call it a trend. I'm an investor at a club in Manhattan. First of its kind in the city."

Investor? I had to force myself not to react, because it was news to me. I needed to stay in character no matter the plot twists. I rubbed Owen's back and gazed up at him adoringly.

"Huh," Josh answered. "I'll have to check it out."

"Oh, you *must*," I purred, really pouring it on. "It's stunning."

Somehow I'd morphed into Katharine Hepburn. All that was missing was a "*dahling*."

"Soph and I are checking out venues in the city, so maybe we can tack on a visit?" Josh said.

My stomach dropped at the casual reveal. I knew exactly what he was implying, but I could tell Owen didn't have a clue.

I wished Cedar would pick up on the absolutely shitty vibes and take off running, so we could end the torture.

"Hold on, you probably haven't heard the news," Josh continued. The man looked downright triumphant.

I forced myself to smile pleasantly as the slow-motion car wreck played out in front of me. There was nothing I could do but cling to Owen as he processed what was to come.

"News?" Owen tipped his head.

I held my breath and stared at him.

"I asked Sophie to marry me. We're engaged."

It only took a half second for Owen to collect himself.

"Oh, no way. Congrats," he replied quickly. The hitch in his voice could easily be written off as surprise, but I knew that it was deeper than that. I gave him a squeeze.

"Yeah, thanks. It's all happening really fast. Too fast." Josh laughed. "But you get it, I'm sure. You're next, bro."

I wasn't about to miss the opportunity to push back. I giggled like Josh had actually said something funny and gazed at Owen. "Oh, I don't know about that. We're having so much fun right now that we're not even thinking that far ahead. We're sort of in this crazy, passionate haze. Just enjoying each other, you know? We're lucky we made it out of the apartment today." I winked at him.

Josh frowned. "Oh."

"Speaking of, we should get back to Cedar," Owen said as he bobbed his head toward the incredibly patient horse.

"Right, of course," Josh said as he backed away. "I'll have Soph reach out the next time we're in the city. She's got your number, right?"

Owen cleared his throat. "Not sure. We'll figure it out. Take care."

Josh touched two fingers to his forehead in a salute. "I'll tell her you said hello."

A parting shot. The three of us watched him walk away.

"You okay?" I asked quietly.

Owen let out a long sigh as he untangled himself from me. "Yup. It's fine. Let's do this."

"Do you want to talk about it?" I pushed.

"Nothing to say."

He was wrong—there was *plenty* of subtext to dissect—but I knew I wouldn't be able to pry anything else out of him. Thankfully, we had the rest of my lesson to focus on.

After fitting me with a helmet, we went through an indoor introduction to basics like posture, steering, and stopping. By the time Owen walked us out of the barn and into the sunshine, we were both fully focused on the mechanics of our lesson and not the run-in with Josh.

I tried to memorize every bit of the sensation of riding, so I could re-create it on the page.

"Where are your eyes, Brooke?" Owen asked. "He's veering a little."

I'd learned that everything I did while riding Cedar telegraphed intent, including something as subtle as where I *looked*. It was overwhelming to realize that minuscule, even accidental behaviors were enough to impact our ride.

Which was more of an incredibly slow saunter than a real ride.

"There's so much to think about." I looked down at him. "Is it crazy to say that learning to ride is like learning to play pickleball?"

He considered it. "I guess there are parallels?"

"There *are*," I insisted. "Like being aware of what my entire body is doing at any given second and trying to be soft when I feel all tight and nervous."

I checked my grip on the reins again.

"Well, I think you're doing great," he said. "You look like a pro up there."

Warmth flooded through me. A compliment from Owen was *earned*.

"I have a phenomenal teacher to thank, then."

I glanced at Owen quickly, because I didn't want to go off course again, and I swear I saw a blush.

The barn was fading in the distance behind us as we walked along a well-worn path by the tree line.

"So do you like it?" he asked. "Riding?"

"It's *amazing*." I sighed. I gave Cedar a pat. "To be connected with this guy . . . it's a little unreal."

The "unreal" aspect would also serve me in *Archer*, which I hadn't been able to stop thinking about. I'd considered where an alicorn's wings would come out of the body in relation to a saddle and how a horn could potentially hinder putting on a halter.

The trees rustled as the wind picked up.

"It's not supposed to rain, is it?" Owen asked as he peered at the sky.

"Not that I saw, but check out the clouds." I pointed at the horizon.

Cedar added to the conversation with a loud snort and head flick.

"Hey, hey, you're good, buddy," Owen said softly to the horse.

Cedar snorted again and then sidestepped.

The wind blew harder, and I saw something flash in the trees in front of us at the exact moment that Cedar shifted his weight back to front.

"Whoa," I said reflexively, leaning down to lower my center of gravity.

Another gust, and the sun reflected off what I could now see was a deflated Mylar balloon caught up in a tree. I was about to mention it when Cedar juked away and the world downshifted into slow motion.

I slid off Cedar inch by inch as he bounced around, but it still didn't give me enough time to grip tighter or right myself. I knew what was going to happen next—ground, meet ass—but instead of falling down and potentially getting trampled, I wound up in Owen's arms.

"I've gotcha," he said as he gripped me tightly.

The combination of the fall and the nearness of him left me shaking with adrenaline.

It was a quick save, which meant that Owen didn't end up holding me cinematically, like he'd just rescued me from a burning building. No, he had a firm grip on one arm near the armpit and the other under my knee so I was horizontal, like we were unveiling our big finish in a jitterbug competition. He let go of my knee when I wasn't expecting it, so I tripped a little as I found my footing.

"You good?" Owen grabbed both of my forearms and held on, ducking down to look into my eyes. "You okay?"

I stared at him, nodding wordlessly as his gaze bounced around my face, his forehead furrowed with worry.

Even though I'd almost taken a hoof to the head, all I could think about was the way I felt with Owen's hands gripping me and his worried face just inches away.

I couldn't catch my breath. It wasn't just due to the fright.

"Well, damn, we weren't expecting that!" Owen said as he pulled me against his body in a tight, comforting hug so quickly that the air whooshed from my lungs.

It was exactly what I needed. The tension in my shoulders eased as I melted into him. I was a little embarrassed at how much I craved the grounding sensation of Owen holding me again. I rested my cheek against his chest as his hands skimmed my back.

Too bad Josh wasn't around to witness it, because we were really selling it.

I couldn't stop stroking his back. Owen was solid in the best possible way. It wasn't a gym-bro, calorie-restricting physique that was hard and unyielding. His arms were strong, no doubt from the hours and hours of pickleball every day, and his chest felt like the perfect place to have a nap.

"I guess Cedar's not balloon-proof," I murmured.

I felt a rumble of laughter from Owen's chest. "Prey animal mentality. That balloon could be a serial killer, you never know."

I didn't want to pull away from him even though the air was blisteringly hot. I caught a hint of Owen's sun-warmed skin, combined with what was probably a deodorant called Major Sage or Midnight Summer. Clean, bracing, with plenty of him mixed in.

Our hug was extending well beyond "I'm concerned for your welfare" and into "I like how your body feels pressed up to mine." One of us needed to pull away.

I couldn't. The buzz blazing a trail through my body was powerful enough to make me adjust my grip a little tighter around him, to reassure him that this was exactly where I wanted to be.

Cedar shifted and whinnied like he was our chaperone, which caused Owen to finally loosen his grip.

He leaned back to look at me. "Should we walk him to the barn, or do you want to ride?"

Owen still had his arms draped around my lower back. Somehow mine had ended up clasped behind his neck, middle school dance–style.

Holy *shit*, I was touch starved. Being pressed against him was enough to wake up a heat I hadn't felt in months.

The corner of his mouth curved into a smile as he studied my face. "You're getting back up there, aren't you? I can tell just by looking at you. That's your determined expression."

Instead of answering him, I ignored logic and just listened to what my body was telling me.

I went up on my toes and pressed my lips to his.

Chapter Eighteen

The car ride home had started off with a brief conversation about the air-conditioning being slow and then settled into a painful silence.

Not at all surprising, seeing as Owen had backed away from the kiss.

No, the truth was he'd actually *pushed* me away.

Sure, he'd been caught off guard by me flinging myself at him at first because I'd given him zero warning. *I* was even a little surprised by it. But within a heartbeat, Owen was matching my intensity, claiming my mouth like the kiss had been his idea.

Then he'd abruptly stepped away from me and pulled the back of his hand across his mouth, like he wanted to get rid of any traces of me. He'd mumbled an apology as he gathered Cedar's reins when I was the one who owed it to him.

I tried to make sense of what I'd done as I stared out the car window, watching the countryside speed past. I was horny, sure, but the roiling confusion inside of me pointed to other motivations. I hadn't just wanted *it*; I needed to admit to myself that I'd wanted *him*.

Based on his reaction, it was totally one-sided. I was mortified. If there was any moment to address my sloppy come-on, it was now.

I took a deep breath. "That wasn't cool of me, Owen. What I did out on the trail. I'm sorry."

I wasn't sure if I actually *was* sorry, because at the time I'd been sort of desperate to see what kissing him was like.

Owen's jaw flexed, and his expression shifted to a frown. "It's fine. No big deal."

"I overstepped. I got caught up in the fake dating of it all."

A shrug in response. "It happens."

He was right; kissing was definitely a part of fake dating, but usually it led to a deeper connection, not mortification.

"Do you hate me?" I asked in a quiet voice.

He made a frustrated noise and glanced over at me. "No, of course not. Not at all."

I wasn't sure what to say next since "Was it good for you?" didn't feel appropriate.

Owen scrubbed his hand across his cheek. "Listen, Brooke, I need to put this out there right now. You came to me for lessons because you're into Kai, and I'll do everything I can to help you make a connection with him. But I'm not about to be your runner-up or help you pass the time until you can get to him. Not after what I've been through. I *humiliated* myself with Sophie. It was disgusting. I swore I'd never let it happen again."

I started to answer him but he kept talking.

"Kind of funny that all went down at the barn. Like history repeating itself, you know? I got burned by the love triangle thing bad, and I promised myself I'd never let it happen to me again."

"But that's not what—"

Owen silenced me with a pointed look.

"I'm sorry."

"Yup. At least you get it. Sophie seemed to enjoy the drama." Owen frowned. "And I was *such* a fool for letting it go on for so long. I kept thinking she'd figure out that I was the better match for her. Pick *me*, you know? And she did, for a little while. She'd complain to me about Josh, how awful he was to her." He shook his head. "Guess she got over that."

"Do you want to talk about . . . the news?" I asked tentatively.

"I don't give a shit that they're engaged," he fired back, sounding like he did. "But seeing him was a reminder of what I let her do to me. I willingly subjected myself to it. I'm still mad at *me* for being such a fool." He smacked his palm to his chest hard enough that I wondered if it hurt.

"Anyway, you get where I'm coming from," he added.

I'd never been in any part of a love triangle, so I didn't actually. I'd written a few, but seeing the collateral damage up close made me never want to again.

"It was a mistake. I'm a mess, sorry," I said quietly, slumping in my seat. "I don't know what the hell I'm doing."

"Yeah, you do," he replied. "You're going to perfect your pickleball game, woo your muse, and write a bestseller. Easy."

I leaned my head against the window. "Yeah, right. Easy."

Plus, I needed to cauterize whatever confusing Owen feelings were waking up inside of me.

"Hey, you learned how to pick hooves today. That'll help with your word count, right?"

I snorted. "Oh, for sure. The bonding scene between Austin and Abby is going to be amazing, cruddy horse feet notwithstanding." I paused. "But after that? I've got nada."

"And that's where our buddy Kai comes in. Speaking of, let's get your first game on the books. I'll text you a list of public courts and you let me know what works for you."

He looked so grim that I wished I could give him a hug. But actually not, since I now knew what it could lead to.

"You're doing too much. Seriously."

Owen met my gaze, softening a little. "I'm helping a friend. Plus, it's sort of fun experiencing the back end of book world. The writer's struggle. How the sausage gets made."

Sausage. Why was I cursed with a mind that couldn't stop conjuring up dad joke double entendres?

"You'll be my first thank-you in the acknowledgments for sure," I said. "You're my pickleball gateway drug."

"Ah, so you're addicted to the *game* now? It's not all for Kai?"

I blushed a little at how shallow it sounded coming out of Owen's mouth. It wasn't exactly "all for Kai," at least not anymore. My feelings for playing had shifted since the first time I picked up a paddle.

"Well, now that I've discovered that I have a tiny bit of coordination, I *do* like it."

"Tiny bit?" Owen scoffed at me. "Please. It's like a switch flipped. I'm getting scared of you."

"Yeah, right." I laughed at him.

"I'm serious. Get a couple of games under your belt and my work will be done. You'll be ready to meet your muse on the court."

I glanced at him out of the corner of my eye, deflating a little. "Done? Like the end of my lessons?"

"Oh, not yet, no," he said quickly. "We still have more polishing to do. But soon."

We both fell silent as we left the open fields and endless sky behind. I felt a little better about the kiss after talking it through. We were going to forget that it ever happened.

I mean, I *could*, if it weren't for the way kissing Owen had made me feel. In the moment? I'd been hungry, a little reckless, hoping it would go on forever.

And now?

I let my eyes stray to Owen's hands on the wheel. I could still feel the heat of them on my back. It wasn't even a long kiss, maybe five seconds, but I was still dealing with the aftershocks racing through me any time he looked at me.

I'd been caught up in the moment; that's all it was. My body had merely been reacting to the near-death experience of falling off a horse and then repackaged the cortisol stress hormones into lovey-dovey dopamine. My breakup with Leo had killed my libido—I hadn't recharged my vibrator in months—and the whole kissing-Owen thing was just a biological response after being deprived of pleasure for too long.

"Hey." Owen gave me a soft punch to my shoulder. "You look stressed out. It's all good, don't worry. You'll get that muse, I promise."

"Thanks, Coach," I managed, trying to suppress the tumult of emotions he'd woken up inside of me.

Chapter Nineteen

"Okay, this book is dark as hell," Meredith leaned over and whispered to me. "I'm only a couple of paragraphs in and the witches are already doing blood rituals on catcallers."

"That's Nia, fighting the patriarchy the old-fashioned way."

We were in the front row at Dog Eared Books for Nia's *Speak Softly* book launch, and Meredith's quick skim of it was clearly turning up gems. I'd read an ARC and knew exactly how psychopath-adjacent my friend came across on the page. What the world didn't realize was that the author who knew her way around creative murder weapons, morgues, and mausoleums took notes in a Lisa Frank notebook with a Hello Kitty pen.

I turned to glance at the rows filling up behind us. We'd arrived in Brooklyn early so we could get seats up front because the ticketed event had sold out almost immediately. Based on the crowd size and stacks of books at her signing table, Nia was probably on her way to bestseller status.

Meredith closed the book in her lap primly and turned to me. "So when's *your* book party?"

"Stop." I rolled my eyes at her.

"I'm serious. The only thing holding you back from all of this is you."

"Um, no, trust me, there are many, many, *many* roadblocks before this destination."

"But you're still working on the romantasy idea, right?"

I frowned and hunched my shoulders. "Yeah, and it feels like I'm cheating on Austin."

She frowned at me. "Oof. So *The Rancher's Backdoor Baby* is breech?"

"Stop it; that's gross." I laughed as I bumped against her. "And yes, I'm suffering for every word I write."

It felt like voodoo to keep pinning my hopes on some magical connection with Kai, but I was getting desperate. The words were *not* coming, and the clock was ticking. Piper had gotten back to me about the pages I'd sent her with less than encouraging feedback along the lines of "sorry, not feeling this" and "I can't tell where you're going in this chapter."

I'd never, ever reneged on a contract, but at the rate I was going, it felt possible.

Although Owen had all but promised a save in the form of a Kai connection on the horizon, I tried to envision how everything would fall into place once it happened.

We'd meet at CPA for a game or two, which, *terrifying*.

I'd serve like a pro and dink the hell out of every shot. I'd be in the zone enough to not just play well, but also strategize my moves.

Kai would be frustrated by my prowess at first since we'd be on opposing teams, then impressed, then enamored.

We'd finish and Kai would be drawn to chat with me about my killer backhand. Another team would come to claim our court, and we'd make plans to continue our conversation over drinks.

Drinks would turn into dinner, then nightcaps, and the evening would end with a toe-curling kiss, a promise of more to come.

The next morning I'd wake up with a renewed belief in happily ever afters, thanks to the world's best date the night before, and when I sat down at my laptop, I wouldn't stop until I'd added four thousand or so flawless words.

At least that was how I hoped it would go. There were quite a few variables that I couldn't control, as well as one I could—my performance—and they all made the scenario that much more challenging.

"*Great* crowd," Meredith said as the quaint shop filled between the bookshelves.

"That's Nia. She's a force."

"Getting close to standing room only." Meredith turned around and craned her neck. "Hey, is that Bucket Hat sans bucket hat?"

Owen and I hadn't spoken in the few days since the inexplicable kiss. I still needed to pick a date for open play on a public court.

I turned around, and sure enough, Owen was standing in the back, bareheaded and chatting with a petite, gray-haired woman.

I gasped at the sight of him in a white linen button-down with his dark baby mullet tamed. Despite the omnipresent hat and slobby clothing at CPA, he clearly knew how to dress in the real world.

"That's weird. Why is he here?" Meredith asked.

For an instant, I considered that it was because he knew I'd be at the signing, but we'd never discussed my connection to Nia.

"He's a big reader. Maybe he likes her stuff?"

I could see how he'd be into the haunted house vibes of

Formido, but *Speak Softly* was about a different kind of terror. Nia had told me her publisher had pushed back because of the tonal difference between her first and second books, forcing her to go to battle for the dark feminist horror novel. Given the prerelease reviews for *Speak Softly*, Nia had been right to fight.

"I'm sorry"—Meredith leaned closer to me, still torqued around in her chair and staring—"but he looks *good*."

I ignored her and watched Owen chat with the woman, hoping to catch his eye so I could wave at him, but he was too engrossed to glance away from her.

The store's marketing manager came out to introduce a yellow-jumpsuited Nia to the crowd, and Nia proceeded to charm her audience for an hour straight. When it came time for questions, everyone seemed too starstruck to speak first, so I raised my hand to ask about her writing process even though I had a front-row seat to it.

I could almost *feel* Owen's eyes on the back of my head after I'd asked the question.

Once Nia finished, everyone lined up to get books signed. I was well acquainted with the process, so we managed to maneuver our way to the front of the very long line. A quick congratulatory hug and photo later, Meredith and I were munching on book cover cookies—creepy because the cover featured a phallic-looking mushroom—plotting where we wanted to have dinner.

"Bucket Hat incoming," Meredith said behind her hand because her mouth was full. "Hope it's not too awkward for you post-make-out sesh."

"It was a split-second kiss, *not* a make-out," I hissed. I squared my shoulders, fixed a smile on my face, and turned to greet Owen. "Hey there!"

"Well, this is a surprise." He grinned at me, then turned to Meredith. "Good to see you again. How's the foot?"

"Hiya." She bobbed her head and pointed at her boot. "Home stretch. Thanks again for all of your help when it happened."

"Of course, glad you're doing better. Colton really misses playing with you."

The sweet-faced older woman appeared at Owen's side, clutching *Speak Softly* against her chest.

"Oh, hey, you're done already," he said to her. He refocused on us. "This is my mom, Cynthia. Mom, this is my pickleball student Brooke and her friend Meredith."

"So nice to meet you both," Cynthia said warmly as she shook each of our hands.

Cynthia had sparkling eyes and a smile that didn't quit, and I liked her immediately.

I nodded toward her book. "Did you read *Formido* as well?"

"I did, and it was terrifying." She shivered her shoulders. "I can't wait for this one."

"I read an early copy; you're going to love it," I assured her. "What about you?" I asked Owen.

"I did. I read anything my mom tells me to read. She has impeccable taste."

Cynthia chuckled at him.

"You guys, I have a great idea! We were just talking about grabbing dinner," Meredith said. "Why don't you join us and we can keep the book talk going?"

I shot her a look for being an instigator.

"Oh, I would love to, but I need to catch the train back to Jersey. I know this guy is hungry, though," Cynthia said as she glanced up at Owen. "He's always hungry."

I felt something spark in my chest when his eyes landed on

me, like he was looking for some sort of approval from me before inserting himself in our evening.

"Yeah, join us," I said quickly, because a meal with Meredith could smooth over any residual kissing weirdness with Owen.

"That'd be great, thanks." He bobbed his head. "I'm going to walk my mom to the station, so text me where you're going and I'll meet you there."

"Oh, stop," Cynthia tutted as she flapped her hand at Owen. "You don't have to walk me."

"Mom, I'm walking you," Owen insisted. "It's five minutes away; it's fine."

We said our goodbyes, and Meredith decided on a restaurant with an outdoor patio since the heat of the day had mellowed to tolerable. The sax-heavy sex music and dim lighting in the place clued me in that we were making a mistake as we followed the hostess outside.

"Mere, this is a first-date restaurant," I complained in a low voice. "Look around—it's all couples."

"Whatever." She shrugged. "The drinks are supposed to be amazing. And tonight we're a throuple."

The hostess seated us at a table in the middle of the patio, and it felt like we were under a spotlight despite the romantic lighting on the rest of it. I glanced around hoping to find a more secluded option, but every table was filled with moony-eyed couples.

"There he is." Meredith waved her hand over her head. "Over here!"

I followed her gaze and once again felt something spark to life inside of me as Owen threaded through the tables, while every woman and a few men turned to watch him. He lit up when he spotted us.

"Hey." He plopped down in the chair next to me. "Thanks for letting me crash your meal. I'm actually starving."

"Um, I'm sorry to report that it's tapas." Meredith held up the menu. "Are you okay with small plates?"

"Half a dozen small plates equals one normal one. Yeah, I'll make it work." He chuckled.

Before long, our table was crowded with deliciousness that was more than enough to fill all of us.

"So how's our student doing on the court these days?" Meredith asked as she struggled with a shrimp tail. "She's way too modest about her game."

I slid my eyes to Owen right as he did the same. Perfectly in sync, on and off the court.

"Brooke is someone who thought that she was an underdog," he mused, watching me. "We had to take care of some faulty wiring, and now she's basically unstoppable. I'm seriously impressed."

"So you *are* good." Meredith fake-glared at me. She glanced back at Owen. "She's always like, 'I'm not ready to play a real game; I need more sessions with Owen.'" Her voice went whiny as she impersonated me. "But now I know the truth. She's having fun with you."

His expression softened as he turned to me. "So you really are enjoying the lessons, huh?"

I shifted in my seat. "Well, yeah. Of course I am."

We shared a flicker of a moment as we both seemed to consider how far we'd come in just a few weeks.

Meredith pushed on, oblivious. "Every time she gets back from the club, she goes on and on about what a great coach you are." She looked over and winked at me.

Okay, so not totally oblivious. I felt my face go hot.

"Well, thank you, that's nice to hear," he replied softly, looking down at the tiny, empty plate in front of him.

"A good coach can make or break you," Meredith continued. "I did gymnastics in high school and my coach was *the worst*. She's the reason I quit."

"I feel that." He sighed. "Been there with my college tennis coach."

Once again, I wished that I could dig deeper into Owen's backstory, but he kept his life zipped up. I guess I was used to having guys spew their autobiography at me without any prompting. Maybe I was enjoying the foreign feeling of being the center of attention during our sessions?

Then again, maybe I was as pathetic as a guy at a strip club, convinced the dancer was into him instead of realizing that he was paying for the pleasure of her company?

"Right, Brooke?"

I'd been so in my head about what I was to Owen that I didn't hear what he'd said.

"Sorry, what was that?"

Meredith leaned closer to me, wearing the world's biggest shit-eating grin. "He said you're going to sign up for the New York Parks Pickleball Tournament!"

Chapter Twenty

"Oh, no way."

I scooted my chair back from the table, like I needed to move away from the very *idea* of competing in a tournament.

"C'mon, it'll be fun," Owen cajoled. "Plus you need a goal." He paused. "I mean, you already have the Kai goal, but it helps to have something, uh, tangible that you're working toward."

"I love it," Meredith said gleefully. "I'll be in the front row, cheering you on."

"As if I have the *time* to focus on something like a tournament," I snipped back. "I have a pretty pressing deadline to worry about, you know."

Owen stacked the dishes in front of him and put his elbows on the table like he was an attorney entering the negotiation phase. "That's just it; you don't have to worry about it—you just do it. It's nothing more than a way to push yourself and achieve a goal. A deadline of sorts. Which you're used to."

Yeah, I was way too familiar with deadlines, particularly the missing them aspect.

Thankfully, before the argument could continue, our wan, disinterested waitress came back to see if we wanted dessert, which Meredith ordered for us without asking what we wanted like she was a douchey dude trying to impress a date. She started gathering her things the moment the waitress turned to walk away.

"Fun night, guys. I need to head out."

"Wha . . . why? You just ordered the entire dessert menu," I sputtered at the thought of eating a chocolate bombe alone with Owen in a romantic restaurant.

"Colton got out of his dinner meeting early. I'm going to his place, so text me how much I owe and I'll Venmo you, Brookie."

It was then I realized that she'd planned to duck out before the end of the meal, to give me time alone with Owen.

"Don't forget to *say yes* to seconds. Byyeeeeee," she sang as she stood up and tucked her Dog Eared bag under her arm.

I glowered at her as she flitted away.

"She's a trip," Owen said. "How long have you two been friends?"

"College. We hated each other at first. I thought she was a stuck-up Connecticut girl, and she thought I was a weird nerd. Turns out, we were both right, and opposites do attract."

"So you're claiming nerd status?"

I snorted. "You've spent the last few weeks with me—what do *you* think?"

He leaned back in his chair and looked at me like he was seeing me for the first time. "I think you're a puzzle," he said softly.

On paper, it wasn't necessarily a compliment, but the way he said it sure made it feel that way.

The waitress came back and dropped off two cut glass tumblers filled with amber liquid. "Your friend ordered these on the way out. Enjoy."

We'd downed beer and sangria throughout the meal, and the

last thing we needed was more alcohol, but Meredith clearly wanted us in an altered state as we finished the night together.

"Bottoms up, I guess," Owen said as he raised his tumbler and leaned closer to me.

"Cheers," I said as I clinked my glass to his.

Meredith and I had gone to a whiskey-tasting event together, and I had a feeling that she'd hooked us up with something top-shelf. I didn't love whiskey, but I wasn't about to let it go to waste. I took a sip and watched as the hostess led another couple to a table across the patio. The woman was petite, blond, and ridiculously pretty, with her hair slicked back in a low bun and wearing a simple cropped black shirt and jeans in the unstyled-but-definitely-planned way of all great influencers.

I tried not to stare as she and her date took their seats because she looked *really* familiar. Did I follow her on Instagram? I took another sip of whiskey as I glanced at her date, then launched into a choking fit of shock and horror.

It was Leo.

"Are you okay?" Owen asked as I tried not to make a spectacle of myself. He glanced over his shoulder to follow my gaze, then back at me, his brow furrowed with concern. "Take my water."

He handed his glass to me, and I gulped it down in between coughing fits that I tried to keep quiet, because the *last* thing I wanted was for Leo to spot me red-faced and runny-eyed.

I tried to formulate a plan as I collected myself. Dessert hadn't arrived yet, but it wasn't like I could remain at the table, speed shoveling caramel mousse in my face, with my ex and his perfect girlfriend just a few feet away. Maybe I could slip out, have the waitress box everything up, and meet Owen on the sidewalk?

"What's going on?" Owen asked when I could finally breathe normally again. "Who are those people?"

Had I been *that* obvious, or was Owen just that perceptive?

We leaned toward each other at the same moment.

"My ex," I whispered hoarsely. "That's Leo."

Owen's face went stormy as he seemed to process that my backstory was invading our present. The ghosting, resulting writer's block, Kai, and our pickleball connection all stemmed from the handsome man across the patio.

I stole a glance at Leo, who was unfortunately positioned so he'd see us if he could tear his eyes away from Isodora. His superpower was his ability to get away with extreme amounts of bullshit because he was so damn *adorable*. Dark hair, light eyes, and a mischievous smile that suggested all sorts of naughtiness. Old ladies thought he walked on water.

"Is this the first time you've seen him since . . . ?"

I nodded mutely.

"Well, you look amazing," Owen said. "No matter what, you've got that going for you."

It was the kindest thing he could've said, because my first reflex was a quick inventory of my outfit and hair. I'd fixed myself up for Nia's event in summery pink, and Owen had noticed.

"Is he watching us?"

Owen tried to surreptitiously peek over his shoulder, then opted to swing his chair over so that he was closer to me and had a straight line of sight for easier spying.

"Not that I can tell."

The waitress interrupted us again, this time to deliver a tray of desserts that had a hissing sparkler sticking out and "Happy Birthday" written in chocolate on the plate. Flying under the radar was impossible now, because the stick of dynamite shooting fire on our mousse was the equivalent of a searchlight on the dim patio.

"What?" I gaped at Owen. "Is it your birthday?"

Then it hit me. Meredith.

"Happy birthday to *both* of you," the waitress said in a louder voice than she'd used all night, which made a few people turn to look at us. A woman at the next table clapped.

I couldn't bear to check if Leo was looking over, but how could he not? It was a spectacle, and all we needed was for the waitstaff to come out and sing to us. I doubted Leo would know that it wasn't actually my birthday. He'd asked me about the date and then recorded it in his phone, but we'd never shared a November.

"He's watching," Owen whispered to me through a smile. "I think it's payback time."

"Huh?"

The corner of his mouth kicked up. "You fake dated for me; now it's my turn to do it for you. It's only fair."

I gripped the whiskey glass in my hands so tightly I worried it might shatter. "Oh, you don't have to . . ."

"But I *want* to."

There was subtext in those four words that I couldn't decipher. I felt his eyes resting on me while I weighed what to do next.

"Kiss me," Owen murmured.

"*What?*" I panic-whispered.

"I said kiss me. *Now*."

The directness in his voice sent a shiver through me. He was issuing a command like we were on the court, only a billion times sexier. Despite everything we'd discussed about broken hearts and love triangles, we were about to kiss.

Again.

I must've nodded, because the next thing I knew Owen was moving closer to gently palm my cheek. My stomach went into a free fall at how damn *convincing* he was as he lovingly stared into my eyes.

"Happy fake birthday, B," he murmured as he slid closer still, his thumb caressing my cheek.

So real. Heartfelt. Believable.

"Ha-happy fake birthday," I whispered, frozen by his very convincing seduction.

Turns out Owen was ridiculously good at make-believe.

He placed his other hand on my face and drew me to him, his eyes on my mouth like *I* was the dessert that he couldn't wait to taste. My breathing went shallow and my heart thudded as we relished the delicious moment of before.

The noise around us blotted out. Owen moved closer in slow motion, and I held my breath.

Then his lips touched mine tentatively, like he wasn't sure how far to take our performative PDA. A hint of a kiss, just a gentle press of our mouths together, but it was enough to send a shock wave through my body. I started to pull back reluctantly, but Owen slid his hand to the nape of my neck to gently hold me in place.

It was his way of conveying that I wasn't going anywhere. Once again, our kiss wasn't over until *he* decided it was. I was more than happy to relinquish control after what had happened the last time I kissed him.

His tongue traced along my bottom lip. Heat flooded my body as the sleeping need inside of me roared awake again thanks to Owen. I moved my hands to the tops of his solid thighs and squeezed. I felt him smile against my mouth.

Leo was just a few feet away, no doubt watching our little show since the sparkler was still illuminating the entire patio, but all I could focus on was how fucking *masterful* Owen was at kissing me. He teased his tongue against mine as he slipped his fingertips through my hair.

I normally wasn't one for PDA, but Owen had me ready to climb onto his lap and grind against him. We'd gone beyond a "look how happy I am without you, Leo," kiss to borderline exhibitionist. I wasn't ready to stop, and based on the way Owen pulled me closer, he wasn't going anywhere either.

Unfortunately, the sparkler had other ideas. It fell onto the plate with a clank, and I could see the sideways trajectory of the sparks from the corner of my eye.

Owen finally peeled himself away from me. "Whoops." He laughed softly and righted it in the blob of frosting again.

The sparkler continued sparkling while Owen and I stared at each other. A little flushed, breathing heavy, and if it were up to me, ready for more.

"He saw the whole thing," Owen ventriloquized through a grin. "You won this match."

I did feel strangely victorious, in addition to the horniness pulsing through me. I wanted to glance over at Leo, but I knew it was better optics to pretend that I didn't know he was there. Instead, I focused on Owen.

"Thank you. Once again, you went above and beyond."

"Of course, it's our joint fake birthday. We're celebrating." Owen's eyes flicked past me; then he raised my hand to his lips, flipped it over, and kissed the inside of my wrist. "Anything for you."

My breath caught as his mouth grazed my skin. Suddenly I was a naive debutante in a Regency romance, nearly coming undone from a chaste kiss.

"FYI, he's very interested in us." Owen draped our clasped hands on the table, then picked up his fork with the other. He sawed off a hunk of flourless chocolate torte that was next to the spent sparkler. "Let's give him an absolutely sickening show. Vile happiness. Open up, B."

I went a little breathless at the command and did as I was told. Owen slid the too-big bite into my mouth, getting a little bit of the frosting on the corner of my lip in the process. He leaned closer to me, dragged his finger through the remnants ringing my mouth, then popped his finger in his mouth to suck it off, wearing a devilish grin.

"Mm." He lounged back in his chair, his eyes mischievous. "You taste delicious."

A shudder passed through me, because I'd written that very line after my cowboy Beau kneeled between Savanna's legs for the very first time. All I could do was nod as I chewed.

We managed to flirt and eat our way through nearly all the three desserts Meredith had ordered while I stole glances at Leo and Isodora. It looked like they were enjoying a standard-issue dinner. Nothing like the lovefest Owen and I were putting on.

The bill arrived and he reached for it before I had a chance to.

I forced myself not to look over at them on our way out, but I could feel him watching us leave, hand in hand.

Shockingly, I felt nothing other than hopeful that Owen would find an excuse to kiss me again. No maudlin feelings about seeing Leo, just a fixation on the man beside me.

We wound up on the sidewalk right outside the patio and conveniently right in the line of sight of every person eating there.

Owen leaned close to me, and I caught another hit of his warm, sagy scent.

"Ready for the grand finale?" he asked.

I'd barely bobbed my head when he swept me into his arms, bent me over backward, and kissed me long and hard. I was so caught off guard that my arms flopped limply behind me, until I finally found enough muscle tone to reach up and lock them behind his neck.

My eyes were squeezed shut, but I felt like I could still see the sparkler going off. We kissed for, what, a half hour? A minute? I lost track of time as we melted against each other. When Owen finally stood me up, I wobbled a few steps.

"*Wow.*"

"Yeah, I think that worked." Owen reached for me. "Let's leave as a united front."

We walked down the block silently, holding hands like it was a normal, everyday thing to do. We'd already jogged together, holding hands and cackling, but this was more reserved, like it was our go-to walking scenario. He let go once we reached the subway station.

"Okay, so our next meeting is at Jimmie McDaniel Park, right? You ready?"

My mouth dropped open, because I expected us to go through some sort of play-by-play about what had just happened at the restaurant. I at least wanted to laugh about the absurdity of our show, to vent some of the very real sexual tension that I was working hard to ignore.

I finally found my voice. "Um, yeah. Sure."

"Inaugural game play," he said. "It's going to be good for you, I promise."

Lately, everything Owen did was good for me.

I could only nod, because how were we having a normal conversation about *pickleball* when he'd just kissed me like that?

Owen backed away from me, pointing at me. "You've got this, B. Next stop, signing you up for the tournament."

I opened my mouth to protest, but he'd already disappeared around the corner.

Chapter Twenty-One

I'd picked the least fancy public pickleball court of all the options for my debut. I wanted to play with friendly folks who enjoyed the game, not serious athletes like the assassins from the Chelsea Pickleball Academy. The court I'd selected was in the shadows of apartment buildings on repurposed tennis courts. There were weeds along the chain-link fence and the view was nonexistent, but the low-key vibe felt perfect for me.

Owen had texted me five minutes before our meeting time to let me know he was running late. He told me to get a feel for the place while I waited since there were spoken *and* unspoken rules at open play courts. I'd expected to find a crowd of eager players when I arrived, but then again, it was eight in the morning on a sunny Thursday, so it made sense that there was only one foursome on the court. I watched from outside the fence, like a kid hoping to be invited in to join.

The group was made up of a deeply tanned guy who looked to be in his late fifties and an equally braised woman who seemed to be his wife, a very focused blonde in what I recognized was an Athleta tennis dress, and a tall, skinny senior in a non-ironic trucker cap. Despite the fact that the couple looked fit and had top-of-the-line gear, they seemed to be losing to the mismatched pair.

Lessons with Owen had allowed me to master the fundamentals and get out of my head, but actual gameplay was still pretty overwhelming. And it moved *fast*. I guessed that the foursome had a history based on how intuitive they seemed with one another.

"That's game," I heard the senior say as the ball bounced in the farthest corner of the court.

He and his partner touched paddles; then they met their opponents to do the same across the net.

"I need to run to class, Howard," the blonde said apologetically. "Next week?"

"Yes, indeedy." He flexed his arm to make a muscle. "See you then."

She turned around and spotted me. "Oh, look, you guys can keep going. You're here to play, right?"

I checked behind me to make sure she was talking to me. "Uh, yeah, but I'm waiting for my partner—"

"No need to wait," the older man said. "Come play with us."

"Oh, I'm just a beginner. You guys are really good."

The tan woman made a frustrated noise since they'd lost.

"We were *all* beginners at one point," he replied. "The only way to get better is to get better, and that won't happen with you out there, fence hugging. C'mon in."

I swallowed hard. "Are you sure? I'm a total novice. This would be my first real game."

The tan team groaned in unison.

"Maybe we should wait?" Tan Man said. "I don't have the energy to educate her. Sorry."

I bristled a little. I didn't want his education; I'd had plenty with Owen, as well as the dozens of YouTube tutorials I watched when I couldn't manufacture any cowboy words.

What I *wanted* was my lucky charm. Where the hell was Owen? I checked my phone but there were no new messages.

"Definitely a beginner—look at her paddle." The woman laughed.

Okay, point taken. But still, she didn't have to be so damn judgy. At least my outfit was cute. I'd found a black set on clearance—ruffled skort and sleeveless tank—that made me look like I knew what I was doing. Owen always talked about the sense of community in the game, but I sure wasn't getting it at the Jimmie McDaniel formerly-tennis-but-now-pickleball courts.

But I wasn't about to let them know they were rattling me.

"You know what? I'll play," I said in an overloud voice to make sure they all heard me.

"Atta girl," the older man said. "Get in here."

The blonde winked at me as she passed me on the way out. "Howard's a doll. You're going to do great—don't worry."

I glanced toward the street, looking for a familiar, loping form, but Owen was nowhere in sight.

"Hi, everyone, I'm Brooke," I said with a wave as I walked in.

"Howard." My new partner did a half bow. He reached out his paddle to tap mine, and when I got close to him, I saw that his navy hat said "Professor Pickleball" in embroidered lettering. "The whiny fellow over there is Mark, and that's his wife, Theresa."

They both grumbled in my general direction.

"They're angry because this old man keeps them on their toes," Howard said. He pointed to his leg and I spotted a knee brace. "I might not be the fastest one out here, but I do okay."

"Let's get this going," Theresa said. "What's your rating, by the way?"

She glared at me from under the brim of her pink Joola visor.

"Uh, I'm not sure, but my coach should be here any minute and he'll know. Maybe, like, I don't know, a two?"

Mark stalked closer to the net. "You have a *coach*? Yeah, you're better than a two. Let's go; switch sides."

Howard tossed the ball to me as we walked to the far side of the court, which was thankfully shady. I was already sweating from nerves.

"Your serve."

I managed to catch it. "Me? Why?"

He pointed to the court numbers on the chain-link fence behind us. "Number side always starts, and you're on the right side of the court, so . . . off you go."

I'd envisioned some sort of fanfare before my first serve because it was a momentous occasion, but to the rest of the group, it was just another Thursday. Maybe it was better that the game was unremarkable? Less pressure. And without Owen there, the only person I had to worry about was Howard.

I could hear Owen's voice as I got ready. Grip, stance, headspace . . . I moved into position, drew back my paddle, and—

"*Score*," Theresa scolded me. "You have to say the score!"

I cringed at my rookie mistake. "Right, sorry!"

"It's okay," Howard assured me.

My palms got a little sweatier.

"Uh." My voice cracked. "Zero, zero, start."

I took a deep breath and shifted my weight back and forth.

"You only have ten seconds to serve after you call the score," Mark said. "You should *know* that."

"Okay, right. Zero, zero, start," I repeated. I dropped the ball and managed a perfectly clean shot across the net and into the right side of the court. Owen always did a growly "yessss" whenever I performed well and I half expected to hear it after my gorgeous inaugural serve. I started jogging to the kitchen line.

"Hold up," Howard coached from behind me, still glued to the baseline. "Serve and stay, serve and stay."

I ran backward—another rookie mistake that Owen would lecture me about if he'd seen it—and got into position beside Howard at the line.

Mark bombed the ball back and directly to me, which was great strategy since I was the weakest link on the court. I ran to it and returned my own bomb that cleared the net and promptly flew out-of-bounds.

"That's okay," Howard said with a nod. He walked closer to me. "Mark likes to hit the hell outta the ball, but those bangers really wear him out. Our best bet is to play at the kitchen line. It's easier for me"—he pointed to his bad knee—"plus he *hates* it when I snatch 'em out of the air and drive 'em down the middle."

"Got it," I said with a nod.

For the next eighteen minutes, I tried to put every lesson I'd learned into play. I served, returned, dinked, and sweated alongside Howard and wound up failing him.

"Ten, two, one," Mark said as he served the shot that put us out of our misery.

Game over, an obliterating defeat.

Both teams walked to the net to touch paddles, and I could've sworn Theresa was gloating despite my beginner status.

But I'd done it! We'd lost, but I still felt like a winner for surviving my first real game.

"Anyone have time for another?" I asked, glancing around at them.

Even though I didn't love the idea of facing Team Tan again, I'd carved out an hour to play and I intended to use every minute of it.

Mark chuckled. "What are you, a glutton for punishment?"

"Oh, stop," Howard scolded gently. "I saw some really great stuff out there. And I missed a bunch of shots, so it's not all Brooke's fault. Let's go again."

Mark and Theresa reluctantly agreed, and when I returned Theresa's serve so perfectly that they both whiffed it, the vibe on the court shifted.

Now we were playing.

Howard had a bunch of tricks up his sleeve, including a backspin that Mark missed every time. But I actually managed to hold my own. I found my rhythm, even though I still had to occasionally chant "just push" to keep from hitting the ball out-of-bounds. I wasn't in my head; my focus was on the game and my teammate.

We won game two. *And* game three.

When we tapped paddles I did a little scrunch-nose smile at Theresa that I hoped telegraphed "sorry you lost; don't you *dare* underestimate me" to her.

"I need to call it a day, my friends," Howard said. "Brooke, phenomenal job. I hope we get to play again soon. I'm here most mornings at this time."

I wanted to ask for his number, or since he was clearly over seventy, get his Facebook handle, but I wasn't sure if it would be weird.

"Thank you for letting me join you. It was really fun."

And for the first time since I'd begun my insane journey to learn pickleball to impress the guy to write the words, I realized that, yeah, I was having a damn good time at it.

And not only that, but I was *decent*! Me, the world champion sidelines sitter was good at a sport!

I turned to gather my things and leave and froze when I saw a man and dog sitting in the shade of the lone tree.

"*Owen?* How long have you been there?"

Chapter Twenty-Two

Owen beamed at me as he walked over, letting Marti drag him to me. "I've been here long enough to see you obliterate that last game! Holy shit, you cooked out there."

I wasn't sure how things would feel with Owen post-make-out, but my shockingly good performance on the court was a great redirect. I knelt down to pet a very excited Marti, who rolled onto her back for belly rubs.

"Yes, she did," Howard answered for me on his way by. "You're the coach, I presume?"

"I am." He reached out his hand. "Owen."

"Howard Daley." He squinted at Owen. "Have we met before?"

He was bucket hatted and in his usual T-shirt and elastic waist shorts, which I'd figured out was his pickleball persona. If Howard knew him, it had to be from that environment.

Owen shrugged. "I teach over at Chelsea Pickleball Academy?"

"Hmm." Howard frowned. "Never been there, but you look very familiar to me."

"I have one of those faces, I guess." Owen grinned at him.

But he didn't actually. To me, Owen was one of a kind. Sure, on paper he was just an everyday cute guy who camouflaged his attractiveness in sloppy clothes, but the wattage of his smile and warmth in his eyes made you feel *seen*.

"And who's this?" Howard asked, pointing at Marti.

"Miss Martina Dogratilova," Owen said proudly.

"Ah, tennis! Maybe that's where I know you from?" Howard said. "I used to play quite a bit before the old bones started giving out. Hence my new obsession." He held up his paddle.

Owen nodded. "I played tennis in college, but it's been a *long* time."

He shifted, and I could tell he was getting uncomfortable with the light interrogation.

Howard turned to me. "Brooke, please come back. Like I said, I'm here all the time." He leaned closer to me and glanced toward where Team Tan was packing up. "But they're not."

I laughed. "Got it. Thanks for the invitation. I'd love to."

We waved our goodbyes, and Owen, Marti, and I set off together.

"Why were you late?" I asked, hoping that I didn't sound accusatory. "I was sort of counting on you being here."

The corner of Owen's mouth curled up. "Exactly."

"Huh?"

"I wanted you to do this on your own, without your crutch."

I paused. "Hold on, you no-showed on purpose?"

He spread his hands in front of him. "I'm right here; I didn't no-show. I was just a little late."

Everything started to fall into place. "Oh my god, that's why you brought Marti with you. You don't have your paddle, and you're wearing slides and socks. You never intended to play with me."

"Bingo."

"But . . . you're my coach," I sputtered, spinning my hands in the air.

"And good coaches give their athletes wings," he replied.

I smiled involuntarily at being called an athlete even though I didn't like where the conversation was headed.

Owen paused and turned to me. "I wanted to show you that you're basically where you need to be. You played on your own today and killed it. I think you're ready to fly solo."

My mouth dropped open. Was Owen *firing* me?

"Hold on a sec. You want me to sign up for that tournament thing—"

"Only if *you* want to," he interrupted. "I said I think it's worthwhile to have another goal besides . . . Kai."

"Okay, so I agree. I want to sign up."

My stomach roiled at the thought of it, but in the moment, it felt like the only way I could get Owen to keep working with me. I knew we'd have to part ways eventually, but not *now*. Our mornings together were one of the few times I could stop stressing about my life and just focus on the joy of the moment.

"Seriously?" Owen asked. "You want to do the tournament?"

I nodded my head vigorously to convince both of us that it was true.

We set off down the sidewalk again while Marti scanned the pee mail. "That changes things. If you want to compete, then we definitely need to polish you up a bit. I mean, you were fucking amazing out there, but I saw a few snags. Little tweaks we could work on."

"Exactly," I agreed quickly. "Are you okay to keep things the way they've been?"

Working with Owen had become an important part of my

week, despite the fact that it always took me a couple of hours before I could stop thinking about my technique and focus on writing. Or *ghostwriting*, because my archer story was now a faucet I couldn't turn off.

"Yeah, meeting with you in the morning before we open is fine. I basically live at CPA anyway."

Based on the little I'd learned about Owen, it tracked. I couldn't resist prying.

"Where *do* you live?" I asked.

He paused to let Marti squat. "It's walking distance from the club. I have the perfect commute."

He didn't even give up the cross streets. The dude was Fort Knox. Or an undercover spy.

"So Chelsea?" I pushed.

"Basically. Anyway, let's talk schedule since we have limited hours for the holiday weekend, and we're closed on the Fourth," he added. "I could still meet you if you want to come in, though."

I frowned. "No, I'll be in the Hamptons for the weekend. Meredith forced me into it."

Which wasn't entirely true.

"Nice." Owen nodded and encouraged Marti to move on from a pile someone had neglected to clean up. "I got a couple of invitations to head out there. Lots of CPA members go, but I'm not sure what I want to do."

"There's a chance Kai is going to the party we're invited to," I blurted out. It felt weird bringing him up in the moment even though Kai was the reason for everything we were doing together.

I saw Owen's jaw flex.

"Wow, so maybe this whole scheme was pointless?" He

looked at me out of the corner of his eye. "If you guys run in the same circles, you don't actually need a pickleball connection."

It really felt like he was trying to cut me loose in the gentlest possible way. "Owen, no, not at all. I mean, sure, that was my initial reason to start playing, but I've grown to love it." I forced myself to keep talking, because he needed to know what he'd done for me. "You sort of rerouted my synapses. You made me like a *sport*. My brother's going to pass out when he visits."

"Your brother is coming here?"

"Yeah, an overnight visit," I replied quickly, not wanting to get derailed before I made my point. "Anyway, I owe you. For taking me on as a student, driving me to New Jersey to get thrown off a horse, and for forcing me to do that." I pointed over my shoulder to the courts behind us. "For all of it. You're an amazing teacher and coach."

He smiled but only with his mouth. The rest of his expression was wary. "Thank you. I appreciate that."

We both watched Marti do her thing, marking every raised surface like she owned the entire city. I thought about my time with Owen, how he'd changed me, and an idea started to take shape.

"Hold on. You should write a *book*. About coaching," I said excitedly. "I could be your beta reader, since I have insights into how it feels to be your student."

"A book?" Owen tilted his head. "For who?"

I squinted into the distance as I considered it. "Depends on your message. If you want a big audience, you could adapt your content to business. Like, 'Everything I learned about human connections was forged across a net.'"

He chuckled. "A bit clunky, but I get what you mean."

"No, better idea; you could make it for *salespeople*! Relationship-selling stuff. That's a huge audience. You could tie it in with speaking engagements," I said, getting ahead of myself as usual. "What's your social media like? Publishers love nonfiction writers with huge platforms."

Owen snorted. "Do I *look* like I use social media?"

"Point taken. That'll be an issue, but you can set one up when you go out on submission. I can help you with that. My agent doesn't rep nonfiction, but I can see if she has a suggestion for you. The first step is putting together a thorough outline, which I wish I could help you with but I do *not* use an outline. To my eternal frustration."

"Yeah, how's writing going for you?"

I shook my head at him. "We're not talking about me for a change, but to put it briefly, it's shitty. I mean, my sidepiece book is going amazing, but Austin is treading water."

Literally. I'd left off in a chapter where he was skinny-dipping in a pond on his property and Abby was supposed to catch him there.

"Hold on, what sidepiece book? You're writing two at once?"

I wasn't sure why I hadn't mentioned *The Archer's Paradox* to him. Since he was a fantasy reader, it probably was the sort of thing he'd enjoy. And he'd liked *Rogue Cowboy*, so I knew he could appreciate my writing style.

"I am," I replied. "A new genre for me. Romantasy."

His mouth went into an upside-down U shape as he considered it. "Okay. That tracks."

I turned to gape at him. "Seriously? You really think so?"

"Sure. You do a great job with tone and setting, which are important in fantasy. And the villain in *Rogue* was evil but still redeemable, which is important if your love interest is a bad guy turned good."

"How did you know?" I asked, then waved my hand in the air and shook my head. "No, stop. This isn't about my book."

"*Books*," he corrected.

"Whatever. *You* are going to write a fabulous, self-helpy book, right?"

"I've never considered it until this very minute."

"Well, get on that, because it's a brilliant idea, and you have a willing partner to help you along the way." I paused. "Just like you did for me. Which is why you need to write the book. Because you help people uncover their inner greatness."

"Wow, and here I thought I was just teaching dinks and drops." We paused at a busy intersection. "Where are you headed?"

I glanced around to see where we'd ended up. "Uh, honestly, I was just walking with you two." I bent over to pet Marti. "I need to get to work."

"Yes, you do. Good luck with *both* books, and I guess we'll talk after the holiday?"

"Definitely." I started backing away from the pair. "Have a great Fourth."

"Safe travels. People get crazy, so be careful." Owen's dark eyes were locked on me like I was leaving for good. "Hope you and Kai get a chance to connect, but if not, I've got you."

Even though I had Kai in my sight lines, I sure liked the way "I've got you" sounded coming out of Owen's mouth.

Chapter Twenty-Three

"Why are we waiting in a line that's twenty people deep for bagels?" I quietly complained to Meredith and Colton. "There's a bagel shop on every corner at home."

"Yeah, but they're not *Goldberg's* bagels," Colton said. "You gotta do local shit when you're in Sag Harbor."

I glanced around at the crowd. "Are there actually locals around here, or are they too smart to come into town during a holiday weekend?"

The two of them fit right in among the fancy folks queued up on the sidewalk for breakfast sandwiches, although more than a few people looked like they could use some hair of the dog. We'd arrived the night before, so late that it technically could be qualified as early, which meant we'd gone right to bed. *Tonight* was the big night.

"I'm just so happy to be naked," Meredith said, wiggling a Tory Burch flip-flop in the air. "Perfect timing to be boot-free."

"You still need to take it easy," I cautioned. "Sneakers would be a better choice."

"Yeah, yeah, I know," she grumbled. "Just let me be cute for this weekend, okay?"

Colton pulled her close and kissed her on the cheek. "Never not cute." He squinted across the street to where another crowd was forming. "Is that one of the Housewives? The one who sings about Pinot Noir and fancy cars?"

I craned my neck to see. "Yup, that's her. First celebrity sighting of the weekend. Colton is officially on the leaderboard."

I loved that despite all of Colton's finance-bro energy, he wasn't afraid to embrace the goofy stuff we enjoyed. Bonding over showmances and villain edits made it easier being their third wheel.

"So beach day today?" Meredith asked as we inched forward. "Perfect weather for it."

"Don't hate me—I know it's ridiculous—but I need to get some writing done," I replied.

"Oh, come on, it's a holiday weekend," Colton whined. "Come for a half day at least."

"He's right," Meredith piled on. "You can take a couple hours to recharge and then do it."

I shook my head. "Not possible for me. I'd sit there and stress about not working and wind up having a crappy time. But if I write first and manage to kick some ass, *then* I'll meet you." I paused. "I'll do it poolside, so it feels a little vacationy."

Meredith pushed her sunglasses on her head and looked beyond us. "Um, I think you're going to have a very successful writing session."

"Yes, exactly. Thanks for manifesting it for me."

"No," she hissed. "*Muse* alert!"

I froze. "Where?"

"Coming up the sidewalk behind you."

Colton went on his tiptoes and craned his neck as if he'd

never taken part in a covert gossip mission in his life. "I know the guys he's with. One of them is a host for tonight."

Meredith squeezed my arm. "Which guarantees he's going to be there."

I leaned closer to her, tilting my head back and smiling widely. "Teeth and nose check, quick!"

"All clear, you're good."

The three of us stood there watching Kai and his friends amble closer. I hadn't seen him in ages, but the butterflies were back in full force.

Muse status intact.

"So do you want me to say hi or . . . ?" Colton asked, glancing between us.

Meredith rolled her eyes. "Do you even understand the responsibilities of a wingman? Seriously, Colton. *Yes*. Of course."

"Please," I added.

Meredith undid the top button of my green stripey blouse and pushed the collar open, then adjusted my twisted gold necklaces. "Perfect. You look adorable."

"Thanks."

"Okay, incoming," Colton said under his breath, stepping out of line to intercept the trio. "Heyyyy, who let the troublemakers in?"

They went through a series of handshakes and backslaps before turning their attention to us. "Guys, meet my girlfriend, Meredith, and our friend Brooke." He turned to point at them. "This is Tyler, Zach, and *Kai*."

He practically wiggled his eyebrows at me as he said the name. I wanted to punch him for his lack of chill.

"You again." Kai smiled at me. "We keep running into each other. You're a member at CPA, right?"

"We all are," Meredith lied for me. "But the last time I was there, I fractured my foot. We ran into you in the lobby, remember?"

"*Right*, of course." He nodded. "Grip was taking care of you."

"Yup, Brooke's taking lessons with him now," Colton said. "Twice a week."

"He said she's really good," Meredith added.

They were a combination of hype man and PR strategist, and I loved them for it. All I had to do was try to look cute.

"Oh, no way," Kai said with admiration in his voice. "Gripper is the best. And you must be good, because he's super picky about who he takes on. I practically had to audition to get him to work with me! He off-loads to Brandon if he doesn't think you're good enough."

It was news to me.

"You folks ready to get crazy tonight or what?" Tyler tried to punch Colton in the stomach, but he ducked away too quickly.

Meredith and I exchanged a look. We'd already agreed to bail if the party wound up going *Wolf of Wall Street*. My hope was to get my Kai time early enough that things were still sober and civil, although thanks to the unexpected meeting, I had a head start.

"We're ready to enjoy a fun evening," Meredith answered with a prim smile. "The weather's perfect, the company is great—"

"The drinks will be flowing," Zach added. "Plenty of party favors too."

I glanced at Meredith again. Yeah, I definitely wasn't down to hang with a bunch of strangers tripping balls. I glanced at Kai to see how keen he seemed to just say yes to illicit substances, but he didn't respond.

"Did you guys eat breakfast? Want to join us?" Colton asked.

The people in line behind grumbled at the possibility of three extra people between them and their bagels.

"Would love to," Kai answered as he glanced my way, "but we need to run a couple errands to get ready. We can hang tonight and gossip about the Big Gripper. He's supposed to come, by the way. I invited him. Last minute, but he said he might make it."

My mouth dropped open. Owen was going to be at the party too? That made my mission even easier!

"Later," Zach said, reaching out to do a complicated handshake with Colton. "Nice to meet you both."

We waited until they were out of sight to begin the download.

"He was *totally* checking you out," Meredith said under her breath.

"I saw it too."

Same. It was too obvious *not* to notice it.

"So how does this muse thing happen? Explain it to me," Colton said as we moved forward a half step. "Is it like a bolt of lightning?"

"No," I answered quickly, even though it sort of was. "I can't figure it all out myself. It's sort of hard to believe that this is my first time dealing with major writer's block."

"Thanks, *Leo*," Meredith sneered.

"Yeah, I never liked him," Colton added.

"Usually I'm in the right headspace to churn out the happiest of happily ever afters," I continued. "But what Leo did to me . . . it broke me."

We all jealously eyed a family walking out of Goldberg's digging into their bagels.

"And Kai fixed you, like that?" Colton snapped his fingers.

"Hardly." Meredith laughed, since she was well acquainted with my ongoing struggle. "But he has the *potential* to."

"Exactly." I nodded. "He's like my embodiment of hope. After feeling absolutely devastated, all of a sudden my heart woke up when I saw him."

"Cue the prolific writing?" Colton asked.

I gave him a wry smile. "That's what I'm banking on."

Colton winced. "Damn. That's a lot of pressure on a regular-ass guy. What if he turns out to be shitty?"

Meredith gave me a pointed look.

"I'm not considering that an option."

He cocked an eyebrow at me and let out a low whistle.

"I mean, it's looking pretty darn positive." Meredith slid her arm around my shoulder as we moved closer to the door. "And now I totally support you being a loser and working today. Based on what just happened, the words are going to *fall* out of you."

Two hours later I was discovering just how wrong she was.

I had everything on my side: a full belly, an absolutely stunning poolside setting beneath a cloudless sky, with bay breezes blowing in, and the promise of something magical once the sun set.

Nothing was working for me. My finger was basically camped out above the backspace key. I was desperate to give Austin and Abby some quality time, not only because of the ticking clock but also because I loved the two of them together. They deserved an HEA, but before I could get there, I needed to put a baby in Abby so they could break apart over the unexpected pregnancy, then come together.

The problem was, they needed to have sex in order to make the damn baby.

I fell back in the chair and hugged my knees. Kai was *right* there, closer than he'd ever been, which should've ignited all sorts of sexy possibilities inside of me. We'd flirted, with witnesses! Or he'd flirted, and I'd received it frozen and wide-eyed. But still, it felt like we were on our way to *something*.

So why was I still stuck?

I glanced over at the sunny-yellow notebook next to my laptop. As I was falling asleep, I'd come up with a solution to my alicorn-taming problem that created an opportunity to introduce a new ally character. She was the perfect catalyst for a reveal a few chapters later, and I'd already taken notes to fully figure her out. It was fine for her to hang out in the wings, named, fully formed, and ready to take part in some fun and games, until it was safe for me to open up my *Archer* manuscript. Which, given my rate of Austin output, was never.

But tonight, everything was going to change. Kai and I were at chapter one of our very own HEA. The fluttery, delicious unknown that started every great romance. We'd begin the evening as acquaintances, and if I had my way, we'd end it half dressed.

I frowned as I thought through the actual logistics of the night ahead. A drunken holiday rager wasn't exactly a great launching pad for sexy-yet-tender moments. But maybe he'd be the type to appreciate escaping the madness for some beverages under the moonlight?

Who knew what he was into? The fact was, Kai was a stranger to me. A hot-as-hell stranger, but still, an unknown outside of his pickleball prowess. There was a gigantic chance that I was pinning my work output on a fantasy version of him. For all I knew, he could hate dogs, be rude to service workers, and think the Earth is flat.

I glanced at my pitiful word count. All I could do was bank on my gut being right and hope that my fading creative spark would eventually become a bonfire.

Chapter Twenty-Four

I think someone forgot to tell them that the Hamptons white party is o-v-e-r," Meredith whispered to me as she nodded toward a cluster of girls in white dresses.

Meredith was in a pale blue short set that showed off her perfect stomach, which was essentially a calling card for her work. I'd opted to be anti-theme in a yellow print dress I'd gotten a couple of years ago. We'd both wisely opted for sneakers given it was an outdoor party.

"I prefer all white to the screaming eagle patriotism." I shifted my eyes toward a shirtless guy wearing a red, white, and blue top hat and a flag tied around his neck. I sighed. "It's going to be a long night."

Colton had already disappeared to do shots with his work friends, leaving me and Meredith to plot our battle strategy.

"A long, *good* night," she said as she looked around the crowd on the manicured lawn. "A muse-tastic night."

I stopped myself from admitting that the two thousand words I'd added today poolside were in the wrong manuscript.

"This place is amazing, but it sure doesn't give the classic Hamptons vibe," I said as I eyed the glass and steel monstrosity in the distance behind us that looked more like a villain lair than a home.

"Yeah, not my thing at all," Meredith agreed. "But you can't beat the view."

We both turned to admire the pink sun sinking into the water.

"I really hope Colton keeps his clothes on tonight," she added. "Drunk skinny-dipping is sort of his thing."

I laughed. "Yeah, I'd prefer to not see your boyfriend naked."

A woman in a clingy red silk halter dress and killer arms stopped in her tracks when she spotted Meredith.

"Harmony Pilates!"

"Yup, that's me." Meredith smiled at her. "I thought you looked familiar."

It was her usual feint, because Meredith saw so many body parts during class that it was almost impossible for her to keep track of people.

"Oh my god, I *love* your class. I usually go to Spirit on the Upper West Side, but I've done a few drop-ins with you," the woman said.

They descended into Pilates speak so I peeled off in search of a drink. The hosts had gone all out and set up three bars around the vast property, along with a dance floor and stage where a club DJ was staring intently at his phone. So far, he'd only been playing lo-fi house music, but I had a feeling he was cueing up a playlist of bangers for when the sun went all the way down.

I squinted at the liquor displayed behind the bartender as I waited in line. No surprise, it was all top-shelf.

"Hey, virgin."

My heart contracted as I turned around, because of course it was Kai in all his tanned, bright smiling glory. Mercifully, there was no one else in line behind us, so the only other person to witness my gape-mouthed stare was the bartender.

"Oh, hi!" I finally managed once I'd collected myself.

He jutted his chin toward the bar. "What are we drinking tonight?"

We? Be still my heart.

"Um, what are we in the mood for?"

He gave me a wicked grin and pumped his fist in the air. "Shots, shots, shots, shots—shots—shots!"

His puppylike enthusiasm was adorable.

"Well, okay then." I laughed. I turned to the bartender. "I guess we're doing shots."

The dour-looking guy did *not* look impressed to be serving us. "And what kind?"

"Uh . . . do you have any Yamazaki 18 back there?" Kai asked.

"We do not," he answered.

"How about Pappy 20?"

I'd never heard of either, but I assumed it was because they were ridiculously expensive.

He put two shot glasses on the bar in front of him and poured as his answer. I noticed that his tip glass was already full, so there was no reason for the grumpiness. But then again, he was working a party in the Hamptons filled with finance bros and their influencer girlfriends on a holiday weekend. It tracked.

Kai handed me a glass, then lifted his toward me. "Happy Fourth."

We clinked them and threw back our drinks simultaneously, then slammed the empties on the bar.

"Wow, you downed that like a champ." He lifted an eyebrow.

It burned my throat, but I refused to even sniffle.

"I'm no stranger to liquor." I shrugged, until I realized how it sounded. "Not in an alcoholic way, of course. I can appreciate it, is all."

"Good to know. Not every woman can handle the hard stuff."

I had to clench my teeth to keep the dad joke inside.

Kai was already diagnosing me as a not-like-the-other-girls cool girl even though it wasn't how I identified. Whatever, it seemed to be working for me.

It took a few seconds for me to come to terms with the fact that after manifesting this moment for weeks, it was actually happening. Kai and I were *hanging out*. We had an ongoing virgin joke, and we'd done a shot together.

Was he in love with me yet?

And almost as important, was my muse back?

"What's with the yellow?" Kai pointed at my dress. "You look fantastic, but you should be wearing the team colors. Happy birthday, America!"

He gestured to his button-down featuring a red, white, and blue popsicle print; red shorts; and boat shoes. Post-shot was not the appropriate time to get into the fact that I was a citizen of our country, not a rabid fan, especially given the political climate.

"I don't know. I just wanted to wear this. And I sort of forgot, to be honest."

"Well, you're making it work." Kai grinned at me, and I felt my cheeks go warm at the compliment.

The party lights under the tents came on and the DJ seemed to take it as his cue to level up the music.

"Nice. Hungry Man is amazing," Kai said as he bobbed his head. "I saw him do a set in Ibiza, and it changed my life."

I laughed, only to realize that he was serious. I'd never been to Ibiza and it was my first exposure to "Hungry Man," so who knew? I was banking on connecting with a stranger to mystically help my writing; maybe a life-changing DJ set should also be within the realm of possibilities?

A group walked over to the bar, so we stepped away to give them room. I held my breath, waiting for Kai to go find someone more exciting to talk to, but he seemed totally focused on me, to my delight and terror.

"Let's sit." He pointed to a grouping of teak furniture that was off to the side, with thick navy cushions that did *not* look weatherproof. "But first . . . another drink. What can I bring you?"

"Gentleman's choice," I said coquettishly. I heard Meredith's voice in my head, cautioning me about accepting open drinks from strangers, so I craned my neck to watch him take the glass of wine from the unhappy bartender.

His hand remained on the stem the entire time.

He served it to me with a flourish. "Starting the night off nice and easy."

"Minus that shot," I reminded him.

"Nah, it was nothing more than light pregaming; you're good." He dropped down beside me on the couch. "So what do you do when you're not living it up in the Hamptons, Brooke?"

After imagining it for weeks, my name coming out of his mouth didn't seem real. I was thankful for the shot warming my belly and taking the edge off my nerves. I took a gulp of my wine.

"I'm a writer. Mainly romances."

"Nice." He nodded. "I gotta admit, I'm not much of a reader. I get bored." He paused. "Is that bad?"

I realized that my expression must've shifted from liquor-drinking cool girl to mild horror.

"Maybe you've been reading the wrong books?" I offered quickly. I took another gulp of wine that brought my glass down to a quarter full. "What sort of stuff are you into?"

"Nothing that's in a book." He laughed. "So talk to me about pickleball. When did you start playing?"

"Oh, it feels like forever ago." I sidestepped the question with a half-truth.

"I get that." He nodded approvingly. "It's an addiction. How's your game?"

I was about to say something self-deprecating, but Owen's advice stopped me. Plus, I was sitting next to a person who needed to believe that I was better than I really was.

"It's, uh, evolving all the time. Definitely improving. I'm signing up for the Parks tournament."

"Aw, that's adorable—good for you," he said. "That's a great beginner tournament."

"Beginner?" I frowned at him. "It's all levels."

"Right, but it's not officially sanctioned by any of the pickleball associations. It's just a community thing."

"Owen suggested it," I said as explanation.

"Well, I'd never question the master's wisdom," Kai replied. "If Gripper wants you to enter, you do it."

I took my last gulp of liquid courage. "You and I should play sometime."

I snapped my mouth shut as soon as I said it, surprised by my own audacity. The invitation hung in the air for what felt like hours when it was probably only a half second.

"Yeah, I'd love that," Kai said agreeably. "I'm not at CPA as much as I want these days—"

He was interrupted by a red, white, and blue ambush that made us both jump.

"Bro, we're taking the Jet Skis out!" one of the three guys said. "Come on."

Kai frowned at him. "Isn't that illegal after dark?"

"Brayden plays golf with the chief of police; I think we're fine," replied a guy in flag shorts. "And we're all sober, right?"

He looked around the group and they laughed.

Kai glanced at me expectantly as he stood up. "You in?"

I ran through a split-second decision tree, with one path leading to being wet and half naked pressed up against Kai and the other ending up with someone in the hospital because drunk Jet Skiing in the dark had to be about the dumbest idea ever.

"C'mon," he teased. "It'll be fun."

The smile he gave me made me seriously consider stripping down to my underwear at a party filled with influencers.

"Darn it, wish I could but I didn't pack a bathing suit," I said, sounding convincingly disappointed.

"Suits optional," a floppy-haired guy said as he backed away. "Let's do this."

Kai paused. "Last chance . . ."

The pull to join them was almost impossible to resist despite the risks. Jet Ski hijinks in the dark felt like a sexy, dangerous plot point I'd never considered.

"You guys go ahead. I'll come down in a minute," I replied.

"Promise?" Kai pointed at me as he backed away with the terrier triplets.

I smiled prettily and nodded. "Yup!"

They disappeared into the darkness, full of golden retriever energy. I finally exhaled and leaned back to stare at the night sky, filled to the brim with warm, fuzzy, delicious *hope*.

The noise level was increasing now that it was fully dark and the crowd was lubricated. After rehashing every second of the interaction with Kai, I finally collected myself and set off to find Meredith again. I glanced to the dance floor, fully expecting her to be throwing her ass in a circle in the middle of it, but I only spotted Colton jumping around with his friends.

I stood next to a hydrangea bush that was almost as tall as me, scanning the crowd.

"Mission accomplished?"

I spun to find Owen peering at me in the darkness.

Chapter Twenty-Five

"Oh, *hey*! I heard you might be here." I jumped up, throwing my arms around him uninvited thanks to my fizzy, alcohol-fueled mood.

Owen circled his arms around me slowly, like I'd forced him into touching me. He squeezed me briefly, and I let go the moment I felt him loosen his grip. But not before I was wrapped in a mist of his warm scent, which triggered memories of the last time I'd been that close to him.

Which wasn't something I needed to be thinking about two drinks in with Kai in my crosshairs.

"Nice dress," he said.

My stomach dipped at the approval in his voice.

I looked him up and down and realized that I was meeting yet another version of Owen as well, one that understood the unspoken Hamptons dress code. He was in a red gingham button-down, dark shorts, and spotless white sneakers, looking just as coastal preppy cool as the rest of the finance bros. His hair was even a little more slicked down than usual.

"Thanks. And you're hat-free." I pointed to his head. "I'm getting spoiled seeing all of your face."

"The Big Gripper hat is my security blanket at the club," he said, confirming what I already suspected. "Anyway, did I just see the man of the hour trotting away with his pack?"

I couldn't hide my smile. "Yeah. We did a shot together."

I caught a brief frown before he rearranged his expression to his usual Owen placidness.

"Well, okay, that's fantastic," he replied. "Did you make plans to play?"

I cocked my head. "Sort of? *I* actually brought it up, but then he got pulled away to go Jet Skiing. Which . . . bad idea in the dark?"

Owen frowned hard. "I sure wouldn't."

"Should we wander down to supervise?"

He regarded me for a minute, and I worried that he'd say no for some reason.

"Yeah, but let's grab drinks first. What can I bring you?"

I could already feel the effects of the shotgunned alcohol, but I wasn't ready to quit drinking for the night.

"It's a celebration, so how about prosecco?"

He bobbed his head. "Got it. Wait here."

My phone buzzed in my pocket, because of course my dress had pockets. No surprise, it was Meredith, asking where I was. We were pros at navigating social scenarios solo, then joining up again when the time was right. Meredith called it "doing laps."

> By the hydrangea bar. You okay?

Perfect. Do you need me?

> Nope. Had a successful Kai moment and I just ran into Owen, all good.

😍

He handed me an overfull glass before I could text her back.

"Are you having fun?" Owen asked as we headed for the beach.

I fell in step next to him. The lights and noise faded behind us, and fireflies lit the way as the grass turned to sand.

"We sort of just got here, but yeah. I guess."

"Oh, come on, you made the Kai connection. I figured you'd be over the moon."

I loved that he used the same expression as my dad to describe happiness.

"I'm still in shock that it happened."

"I'm not. Why wouldn't he chat up someone like you?"

"Because I'm not a 4.0 pickleball player." I laughed, bumping my shoulder against his. "You told me yourself that's his criteria."

"Revisionist history." He cocked an eyebrow. "I never said that was his criteria for hanging out with someone. You told me you wanted to *play* with him. Remember?"

"Fine." I sighed. "You're right, I did."

"And now you're ready." Owen paused. "Ish."

We both went silent as we considered what that meant.

"No sign of the death wish crew." I gestured down at the empty docks. "I guess someone talked some sense into them?"

"Or they couldn't find the keys." He snorted softly.

"Wanna walk all the way down? It's pretty out here."

Owen glanced back toward the chaos of the party. "Definitely."

I felt my shoulders unfurl once we hit the end of the dock. The bay breeze did its thing, sending a wave of goose bumps up my arms even though the night was warm. Based on the sounds echoing from various parts along the shoreline, we weren't the only ones celebrating.

"Let's sit for a minute," I suggested.

"Okay, but not for too long. You need to seal the deal tonight."

Owen seemed even more preoccupied than usual with my connection to Kai.

We both lowered ourselves to the edge of the dock, letting our legs dangle off the edge. I took a sip of prosecco, and when my head went that much woozier, I finally figured out that I needed to slow down.

"Sealing the deal will be much easier now that Jet Skiing is off the table," I said. "*How* did they think they were going to manage it?"

"*Psh*, it probably would've been fine." Owen swiped his hand through the air. "Bad things don't happen to people like Kai."

There was an edge to his voice.

"What do you mean?"

"Ah, right, you barely know him." Owen took a sip of Wave Chaser IPA, then looked over at me. "Kai lives his life on easy mode."

It was the first time I'd heard Owen say anything less than positive about Kai.

"Seriously?"

Owen nodded as he took another swig from the can. "Can't you tell? He's got that charmed-life vibe."

It *almost* sounded like Owen was jealous.

My eyes had adjusted to the inky-black darkness, so I could pick up on his drawn expression. Eyebrows furrowed, mouth downturned.

"Is that a bad thing?"

My heart thumped as I waited for him to answer. Had I been chasing down a faulty muse this whole time?

"No." He shook his head. "Not at all. It's a *good* thing. He's lucky. He was born under sunny skies. Unfortunately, that's not everyone's experience." Another long sip from the can. "It definitely wasn't mine."

He put it out there, so it was totally fine for me to push a little. "What do you mean?"

"Winning is in his bloodline. Kai went to Yale. So did his father, and his grandfather, and his great-grandfather. Kai graduated and went to work for the investing firm his dad founded. From what I can tell, he's never known struggle." Owen paused and the corner of his mouth kicked up. "Okay, maybe *I* make him struggle on the court, but that's not a real-life challenge."

"Well," I began, "you can't know the entirety of a person based on a few pickleball lessons."

"We've been working together for a while." He shrugged as he finished off the beer. "You'd be surprised how much I can figure out during lessons. Obviously, I can read my clients' physical abilities, but there's more. Does he respect my time? How does he respond to corrections? Does he get angry when he makes a mistake, or is he more frustrated? Does he have fun while he's playing? Is he able to put my constructive criticism to work? Does he gloat when he wins or pout when he loses? Coaching gives me a snapshot of the best and worst of a person, so even though I *don't* know the entirety of my clients, I sure get a good sense of them."

"So is he . . . a dick?" I asked tentatively.

"Nope." Owen shook his head as he stared out into the black water. "Not a dick at all. He's just . . . simple. And I'm not saying that he's not intelligent or anything. I mean, simple like . . . he doesn't have the nooks and crannies that make up a real, lived life. He's smooth, like marble."

"Well, marble is beautiful and strong," I offered, feeling a little bad that Owen was dismissing Kai.

"And expensive and easily stained. It needs lots of special care, like sealing."

"So if Kai is marble, what are you?" I asked.

"Me?" Owen chuckled and looked down at the can in his hands. "I'd say I'm . . . a brick."

I barked out a laugh.

"It's true." He shrugged. "Bricks are ubiquitous. You'd never pick up a brick and think, 'Yup, gorgeous.' But you know that a brick gets the job done."

I leaned away and squinted at him. "I'm sorry, did you just call yourself a basic brick?"

He shrugged again. "Sure. And I don't have a problem with it."

"Bricks are rough and scratchy," I said.

"Still works for my background."

I polished off my prosecco. "Do tell."

"On paper, it looks great," he said slowly. "Went to Princeton, played tennis. What most people don't know is that I was the first person in my family to go to college, so yay for an Ivy, but my folks would've been just as proud if I'd graduated from a community college.

"My dad was a mechanic and my mom was a hairdresser," he continued. "They *worked*. They sacrificed for me. The only reason I got into tennis as a kid was my dad. His specialty was classic cars, and one of his regular customers had an old Corvette. Turns out he was the tennis pro at a local golf club, so my dad convinced him to trade lessons for me for repairs. And I guess I had a knack."

"He was your first coach?"

Owen nodded. "Yeah. I got so lucky with Scott. If it weren't for him, I wouldn't be where I am."

"Where exactly is that?" I asked before I realized that it was a loaded question. But I wanted to know how Owen went from Princeton athlete to pickleball instructor, with a detour for cheesemongering.

"It's . . . well, for now it's where I need to be," he said in a way that didn't invite more prying.

"And does that place include a book?"

He let out a soft snort. "You're relentless."

"I'm serious! And I think you like the idea, deep down."

He leaned against a post beside him and stared at me for a beat, a little cliff-hanger. "I do."

"Let's *go*!" I cheered and pumped my fist. "I knew it! This is perfect; now the student is the master."

"Excuse me?"

"You coached me—now it's my turn to do it for you."

"Yeah, we'll see."

I slammed my prosecco glass down on the dock beside me. "You have done *so* much to help me on my pickleball journey; the least I can do is support you as you try something new that I happen to know a thing or two about."

"That's the issue here; I don't try. I *do*," he said, refocusing on the navy horizon. "Once I start something, failure isn't an option."

It sounded more like conviction than bragging.

"That's the best attitude because publishing will break you if you let it."

He glanced over at me. "Are you broken?"

My heart expanded at the concern in his voice.

"A little . . . yeah. My debut novel didn't get picked up, and that hurt like hell. Total crisis of confidence, hence the ghostwriting."

"Ah." He nodded. "Now I get it. I was wondering why you don't publish under your own name. Will that change?"

I smiled involuntarily at the thought of *Archer*. "I'm working on it."

"Good. You deserve to have your name on the cover."

I could tell that the conversation was about to shift to my muse hunt, and I didn't want to discuss Kai with him anymore.

I glanced over my shoulder at the party raging on behind us. "I heard the fireworks show is going to be ridiculous. Colton said they shipped a bunch over from Italy."

"Yeah, it's going to sound like a battle zone soon. Glad Marti's back in the city with her dog walker; she hates noise."

"Same, Marti, same," I agreed. I sighed and looked back at the crowd. "I should probably get back there. I'm feeling antisocial."

I slid my phone out of my pocket to check the time and placed it on the dock beside me.

"Yeah, Calliope awaits," Owen said.

We shared a moment of silence, because once we walked back, we'd get swept up into the madness, and there was a good chance we wouldn't connect again.

Which bummed me out a little.

I leaned over to grab my prosecco flute but misjudged the distance, accidentally knocking it off the dock and into the water with the world's tiniest splash.

"Well, shit!"

I switched to my knees and leaned off the dock to try to grab it.

"Leave it," Owen said. "I'm sure no one will miss it."

"But it's *right* there," I said. I gripped the post next to me and stretched out my arm to where the glass was still bobbing along the surface.

"Brooke, seriously, it's a catering glass that probably cost—"

I didn't hear his estimate as I fell headfirst into the bay.

Chapter Twenty-Six

I was laughing when I came up for air.

The water was bathtub warm, and in any other scenario, I'd invite Owen to jump in and join me so I wouldn't be the only idiot going for a dip in my clothes.

He leaned off the dock, the worry creasing his face obvious even in the dark. "Are you okay? Can you swim?"

He reached his hand down to me as if he could hoist me out of the water like a superhero if I grabbed on.

"Oh my god, I'm an *idiot*," I sputtered as I treaded water. "But yes, I can swim."

"There's a ladder right there." He pointed down the dock. "Do you need help?"

"I'm okay."

"Don't forget the champagne glass." Owen finally cackled a little.

"Stop." I pouted as I swam the few strokes over to the ladder. "I was trying to avoid littering."

My sundress and sneakers made swimming more challenging. I made it to the ladder and grabbed on, then paused when I figured out what was going to happen next.

I hadn't worn a bra, and my pale-yellow dress was now essentially see-through.

Meredith had convinced me that I didn't need one and that the crisscrossed straps in back would be ruined with a bra peeking through them. The minute I hoisted myself out of the water, Owen would have a front-row seat to my nipples.

"What's wrong?"

I took a deep breath. "Nothing."

I climbed the ladder awkwardly, because the alcohol combined with wet sneakers made me keep slipping off the rungs. Owen offered his hand to me when I got to the top and I took it reluctantly, because I needed to cover my *very* alert nipples. The second he let go of me, I crossed my arms over my chest.

"Are you cold?" Owen asked me, ducking down to study my face.

I shook my head. "No, I'm fine, just sort of mortified I did that."

He tried to hide a smile. "Gotta admit, it was amazing. You sliced into that water like an Olympic diver."

"Sure, face-first into the drink. So elegant of me."

I looked down at myself and discovered that my dress was see-through *and* vacuum sealed to my body. As in, Owen, please meet my pink underwear/panties/knickers. I pulled my dress away and I swore it made a suction sound.

I looked up at him and discovered his eyes traveling down my body as I wrung out the hemline. Not gawking, though. He was watching me with awed appreciation.

"Do I have mascara everywhere?" I swiped beneath my eyes self-consciously. "I'm a mess."

"No." He shook his head slowly, still watching me. "You look like a mermaid."

Owen sounded awestruck, like he really believed that I was something beautiful and otherworldly.

"I promise not to lure any sailors to their deaths tonight." I held up two fingers in a mer-swear.

"Too late," he said softly.

My heart fumbled at his Kai reference.

Or did he mean something else?

"My phone!" I exclaimed out of nowhere, slapping my hips even though I knew it wasn't in either pocket. I remembered leaving it on the dock and ran back to get it. He watched me walk back, and despite me feeling like a sea hag, Owen somehow seemed to like what he was seeing.

"What now?" he asked.

I glanced back at the crowd on the lawn. "I mean . . . I don't want to leave, but I also don't want to *not* leave, you know?"

"Same."

"I still have some wooing to do, after all," I added. "I have to at least get his number, since we had a moment, which means that it won't be too awkward to follow through about playing pickleball."

Owen cleared his throat. "Exactly. If you want, I can drive you to where you're staying so you can change, and I'll bring you back."

As always, going above and beyond.

"No, that's okay. I don't want to interrupt your night. I can get Colton to do it."

"Colton?" He laughed. "Last I saw him, he was three shots deep. C'mon, I'll drive you. No big deal."

I was dripping, and yes, a little chilly despite the midsummer heat, so the faster I could get into dry clothes the better. I scanned the crowd, trying to find Kai in the sea of popped collars.

"Actually, that would be great, thanks. But if you do it that means even more author support as you write your book. You keep saving my ass; I need to return the favor eventually."

We started down the dock and I stared at Owen's profile, waiting for him to answer me.

"Life isn't quid pro quo," he finally said. "I'm not keeping a tally, I promise you."

"Yeah, but I am," I replied quickly. "And it's ridiculously lopsided. I don't like feeling like I owe someone."

He stopped suddenly and pivoted to me, frowning. "Seriously, you don't owe me anything, Brooke. Friends help friends, right?"

The way he said "friends" sounded almost accusatory. Owen's expression was stormy, like the levity of me belly flopping into the bay was long forgotten.

"Right," I replied in a small voice. I crossed my arms tighter across my chest and didn't look away despite his glare.

Since I'd met Owen, he'd pushed, and cajoled, and cheered me, but this was an entirely new side of him. All I'd done was offer to help him, yet he was acting like I'd somehow insulted him.

The air between us felt staticky, like I'd get a shock if an elbow strayed too close to Owen.

"If and when I need your help, you'll know," he said. "But I doubt it."

His eyes tracked around my face. I tried to keep my expression neutral despite the nearness of him and my sopping state.

"Okay."

I followed behind him, each squishy footstep a comical soundtrack to a suddenly unfunny moment.

"My car is parked down the street; it'll take a few minutes

for me to get back," Owen said to me once we reached the outer ring of the party. "I'll pull into the driveway, and you can meet me there."

"Yup," I said with a quick nod. "I'll let Meredith know I'm leaving."

Owen disappeared into the crowd, and I pulled out my phone to text Meredith.

> I fell in the bay. Owen is taking me back to change.

The reply bubbles popped up immediately.

> What?!! How? Where are you now?

I looked around at groups of people filming themselves. The lower patio that's filled with people in influencer mode.

> I'm hiding in the bushes.

> Coming

She found me two seconds later and looked me up and down, wide-eyed. "How did it happen? Are you drunk?"

"Not at all. I knocked my glass into the water, and I lost my balance when I tried to grab it."

"I don't know." She cocked an eyebrow at me. "You look sexy as hell; you should stay in that dress."

"I'd prefer to not get a yeast infection from wet underwear, thank you," I said wryly. "I'll be back in a bit."

"I don't know how long we're going to stay actually," Meredith said. "Colton went hard right out of the gate, and he's already pretty wasted. He's in fun mode at the moment, but that's just a few clicks away from 'I'm a golden god' status."

Colton liked re-creating the scene from *Almost Famous* any time he was around alcohol and a pool, and he'd miraculously managed to live through all of them.

So far.

"You're babysitting?" I asked.

"Yeah, but it's okay. He's been working hard and he needed to blow off some steam. This is his jam and these are his people." Meredith leaned closer to me to whisper in my ear. "Speaking of people. *Incoming.*"

She jutted her chin across the patio and widened her eyes. It was Kai, strolling by solo.

"Oh, not now! I look shipwrecked," I said, retreating farther into the shadows.

But it was too late. Somehow, his gaze was drawn to me, almost like he'd been seeking me out. He brightened, waved, and headed over.

"Want me to leave?" Meredith whispered out of the corner of her mouth.

"No, that would look weird; stay and talk to him."

"Uncross your arms." Meredith giggled. "Show off those nips!"

I glowered at her, then rearranged my face into a smile.

"Hey, what happened to *you*?" Kai looked surprised but also not, given the way things were starting to ramp up all around us. "Someone push you in the pool?"

I laughed and hoped I sounded cute and not hysterical. "No, I fell off the dock." I rolled my eyes at my ridiculousness.

"Maybe it's time to stop doing shots and switch to sparkling water?" Kai joked.

I didn't want him to think that I was already so sloppy at the beginning of a long night.

"No, I'm barely tipsy. It's a long story, but I'm fine."

Meredith furrowed her brow. "You know what? My ankle is actually starting to ache a little. I'm going to head over there and sit for a bit." She pointed to an area where there were zero chairs. "Nice to see you again, though."

Meredith was a lying liar, and I loved her for it. She waved and disappeared.

It hit me that Owen was probably waiting for me in the driveway. I needed to make something happen with Kai *now*.

"I'm going to run home and get out of this." I plucked at my dress. "I'm coming right back, but why don't we exchange numbers just in case, so we can set up a game?"

"Yeah, I agree. We definitely need to," Kai said as he pulled his phone out of his back pocket. "Who do you normally play with?"

It hit me that not only was I was going to have to fake my way into the Chelsea Pickleball Academy as a member, but I also needed to manufacture a believable pickleball backstory, complete with court BFFs.

"Uh, this summer I've actually been spending time on some outdoor courts. Enjoying the weather, you know? And stretching my skill set by playing with different people that aren't members."

He snorted. "You're a glutton for punishment. It's been hot."

"I play early; it's not too bad." I shrugged.

I'd played early outside *once*, but he didn't need to know that.

"Well, you and I are definitely going to meet in the comfort of CPA. What's your number?"

I gave it to him quickly and crossed my fingers that he'd

send me a confirmation text so I'd have his number as well, but he slipped his phone back in his pocket. "Perfect."

"I think my ride is ready to go." I hitched my thumb over my shoulder.

"Got it," he said with a smile. "Come find me when you get back. We'll hang out."

I grinned back at Kai like a dork because I couldn't find the words to express how badly and how long I'd wanted to hear that.

My heart thumped as I walked away from him. Austin, Abby, and I were *finally* at the start of our HEA.

Chapter Twenty-Seven

The headlights of Owen's car illuminated the front of the house as we pulled down the white stone driveway. "Nice place."

It was an obvious understatement, because the gray-shingled house with a gambrel roof had the old money aesthetic of a true Hamptons classic.

"Yeah, it'll do," I joked. "Come in and check it out while I change."

He came to a stop and put the car in park, motor running. "It's fine; I'll wait out here."

"Seriously?"

"Yeah. You're going to be quick, right?"

I was so fizzy from the Kai moment that I hadn't actually thought through what I needed to do to clean up. My makeup was ruined, my hair was shaggy thanks to the air-drying, and I didn't have anything else cute enough to wear.

"I need to do something with this." I pointed to my head. "That'll take a few minutes."

"Okay, I'll wait," he said as he turned off the car.

"And I'll rush."

I ran to the house and had to enter the code into the keypad three times before I got it right. It wasn't fair of me to make him wait in the driveway like a chauffeur, so I decided to skip the overhaul and work with what I had.

Everything inside the house was white, white, white, and I felt like I was filthy, so I kicked off my wet sneakers at the door and jogged up the perfectly spaced steps to my white-with-orange-accents room at the end of the hall. My first stop was my bathroom for a quick face wash to get off the remainder of my makeup. Not that I wore much, but the traces of it had left little smudges beneath my eyes. Noticeable in the bright light of the bathroom but probably not in the darkness at the party.

My dress had dried to just uncomfortably damp instead of full-on sopping. As I turned around to try to reach the tie in the back, I remembered that Meredith had strapped me into it, laughing about the tightness of her knot. When I tugged at it, I realized that she'd done some sort of complicated triple loop that could've secured a yacht to a dock, because the thing wasn't budging.

I bent over at my waist and tried to pull the whole dress up over my head. Suddenly, it was as tight as a corset. I flipped upright and stared at myself in the mirror, the dress half snagged up in my underwear. I only had one option.

I grabbed my phone.

> OMFG, I'm trapped in this dress!! Could you please untie the knot in back?

It took a few minutes before Owen responded.

> Yup.

> Thank you! Meet you in the foyer

I shoved my hair up in a ponytail and jogged down the stairs. Owen was standing outside, his back to the door.

"Hey!" I flung the door open so abruptly that he jumped. "Come in."

Owen stepped inside gingerly, like he was afraid the place was booby-trapped.

"Lemme see," he said, and I spun around so he could survey the shibari crisscrossing my back. He gave the knot a tug. "The water didn't help; it's basically cemented now."

He was close enough to me that I could feel the warmth of his hands hovering near my back, but I noticed that he took care not to let his fingers brush against my skin as he worked the knot.

"You can't just pull the whole dress off?"

I shook my head. "I tried. Wide ribs."

He snorted softly. "That's a thing?"

"Yup, something brand-new for me to obsess about. My big-ass ribs, in addition to my wonky thumbs, the vein in my forehead, my double chin, my concave ass, and my weird eyebrows."

Owen paused with one hand still tugging the string. "Are you *serious*?"

I glanced over my shoulder at him. "Well, yeah, I think every woman has a list of random things that she hates about herself. I have more—shall I go on?"

"God, no." He resumed fiddling with the knot. "That's some warped thinking."

I didn't answer him because I was too focused on the way his hand was now resting against my skin. Lightly, almost ticklish, but the gentle contact was enough to send warm ripples along my back.

"I can't find a single thing wrong with you," he murmured as he worked, so softly that he might've been talking to himself.

I swallowed hard as he slid a palm beneath the strapping.

"Okay, *now* I see what's going on. It's twisted with another part."

Owen's efforts to maintain some sort of boundary between us seemed to be lost as he focused more on winning the knot war. Every knuckle brush against my back made me catch my breath.

Still so fucking touch starved. Still left quivering from the most basic of human contact.

But then again, it didn't feel basic to me. Owen was now bent at the waist with his warm fingertips brushing against me in unpredictable rhythms. I had to fight to keep from moving closer to him.

"Come this way," Owen said as he tugged the straps and gently leash walked me backward toward a small desk lamp, the only light in the foyer.

I was instantly reminded of the scene I'd written in *Christmas at Whiskey Ranch* where my hero Blaze lassoed a very ornery Nellie and pulled her across the barn to where he was standing. When she kicked up a fuss, he'd flicked the rope around her body again and then secured her wrists together so she was basically helpless. And then he'd kissed her, long and hard, because they both knew it was exactly what she wanted.

After asking first, of course, because I was a consent queen.

Just thinking about the scene made me blush, because what came next involved Nellie bent over a saddle rack with her hands still bound together while Blaze buried himself in her from behind.

Yeah, I could use some of that right now.

I let out a long, slow breath through pursed lips and flicked my eyes back to Owen in the reflection of the mirror above the light.

Owen's movements slowed, like he sensed that the knot was about to pull free and he wanted to prolong the moment.

"Almost there," he said softly.

He pulled at the tangle and the dress went tight against my chest. I glanced at myself in the mirror to confirm that, yes, my nipples were at full attention.

This time not from the cold.

Owen was focused, squinting a little, and lit like a Vermeer painting with half his face in shadow and the other bathed in the golden light. He was as clean-shaven as I'd ever seen, though the hint of scruff remained, like a stain in a coffee cup.

I let out a little sigh. He'd never looked better.

"And there . . . we . . . *go*," Owen murmured as the straps finally pulled free. "Wait, hold on. One last tangle."

He didn't know that I was staring at him in the mirror. I watched him as he gently unwound the thin string from around the other straps, smoothing them to the side with his palms like he was cleaning condensation from a mirror and sending goose bumps racing down my arms. The dress skated down my shoulders and I had to clutch my hands to my chest to keep it from falling off my body.

Neither one of us moved away.

Owen was closer than necessary now that I was free. It felt a little like the way he'd stood behind me at my first lesson, but the stakes were so much higher this time around.

"Did you just shiver?" he whispered, finally catching my eye in the mirror.

I nodded shyly. "You give a mean accidental massage. Your hands are . . . nice. Gentle."

He glanced at my naked skin. "Whoops, still a mess at the bottom."

This time he swept his hand across my lower back, making me giggle. I arched away.

"Ticklish?" he asked with a soft laugh.

"Maybe a little."

We held each other's gaze in the mirror, still close enough to give in to the pull we both seemed to be trying to ignore.

My breathing went shallow. My body was now in furnace mode, kicking out enough heat that my dress would be dry in minutes.

I turned so that we were face-to-face and looked up at him. Given we'd already kissed more frequently than what was acceptable for friends helping friends, it felt familiar being so close to him. His chest rose and fell, like freeing me from the dress was a marathon he'd just finished.

Do it.

The invasive thought was so overwhelming that I had to fight to keep from going up on my tiptoes to kiss him yet again.

Owen's eyes were anchored to my mouth, which felt like a countdown to something.

Any time we kissed, it was *good*. There was no disputing what was fact. And despite all the static around Kai, and Owen's history as the underappreciated third angle of a love triangle, it was about to happen again.

My stomach flipped at the thought of his lips on mine.

"I don't want to kiss you," he rasped as his gaze traveled around my face.

I could hear my heartbeat pulsing in my ears. "I don't believe you," I whispered.

I inched toward him, almost daring him to step back from me. Nothing made sense but somehow everything did.

"You're drunk," he countered without moving away.

"Not even close," I replied, hoping I didn't sound as desperate for him as I felt.

I went statue still, not wanting to break the spell, but inside my body was alive with a pulsing need to *get on with it*. To make the inevitable moment that we were both pretending wasn't going to happen, happen.

"This is the *last* time," Owen growled, then swept me into his arms.

His mouth found mine like the waiting had tripled his urgency, but within the first few seconds, I could sense that this kiss was different. His lips were almost fierce against mine, like he was angry that we were kissing but powerless to stop it. The words "hate fuck" flitted through my head, but it was impossible because I could never hate Owen, and we weren't going to fuck, no matter how badly I wanted to.

Owen reclaimed the naked skin of my back without any of the hesitancy of a few minutes prior, like every inch of me was now fair game. His tongue flicked against my lips, and I stifled a little thankful noise before it could escape the back of my throat.

The only thing holding up my dress now was the tension of our bodies smashed together. Owen's hands slid down to cup my ass, drawing me closer still, until I had zero doubt about what I felt pressing up against me. I slid my hand between us and against his hardness.

"*Brooke*," he whispered.

I kept going, drawing my hand up and down his stiff cock as we kissed. His fingertips migrated down my back to the hem of my dress, drawing it up the sides of my thighs and getting a whimper out of me. He turned me so that my ass was up against the sturdy table, never breaking off the kiss, then picked me up and sat me on top of it and bumped his way past my knees. I smiled against his mouth, then drew in a sharp breath when he pressed his hand against the heat between my legs.

The faintest touch through cotton was enough to send shocks through my body.

"We should stop," he murmured as he moved to take my earlobe in his mouth.

His body hadn't gotten the message. The featherlight touches through the thin fabric of my underwear had me feeling unhinged and desperate for him.

My head fell back as Owen finally slid his fingertips beneath the elastic, and he took advantage of my exposed neck, kissing me from my ear to my collarbone, then back to my mouth.

He wasn't tentative. He was toying with me, teasing me in time with my jagged breathing.

"Owen . . ." I inhaled sharply, my lips pressed against his ear.

My heartbeat was a drumline, loud enough that he could probably hear it.

"Do you want me to stop?" He brushed against my warm heat, and I shook my head and tightened my thighs around his waist as an answer.

"Do you like it?" Owen murmured. He teased his fingers along the dampness between my legs, so gently that I quivered with need.

My head dropped back, and I made a noise that was the closest I could get to a yes.

"I've thought about this so many times . . ." he whispered in my ear, trailing off like he needed to fully focus on the little circles he was making with his fingertips.

Our mouths crashed together again, right as the front door swung open and the massive chandelier above us flicked on.

"Um, *whoops*," Meredith said, eyes wide.

Chapter Twenty-Eight

Meredith and a very drunk Colton tripped up the stairs without another word, leaving me and Owen to squint at each other in the bright light from a safe distance apart.

"Yeah, that was a mistake." Owen sighed as he reached down to adjust his very obvious hard-on. "I'm sorry. Good night."

He strode out the door, leaving me bewildered, horny, and struggling to keep my dress in place.

"Owen." I chased after him once I'd managed to weave the thing back on. "Wait. Let's talk."

He spun around in the driveway, nostrils flaring. Angry Owen, once again.

"Why are you mad at me?" I demanded.

"I'm not mad at you; I'm mad at *me*. That was my mistake." He jabbed his finger toward the house. "It absolutely will not happen again."

"It wasn't a mistake," I countered softly.

He hung his head and stared at the ground. "Yeah, it was." He lifted his eyes to meet mine and held my gaze for a long time before he spoke again.

"Why did you start lessons with me?" Owen asked in a hollow voice.

"To learn how to play pickleball," I offered weakly, because I knew the answer he wanted.

"And?"

Awkwardness flooded through me given what we'd just been doing together.

"To meet Kai," I replied in a tiny voice.

"And what happened with him tonight?" he demanded.

"We talked and—"

"He took your number," Owen finished for me. "So you're well on your way to capturing your precious muse. Your game is good enough that you can stand on your own, so I think my work here is done. You're screwing with my head and I swore I'd never let that happen again—"

It was my turn to interrupt. "Hold on a sec—*you* kissed *me*!"

He sighed and his shoulders drooped.

"How could I not, Brooke?" he asked, his voice full of hurt. "How could I not? You were looking up at me with those eyes, and your skin is just so damn soft . . ."

My mouth was already open, ready to fight back, but I snapped it shut at the quiet admission.

"This is all feeling too familiar," Owen continued, gesturing between us. "I'm here, I'm convenient, but I'm not the one you truly want. So let's just be done, okay?"

I couldn't answer him because he was right and wrong at the same time. It was more than him being convenient. Sure, I was horny, but when we kissed, it transcended what was normal. I was drawn to Owen in a way I couldn't understand. He was unlike anyone I'd ever been attracted to. I wrote the type of men who normally captured my heart, the swaggering, larger-than-life cowboys who oozed sex appeal and knew their way around a grand gesture.

Owen had plenty of confidence since he was basically a god at CPA. And handsome? Yeah, in the best, slow burn–iest sort of way. His sex appeal was unquestionable. But the guy who made my heart flutter, who'd given me all the undefinable hopefulness of a good old-fashioned crush was *Kai*, and I needed to sort that out if I wanted to finish my fucking torturous book.

The problem was I couldn't stop kissing Owen. Or being kissed by him. I craved it more than I wanted to admit. And I loved being with him, on and off the court. I didn't want to lose our friendship, or whatever it was, but I wasn't sure how we could move forward after this latest car crash.

And if it was possible to stop wanting something I couldn't define.

I grasped for the last possible connection that remained between us.

"What about the tournament?"

"You'll do fine," Owen replied quickly, his frown evident even in the dim light. "You're ready."

"You literally just said I wasn't," I replied, throwing my hands up in frustration. "You told me I needed polishing!"

He made an indecipherable noise.

"I'll pay you to keep coaching me," I said, defiantly raising my chin.

"I won't take your money."

"Then I'll beg."

"Brooke." Owen sighed and scrubbed his hand across his eyes like he was over my shit.

I walked closer to him. "This is bigger than the tournament and you know it. You picked up on something fractured in me, dissected it, and helped me get past it. And that opened up a whole new side of me." Tears inexplicably filled my eyes. "Can't we just, I don't know . . . keep going a little longer? I'm having *so* much fun learning from you, and honestly, given how shitty the rest of my life has been, I sort of crave it."

His expression softened a bit. "You crave *pickleball*?"

I opened my mouth to answer but couldn't say that what I craved was the way I felt hanging out with him on the courts.

"I like being sporty for a change." I shrugged a shoulder, trying to make the confession sound nonchalant. "I like being good at something athletic, even if it's just an old-timer sport like pickleball."

"Hey," Owen chastised gently while staring at the ground.

"I like learning and mastering new techniques," I continued. "I *still* don't know how to backspin, by the way."

I caught the tiniest curve of a smile.

"Let's just keep going until the tournament. Okay? Please?"

His arms were crossed and he wouldn't look at me. I held my breath.

"And I still need to help you with your book," I offered gently.

He was shaking his head before I even finished speaking. "Nope. Once we're done, we're done. No cute, encouraging texts about my word count, no coffee shop writing sessions. If I write this book, I'm doing it on my own, because I can't have you in my life cheering me on like some regular friend."

A red chrysanthemum firework thundered in the air above us, an exclamation point to Owen's anger.

"So we're okay to keep going?" I asked tentatively, my heart thumping.

Owen finally looked at me and held my gaze as the sky filled with explosions.

"I'm not sure I can."

I slumped as a series of staticky fizzles went off over our heads.

"I'll let you know," Owen continued.

Relief washed over me. It wasn't a hard no. For now, it would have to do.

Of course, the bedroom I was in had blackout blinds on the gigantic windows—everything was calibrated to give the occupant the most luxurious night of sleep ever—but I woke with the sun regardless. Our plan was to clean up and hit the road in the afternoon, a day early and before the holiday weekend traffic, so we'd have time to de-stress at home before the week began.

I rolled onto my back and stared at the ceiling, feeling hungover even though I'd stopped drinking after the fateful glass of prosecco. The night flashed back like an episode recap on a Netflix show: hanging with Kai, the bay dunk, kissing Owen. I squeezed my eyes shut.

What the fuck was I even *doing*? My life was messy enough; why did I keep wading in and making it worse?

I was in Owen limbo. After *that* kiss and everything that went with it, I wasn't sure how we'd find a way back to feeling okay around each other. I wondered how long he'd make me wait before he rendered his verdict.

I slid out of the billion-thread-count sheets and grabbed my phone and laptop, then headed downstairs. The sun was already popping up over the tops of the trees, and the birds who hadn't gotten the message about spring mating season being over were singing their little hearts out. I put the coffee on and headed to the patio by the pool.

I had at least a couple of hours before Meredith and Colton

got up, possibly more given how wasted Colton had been when he got home, so I could knock out a bunch of words before the party rehash with Meredith. I opened up the document that consistently gave me migraines and scrolled to where I'd left off.

The pregnancy test. I'd managed to get their first time having sex on the page and now it was time to deal with the aftermath. In her hurry to find out if she was just late or if it was something more, Abby had missed the trash can when she tossed out the pregnancy test wrapper, leaving part of it on the ground, only to be discovered by Austin.

The scene took shape in my mind as I glanced across the manicured yard, and the next thing I knew, my fingers were flying over the keys. By the time I paused to drink my now-cold coffee, I'd added close to two thousand words, with no end in sight.

"Good morning?" Meredith called from behind me, her voice cautious.

I glanced over my shoulder at her standing in the doorway, hugging herself. I could tell by her hesitation that she didn't want to interrupt me, but that she was also desperate to find out why the hell I'd been making out with Owen the night before.

"Hey there."

"Can I . . . ?"

She pointed at the chair across from me.

"Please."

It was time for the debrief I'd been dreading. Not that I ever held back from sharing my feelings with Meredith, but this time I wasn't sure how to catalog them, and worse, how she'd react.

"So." She dropped into the chair. "What's new with you?"

I laughed despite myself. "Not much. Just making bad decisions and waking up with an emotional hangover."

"Not a real one? You were sober last night?"

I gave her a tight smile. "Oh yes. I remember every second of last night."

She leaned forward and slapped the table with both hands, chastising and concerned at the same time. "What the *hell*, Brooke? You hooked up with Owen? I mean, I totally get it, and I approve, but what about the mighty Kai? I thought he was the final boss."

I slumped down, embarrassed by my all-over-the-place-ness. "I don't *know*. I'm a trainwreck."

"You do realize that this muse thing is pretty weird, right? I can't say that I understand it now, given . . ." She gestured vaguely toward where Owen and I had been busted.

I crossed my arms over my chest and stared across the lawn. "But it's not weird. Leo crushed my heart, I needed to find a romantic spark so I could actually write a happily ever after, and Kai was it."

"Yeah, he *is* your usual type," Meredith admitted. "Hot and charming. So how did it go with him last night?"

"He took my number and said we need to play."

I expected some sort of celebration at the news we'd all been working toward, but she merely bobbed her head. "Nice."

"What?" I demanded, lapsing into our shorthand.

She pointed to my laptop. "Did it help? Did a hang with your muse last night plus another on the horizon open the floodgates?"

I hadn't made the connection until she pointed it out. "Actually, *yes*. I wrote more this morning than I've written in ages. And I'm happy with it for a change."

Her mouth downturned like De Niro. "Well, okay then. You were right; I was wrong."

"What do you mean?"

She pushed back from the table and stood up. "Kai's great. Ripped from the pages of one of your books. Sexy, charming, and plenty of good chat. But I'm sorry, I was pulling for a different character."

She walked away without another word before I could defend myself, which was fine because we both knew there was nothing more I could say to make it make sense.

Chapter Twenty-Nine

I'd sent the email to Piper about the other two books in the series over a week ago, and all I'd gotten back from her was radio silence. I'd expected some sort of confirmation, given I'd agreed to write them—thank you for your service, Melete—but then again, I was used to her minimalist communication style. I'm sure she'd logged it on the back end of Pro Depot with a quick nod, then moved on to the next task in her endless queue. It was fine, because I didn't even have to think about book two until Austin and Abby were cooing over their newborn.

"Why are you frowning at your screen?" Nia asked me, quirking an eyebrow. "I thought cowboy life was going well."

We were at a hipster coffee shop known for sourcing rare beans from around the world for another writing date. Nia was now an official bestseller in between stops on her tour and already working on her *next* book.

"Was I frowning? Everything's fine. Just pondering."

She nodded sagely. "Ah yes, the writer's favorite pastime. Pondering, followed closely by researching obscure topics that don't add anything to the story to stay busy when not pondering. Anything but writing."

"Exactly," I agreed. "I just finished researching the average weight of Texas longhorn cattle."

"Why?"

"Austin's ex the veterinarian almost got trampled by one, and I wanted to see how devastating her injuries could be. Turns out, those dudes can top out at over two thousand pounds."

"Ouch, no thank you." She winced. "And the *horns*."

"About four feet wide," I added sagely, since I was now an expert in all things steer.

But for a change, I wasn't researching to kill time. I'd had a real need to find out about them, and once I knew enough, I'd gotten back to business. Instead of focusing on my bickering archers, I was making magic happen for Austin and Abby, faster than usual. I was finally on track to hit my deadline if things kept up. And the sex scenes? Scorching enough to make me blush as I wrote them.

I was coasting on the vibes from the Hamptons weekend, trying to ignore the fact that Kai still hadn't reached out to me in the three days since. But it was the post–holiday weekend slog, plus Colton had assured me that he'd heard the Atria Paris office was in town for the week and they were busy with meetings and after-hours events.

I was equally stressed that Owen hadn't let me know if he wanted to keep working with me. Every time my phone chirped, I jumped, hoping that it was him confirming our next lesson.

Thankfully, the little number in the bottom corner of my Word doc kept going up, and that was enough to help me stay in a stable headspace. Just the *promise* of Kai seemed to be enough to keep the words flowing. I could only imagine my output when we actually connected in a real way and not just a drive-by.

"What's happening with the romantasy?" Nia asked.

"Not much at the moment." I hunched my shoulders up to my ears. "I feel like I'm cheating on Einar and Zandria whenever I work on Austin and Abby's story, even though the Liaison book is what really matters."

"Is it, though?" she asked pointedly. "I love what you've told me about *Archer*. What does your agent think?"

"She doesn't know."

"*Seriously?*" Nia frowned at me. "How many words do you have?"

"Plenty, but I don't want to keep throwing half-baked ideas at her. Let's just say I've had a bunch of false starts since we gave up on *Truth and Beauty*, and I feel like I'm coming off unfocused. I want to finish this one."

"So she has no idea you're writing it?"

Nia's cross-examination made me feel twitchy. She was a pro at getting to the heart of an issue.

"No . . ." I admitted.

"Oh, girl." She tilted her head at me. "At least send her a summary to see if she likes it. What if you finish it, and she thinks it's a crap idea? I mean, it definitely isn't, but still."

I knew she was right, but a part of me liked keeping my archers to myself. I still wasn't sure what sorts of adventures they were going to get up to as they tamed alicorns, battled interlopers, and finally stopped arguing long enough to fall in love. But if I shared it and Celeste didn't like the concept, there'd be no reason for me to keep writing their happily ever after, and they'd be stuck in limbo forever.

"Yeah, I probably should," I offered weakly, my stomach free-falling at the thought of actually doing it. "I never thought I'd get this far, so I didn't bother running the idea by her. The story is just falling out of me."

"Okay, that's a great sign. So tell her. Before you add another word to that manuscript," Nia scolded gently.

I knew she was right, but I dreaded the thought of my lovers potentially condemned to purgatory.

"Think of what a lift you'll get when she tells you how much she loves the concept," Nia added as her fingers danced over her keyboard. "Just do it."

She was right. Without buy-in from my agent, I was wasting my time.

My copywriter background meant that writing a three-paragraph elevator pitch for the book was second nature. Nia helped me refine it, and I sent the email off to Celeste before I could decide that I was making a huge mistake. My palms were actually sweaty after I finished.

I hadn't sent her an idea in so long that she was probably going to wonder who the hell I was.

Nia held up her coffee cup. "To good news."

"Yes, please." I clinked against it with mine. "But enough of that. I need to get back to the ranch. At least this book is paying the bills."

"For now," Nia corrected.

We fell silent as I worked on the joyful first sonogram appointment scene, and Nia went back to whatever bloody, gut-churning moment had her grinning as she typed. My phone buzzed and my first thought was of Owen. He'd told me that they were doing a deep clean at CPA during our usual Tuesday morning meeting time, which explained why I hadn't heard from him.

Or at least that was the fiction I was writing about us.

Although if the text *was* from him, maybe he was reaching out to tell me our lessons were done?

I wasn't sure how we were going to go back to normal this time around, if he even considered me worthy of another chance. He'd been generous with me after I'd jumped him at the farm; then we'd *both* agreed to playact our second make-out session for Leo's benefit, which meant that the only lingering awkwardness from it was the way I felt afterward.

The Hamptons kiss was . . . next level. Real enough that it made him angry.

And me confused. And thinking about it when I pulled my buzzing friend from my nightstand at night.

But Owen didn't seem like the type of person to back out of an agreement, and he'd said we'd work together until the tournament.

Three more weeks.

I finally stopped obsessing about if the text was from him or not and picked up my phone to check. It was from Wes, a photo of a pyramid of dark chocolate Hobnobs biscuit packages on a Sainsbury's conveyer belt.

I didn't have to ask what was going on in the photo. He was stocking up on my favorite cookies prior to coming home. I sent back a photo doing a Korean finger heart.

Can you talk

I jumped at the chance to connect with him.

Always.

I walked outside right as the phone rang and tucked myself in front of an empty space for rent. My stomach went into free fall when I looked at the screen.

It was *Owen* calling, not Wes, like I'd summoned him by obsessing about our next steps.

"Hi?" My voice felt shaky as I answered.

"Hey," he said quickly. "Listen, there's a, uh, a technicality with the lessons Meredith got for you. I never logged them as completed in the computer system, so it says you still have unused time with me."

I stared out at the crowds passing by as I tried to make sense of why the Big Gripper didn't have the authority to overwrite their computer system and mark my lessons as used. He *had* to be able to, and if not him, someone else on the team probably could. But if this was the angle he wanted to use so that we could keep going, I was down to play along.

"Oh?"

"Yeah, so I guess we need to finish them."

"Okay, that's great!" I fought the urge to do a little jig. "I mean, if you're okay with it?"

"Sure. Yeah. You've got the tournament coming up, so it makes sense to get some more court time."

He didn't mention Kai, probably because he assumed it was already a done deal.

"Thursday morning?" I asked.

"Yup, that works. See you then."

He disconnected right as Wes called me.

"Hey!" I answered brightly, feeling doubly happy.

"Heeeeeey." He drew out the word, and I could tell in the single syllable that he was just as excited about his upcoming visit as I was. "Anything else you want me to bring you?"

"Hobnobs'll do it. Thanks for remembering."

"You're letting me crash at your place. I didn't want to come empty-handed."

"I'm sort of shocked Mom and Dad didn't cancel the race since you're going to be here."

"I told them not to," Wes answered. "This is Dad's first post-injury race, and I know he's been working hard. I didn't want to fuck with his mojo. Plus they get me Friday, Sunday, and Monday night."

"So what do you want to do while you're in the city?" I asked, already planning half a dozen excursions.

"Uh, first thing I want to do is see you dink, because I still don't believe that you're playing."

I paused for a beat, because what seemed like a simple request complicated things in ways I didn't feel like getting into on an international call.

"You want to play *pickleball*? Dude, your life is sports; why don't we do something that doesn't require sweating? You need to relax these last few weeks before the season kicks up."

His laughter prevented him from responding for a few seconds. "Hold on, are you suggesting you're *that* good? You actually think you're going to wear me out?"

It was a new twist to our sibling rivalry, sporty competitiveness.

I straightened my back and raised up my chin as if he were standing in front of me. "Actually, yes. I am good."

Because I had an amazing coach.

Have an amazing coach.

"Oh, this is gonna be *fun*." He chuckled. "I'm definitely packing my paddle."

"That'll take a couple of hours, so what else?"

"Hang out, eat good food, get your state of the union. I feel like I have no clue what's going on in your life. I get the summaries from Mom, but I know you don't tell her everything."

As close as we were, the time difference and his busy schedule made it tough for us to keep up with each other. We texted memes and photos all the time, but they didn't take the place of a good sit-down. And Wes had always provided my guy perspective, which would come in handy if I decided to dive into the Owen situation with him.

"Well, my life isn't nearly as exciting as yours. No hordes of adoring fans chanting my name on the regular. But I do have some stuff going on."

"Can't wait to hear it. Will I be sleeping on the futon again? Just want to make sure to pack loungewear so I don't scare Meredith."

I stifled a giggle. Meredith had nursed a massive crush on Wes since the first time she met him, and I could guarantee she'd welcome the chance to catch him shirtless.

"Yup. Unless you want my room and I'll take the futon."

He pshawed. "Absolutely not. The futon is fine for us."

My head jerked back. *"Us?"*

Wes's warm laugh made me realize just how much I missed him. "I've been in England too long; it's just an expression. I'll let you know what train I'm taking on Friday, yeah?"

"Perfect," I replied. "Absolutely cannot wait to give you a giant hug."

"Same. Love you."

I could hear the smile in his voice.

"Love you back."

I disconnected the call and stared at my phone. The Owen issue felt more settled, which left me to only have to worry about hearing from Kai now.

Despite what Owen thought, I refused to call it a love triangle because by definition it *wasn't*—no one was in love with anyone—but if I was honest with myself, it was starting to feel more than a little isosceles.

Chapter Thirty

> Hey, it's Kai. Sorry I've been M.I.A. work shit. Still want to play?

I stopped in the middle of the sidewalk like a goddamned tourist and stared down at my phone, because I couldn't believe what I was reading.

It wasn't even seven in the morning, I was a dozen steps away from CPA, and *Kai was texting me.*

My stomach clenched. It was go-time. I needed to come up with a breezy response that suggested interest and not obsession. So basically, I needed to fake it.

A guy behind me sighed heavily as he brushed past me, and I finally regained my city sense enough to move out of the way, clutching my phone like it was an eel that might slip out of my hand. I flattened my back against the slightly pink facade of an office building and grinned up at the sun.

It was happening. *Finally.*

I glanced at the time and saw that I had three minutes before I was supposed to meet Owen at the front door. I'd arrived to one of our first practice sessions seven minutes late, and he'd responded with "Better late than never, but never late is better."

I'd taken it to heart. I needed to sort out my response to Kai, and fast.

Shockingly, I didn't have to cast around for the right words, because he'd made it easy for me.

> Hey! Definitely, what works for you?

I stared at my phone for exactly fifteen seconds, and when nothing came through, I shoved it in my duffel. I needed to get my Owen game face in order before arriving at the front door, because we hadn't seen each other since the foyer debacle.

Of course Kai had to reach out to me now. Trying to play off the fact that Owen and I had kissed *and* fought wasn't going to be easier knowing that the lines of Kai communication were now open.

I wasn't going to tell Owen about the text. There was no need since his role in my muse plot was essentially done. But how was I going to focus on the lesson?

Owen was waiting at the door with Marti at his feet when I got there, as usual. I waved and tried to smile normally despite the swarming butterflies in my gut.

"What's wrong?" He frowned as he held the door open for me, observant as ever.

You mean aside from the fact that your hand was in my underwear less than a week ago, and now we have to pretend that it didn't happen?

"Why would you think something's wrong?"

Marti gave me an obliviously happy hello, but it did little to lighten the mood.

I stepped past him and tried not to inhale, because he always smelled more Oweny first thing in the morning, when his hair was still a little damp from the shower. He'd taken to leaving his hat off during our lessons, which to me felt like the equivalent of seeing a priest without his collar.

Owen shrugged. "You just look stressed. Anything I should know about before we get started?"

It had become his go-to question at the beginning of our sessions, to quickly find out if I had any aches or pains, but this time it felt like he was psychic and prying for proof of his abilities, as if he *knew* something had gone down with Kai a few minutes prior.

I followed behind him, resigned to keep Kai's name off my lips. "Nope, all good." The squeaky echoes of our footsteps filled the silence. "Unless there's anything else we should talk about . . . from the weekend."

"Nothing more to say," he said quickly without turning to look at me.

It was true; he'd made his feelings about the kiss clear.

He walked Marti back to his office while I waited in the lobby, just like every other session. But this one felt like there was a haze of smoke around us, clouding my vision and making it a little heard to breathe.

I was responsible for the bad vibes. We were in an awkward hinterland because I was complicated and needy, and I'd somehow telegraphed my attraction to Owen while spouting off about how badly I needed Kai.

Yeah, I'd fucked up.

Owen came out of the office with his eyes glued to the ground, like he was checking just how clean the deep clean had made the floor. We headed for our court without discussing our goals for the session, which was odd because Owen was all about hitting benchmarks. I almost felt like I was being punished for the kiss that *he* initiated.

And I'd wanted.

He stalked to his side of the court, spinning his paddle in his hand. "Sign-ups for the tournament just opened. We're going to take care of that this morning before you leave."

My heart lurched at the "we." Despite his frustration, he was still looking out for me.

"Okay, thanks." I welcomed more time together to try to find the old Owen.

"*Shit*," he said as he slapped his paddle against his thigh. "Hold on, I forgot something."

I kept busy stretching and stressing as he walked away.

Owen ambled back to me a few minutes later like we had all the time in the world. I peeked at him while I balanced on one leg to stretch my right quad but couldn't see what he'd gone back to fetch. I switched legs and turned a little, so it wouldn't look like I was staring at him.

"I got this for you."

I refocused on Owen as he pulled a second hidden paddle from behind the one he was holding and handed it to me. Compared to my cheerful pink-lemonade paddle, the sleek blackness he was offering me looked like a weapon.

My mouth dropped open as I took it from him. "Seriously?"

"Yeah." He nodded. "I couldn't have you repping CPA at the tournament with that shitty paddle of yours. You need to get used to playing with it over the next couple of weeks."

I bit the inside of my cheek because I felt my eyes welling up at the unexpected gift. How long ago had he bought it? Given our crap current scenario, he could've skipped giving it to me and kept it or returned it. Despite everything we'd been through, he still wanted to help me win.

I sensed the difference in the paddle the second I curled my palm around the handle. The ergonomic grip felt like it was bespoke. The paddle was black on black, with a shaded repeating box pattern on the hitting surface. It was serious, elegant, and 100 percent Owen.

"This feels expensive," I said, giving it a few test swings through the air.

I didn't mean to be funny, but it got a chuckle out of him. "You're right—it is. But I get a pro discount, so don't worry about it."

I didn't think I could feel any worse about everything, but the unexpected gift proved me wrong.

"Owen, thank you." I stared at him and hoped my eyes weren't too misty, because it felt silly getting choked up over a pickleball paddle. "You're setting me up to be unstoppable."

He shook his head, the dark waves dancing at the back of his neck. "It's a tool, Brooke. It's all about how the operator uses it. Let's get out there and give it a try. Paddles are a personal decision, but I know how you play. I'm pretty sure you're going to like it. And I bet your backspin is going to shape up, big-time."

I hypergripped the paddle, just like the old days, because I needed to feel some sort of anchor.

"Today we're focusing on reset shots," he said as he fished a ball out of his pocket and retreated to his side of the court. "Newbies usually get worked up during their first competition, and this strategy is an easy way to take a breath. It'll help to neutralize the other team's aggressive shots."

I felt like my whole life could use a reset.

I tried to focus as Owen went on to describe the proper grip (soft, no surprise there), paddle position, swing path, and target, but all I could think about was how mechanical he sounded as he coached me. It felt like I was any old student who rolled in off the street for a lesson. He could've been reading from a manual.

I wanted to go back to the way we used to be.

Still, we were yoked together until the tournament, and if I wanted to do at least passably well, I needed to drink in every fake, unused lesson. After all, I wanted to make him proud. To show him what a difference he'd made in a dork with two left feet.

Although if I was honest with myself and sidestepped modesty, my new paddle wasn't the only weapon in my arsenal. The reset shots I consistently managed were good enough to almost unearth the old Owen. He looked impressed but not surprised.

He seemed *challenged* by my game.

By the time we finished, we were both sweaty.

"Okay, let's get you signed up," Owen said after he drained half his water bottle.

Yeah, I was ready, without any hesitation. I wasn't nervous about the tournament; I was *excited*.

I followed him behind the front desk to his office, a new space for me to scope out. After greeting Marti, I surreptitiously eyeballed every wall and surface in the place, only to discover that it offered zero clues about Owen aside from a box filled with power cords and a couple of thank-you cards perched behind his laptop.

Would I end our time together with a card too? The idea of it made me preemptively sad.

"I'm signing you up as 'needs a partner,' right?"

I paused. I hadn't even considered that part of the equation. "Well . . . can't *you* be my partner?"

I realized it was a stupid question the moment I said it.

"Different skill levels," he reminded me.

As if I could forget.

Owen explained that the tournament was double elimination, which meant that even if my TBD partner and I lost our first game, we'd still have a second consolation game to play.

"I wish the timing was a little earlier, because my brother's visiting this weekend and he'd be the perfect partner," I said.

Owen looked up from his laptop. "The one with Barnham?"

I nodded. "Yeah, my one and only sibling. He wants to play with me while he's visiting, so I figure we'll go to Jimmie McDaniel and goof around."

"Supposed to rain on Saturday," Owen said. "Play here."

My heart fumbled at his nonstop generosity, but I didn't feel like I deserved it any longer. I started to manufacture an excuse, but he interrupted me.

"I'm serious," he continued, like he could read my mind. "Depending on what time you want to come, I'll play with you guys. I love Barnham; it would be cool to meet him. It'll be easy to find a fourth."

So Owen was a *fan*. Playing with us would be partly for him.

"I'd love that." I beamed at him, envisioning how well he and Wes were going to get along. "Thank you."

I made a mental note to tell Wes to bring a Barnham stadium shirt for Owen.

"Let me give you my credit card for the registration," I said as I shuffled through my bag.

He slapped his laptop closed. "Too late, all good."

I froze. "*Owen*. Come on, why did you do that?"

His eyes were snagged on mine as he seemed to weigh what he was about to say. "Because it's my turn to call in a favor."

I squinted at him, unsure what he meant.

Owen leaned back in his chair, watching me with an unblinking stare. "I drafted the full chapter outline for my book, and I want you to read it."

Chapter Thirty-One

The text from my mom was a blurry close-up of her, my dad, and Wes with their faces pushed together and beaming.

> Package delivered. Wish you were here!

I had a feeling I'd be getting a few dozen more photos as the visit progressed, as well as a FaceTime call. I threw my phone to the far end of the futon, because I wasn't even supposed to have it within reach thanks to my word count goal.

For the wrong book, as usual.

Einar and Zandria needed to kiss. *They* wanted it (even though they would never admit it, even to themselves), *I* wanted it, and I was convinced my future slow-burn readers would want it. I'd paused the story in the perfect spot during the Hamptons weekend, with the two of them locked in a fight about Zandria's risky behavior and Einar's tendency to be overprotective of her. It should've been a home-run chapter to write—I'd been waiting for it since I introduced them to each other—but my fingers wouldn't budge.

I was sitting on the very futon I needed to be outfitting with clean sheets for my brother's visit, determined to at least start the scene. Meredith had an appointment to check out the potential studio space the red dress Hamptons woman had told her about, so I could work uninterrupted. I'd already nailed the cowboy chapter where Austin and Abby outlined the parameters of their fake relationship since her pregnancy was starting to show, which gave me free rein to focus my energy on the story I *really* wanted to tell.

But I was stuck.

Rather than obsess about it, I decided to focus on cleaning the apartment. It was Friday afternoon, which meant my inbox was a wasteland of nothingness, but I checked again before I started tidying up.

The last thing I expected was a reply from my agent, Celeste, about *The Archer's Paradox*.

The "flight" part of my fight-or-flight response won, and I jumped off the futon to pace circles around my apartment. It was close to 90 degrees outside and our window air conditioner was straining to maintain a not-so-cool 80, but I suddenly craved a hoodie. I talked myself through the various options contained in the email as I stress-walked.

A rave.

A "not feeling it, so sorry."

An "I'll get back to you soon."

Part of me wanted to wait until my visit with Wes was over before seeing what Celeste thought, but I knew I'd wind up distracted until I had a read on how she felt. I dropped back onto the futon with a shaky breath and grabbed my laptop. If the news was bad, Wes could console me. If it was good, we'd celebrate.

Celeste was only a few years older than me, and she was a newer agent without any hits in her client list. When she fangirled, you knew it, and based on the number of exclamation points in her email, she loved the idea of Einar and Zandria as much as I did.

My eyes swam as I tried to read through her message. The final line? "Send me those pages *immediately*!"

Yeah, I was about to have the best weekend ever.

Wes was easy to spot in a crowd, even in Manhattan. He'd always had an aura around him that made people take note, long before he was a semi-famous footballer. He had a way of walking through the world that telegraphed confidence *and* kindness. He was almost intimidatingly good-looking, but he was so quick to smile that it defused any nerves. He had his father's ebony skin and thick eyebrows and our mom's beautiful smile. Wes turned heads because of his good looks and also because his face regularly appeared on TV screens around the world.

Here in New York, it was probably due to the former. Sure, he was occasionally recognized, but when he visited he tended to bank on the fact that Barnham wasn't as popular as Chelsea or Manchester, so he could skip his usual cap and glasses incognito act. I peered into the Saturday morning crowds streaming through Penn Station, trying to spot him before he saw me, so I could hug him into submission. We were meeting in front of Hudson News, and of course *Speak Softly* was displayed front and center. I snapped a selfie with it to send to Nia.

Someday, I vowed to myself, *The Archer's Paradox* would be on the marquee display table next to the rest of the bestsellers. I stared at the books, trying to visualize mine nestled among them, willing it to be.

Someone reached past me to grab a book in the center of the table. It was an obnoxious, "you're in my way" lean that pushed into my personal space. I frowned and moved to the side, shooting the guy a glare.

"*Wes!*"

I crashed into him as he laughed at my obliviousness.

"Took you long enough," he said as he squeezed me tightly. "I've been standing here for like five minutes."

I always forgot just how far away England was until we were back together again. We'd learned to ignore the fact that we didn't connect as often or as deeply as we used to, but whenever I saw my brother in person, I was reminded how much I missed being part of his everyday life. I held him for a long time before I pulled away.

I stared at him like I couldn't believe he was really standing in front of me.

I frowned and pointed at his upper lip. "Hold up. A *mustache*? Seriously?"

"You don't like it?"

I shook my head. "Sorry, not a fan."

"Just having some off-season fun," he replied as he smoothed it with his thumb and pointer finger. "It'll be gone soon."

Of course, on Wes it looked amazing. He was dressed like he'd traveled from Maryland on the Orient Express and not Amtrak, in a black blazer, black linen button-down, perfectly tailored white pants that were somehow spotless despite the public transportation, no socks, and horse bit loafers. He'd always been stylish, but he usually opted for hybrid workout pants and T-shirts when he knew he wasn't on display. Wes was clearly in his fashionista era.

"If I'd known we were catwalking, I would've dressed accordingly," I said, nodding to his outfit.

I'd gone for jean shorts and a sleeveless white T-shirt.

"Stop, you look great," he chided. He reached over to tweak my bicep. "Fit, even."

"'Fit' in the UK slang way, or 'fit' like I've been working out?" I tossed my hair and preened.

"Both, actually." Wes glanced around the claustrophobic station, his expression worried. "Hey, before we get going, there's something I need to tell you."

A lump preemptively formed in my throat.

"What?" I demanded. "Is it Mom and Dad? Are they okay?"

"Yeah, they're fine." He nodded. "Great and annoying, like always. It's, uh, about me."

He squinted into the distance like he was looking for something. I glanced over my shoulder to follow his gaze and saw a group of girls dressed alike in sparkly clothes, obviously in town for a concert at Madison Square Garden later.

"Tell me. You're freaking me out."

His eyes bounced between me and the shifting crowds.

"I met someone."

It was the least traumatic thing he could've revealed to me.

"Wes! That's amazing. I can't wait to hear all about her." I paused. He seemed unusually fidgety, so I made room for an unexpected confession. "Or him."

He finally managed to focus on me, laughing. "I met a *woman*," he clarified. "And I fell in love. And I'd like you to meet her."

Wes was getting more jittery by the second, but then again, he'd always been a serial dater. Telling me that he'd found the one was a huge deal.

"Oh my god, of *course* I want to meet her," I exclaimed.

"Let's get out of here and talk about it over lunch. I picked this great—"

A stunning, dark-haired woman materialized out of the crowd beside Wes. She clasped his arm and smiled shyly at me.

I froze as I pieced together what was happening.

"Brooke, I'd like you to meet my fiancée, Claudia Esparza."

"Hi," she said, beaming at me. "I'm *so* happy to meet you."

The chaos around us faded to ambient noise as I stood there dumbstruck, glancing at the world's most beautiful pairing with my mouth hanging open.

"*Fiancée?*" I squeaked out, still frozen in place.

They laughed in unison, and I was faced with two sets of perfect, blindingly white teeth.

"I told him that he needed to let you know before we arrived, but he wanted to double-surprise you." Claudia chastised him with a fake punch to his side.

I cataloged her quickly. British accent with a hint of something else. Skin so perfect that it looked filtered. Tall but still a few inches shorter than Wes. A bob that would make anyone else look like Lord Farquaad. And eyes so filled with love for my brother that I didn't even question the mechanics of how this speed-run engagement came to be.

I barreled into her, hugging her tightly enough to make her laugh. *"Fiancée!"*

"Oh, good," she said softly as we embraced. "I'm a hugger too."

"You smell like apricots," I said as we pulled apart, because I wasn't sure how else to express my amazement at the goddess my brother had scored.

"And *you* are stunning," she said, still gripping my arms. She beamed at Wes. "I see the resemblance."

I grabbed her hand. "The ring! Oh my god, it's incredible."

It was a dream of a thing, a gleaming, nearly dime-sized diamond on a silvery band.

"It's good, right?" Wes boasted.

Claudia giggled.

"Beyond," I said, bringing it closer to my eyes to admire it.

The ring on my surprise sister-in-law-to-be woke me up to a logistical issue.

"Wait a minute . . . the two of you . . . in my shitty little apartment? You should get a hotel!"

"*Ab*solutely not," Claudia said with authority, glancing at Wes for backup. "We agreed that since this is a whirlwind introduction, we should sop up every last second of togetherness. It'll be like a kid sleepover. I have five siblings. I'm used to waiting in line for the loo." She paused to frown. "As long as your roommate doesn't mind."

"God no, Meredith is very much a 'more the merrier' type of person. Plus she's closing at work tonight, so she won't be home until late."

"We should stop by and annoy her after dinner," Wes suggested.

I knew Meredith would love the chance to study the clan while she mixed cocktails.

"Well, this changes my agenda for the day," I said, my heart sinking a little at the realization. "I guess we're skipping pickleball?"

"Fuck no," Wes said adamantly. "You playing a sport is *huge*. I need to see it with my own eyes. And Claudia plays with me all the time; she's really good."

"I'm merely decent," she added. "But I do love it."

"Don't you guys want to tour the city?" I pushed. "Claudia, have you been to New York before?"

"Oh, I *lived* in New York when I first started out," she said with a smile. "No need to cart us to the Empire State Building or Macy's. Being here feels like coming home."

"Claudia's a model," Wes explained, as if it weren't obvious by her lush, otherworldly features and willowy build.

"Of course you are." I beamed at her.

Wes eyeballed a man cradling pantyhose stuffed with what looked like birdseed ambling past us. "Can we get out of here? I'm verging on overload."

"Yup, I just need to send a quick text," I said as I pulled out my phone.

So far, we were on track for our game at CPA this afternoon, but I wanted to let Owen know that we no longer needed a fourth. Claudia joining us felt like a leveling of the matchup, unless she was a sniper being modest about her skills.

But now it felt like a double date.

I was so busy obsessing about the optics that I didn't notice the little boy working his way over to Wes until my brother was kneeling to chat with him.

"You know me from the video game? Is that so?" I heard Wes gently ask the boy. He looked up at the man accompanying the child to acknowledge him with a smile, then shifted his attention back. "Do the two of you play *FIFA* together?"

The boy bobbed his head eagerly, finally breaking into a smile.

It had only taken about ten minutes for one of the many video game–obsessed kids to identify my brother from his avatar player status.

But I had a feeling that little gamer boys wouldn't be the only ones fanning out over my brother.

Chapter Thirty-Two

CPA during regular business hours felt like a foreign country. I was used to quiet mornings with Owen, not the chaos of a busy Saturday afternoon. Nearly every court was in use, and I could see a crowd waiting at the smoothie bar.

"Damn. Swanky place," Wes said as we ducked out of the rain and into the lobby.

"Not at all what I was expecting," Claudia added, swiveling her head to take in the living plant wall and lounge chairs in one of the hangout spaces.

I puffed up with pride like I was actually a sustaining member, until it struck me that I was enjoying the perks of the club without paying a penny.

Yeah, I was actually a leech, and Owen would probably be glad to get rid of me once my lessons were officially marked complete. I stuffed down any thoughts about the end of the line and forced myself to focus on the moment.

"Wait until you see the locker rooms," I replied.

My worlds were about to collide, and I was feeling shockingly okay about it. Probably because Wes was one of those people who took the spotlight trained on him and bounced it outward, making everyone else the focus. He knew how to make people in his orbit feel comfortable and important, from the littlest fanboys to the moms with crushes.

Everybody loved Wes and everybody loved Owen, for different but related reasons. They'd be besties within three minutes.

We'd planned to play a few games and then get ready at CPA for a big night out, which included cocktails, then dinner at a fancy restaurant Wes picked, then ending up at the bar to hang with Meredith.

"You remembered the stadium shirt, right?" I whispered to Wes.

"Damn straight." He grinned back. "I need to thank the man who coached you to greatness."

I was about to say something sarcastic about being less than great, but Owen's voice echoing in my head reminded me to speak about myself as if I were talking about a friend.

We were twenty minutes early for our assigned time, partially because Wes wanted to fight for the right to pay for the games. The guy at the front desk glanced up at Wes and briefly widened his eyes, which was the normal Manhattan trying-to-play-it-cool-in-the-presence-of-a-minor-celebrity response.

"Oh, hey," he said, quickly looking at Claudia and me and determining that Wes was the only VIP. "Checking in?"

I pushed up to the desk beside Wes. "Yup, we're the four o'clock on court twelve."

"And we still need to pay the guest fee," Wes added with his signature smile.

The guy nodded and refocused on the laptop in front of him. "Actually, you're all set, no payment necessary. Do you need a tour? I'd be happy to show you around."

Since I was rarely there during business hours, he didn't know that I was just as qualified to give the tour.

Owen appeared from his office, no doubt because he'd been watching the CCTV for us.

"Not necessary, Marcus, I've got this."

I tried not to stare as he stalked toward us, because it was yet another Owen I wasn't acquainted with. Not the Brooklyn book-signing version or the vacation-casual Hamptons-party guy, but a naked-headed pickleball *god*.

He was wearing a dark gray slim-fit T-shirt that looked like it was made of wicking fabric and black shorts that actually fit his body instead of swimming on it, which were short enough to show off shockingly defined thighs.

I cleared my throat and looked away before he could catch me admiring him. It was better for both of us that I'd never met this side of him when we were sweaty and alone.

"Hey, folks, welcome to the Chelsea Pickleball Academy," he said, hand outstretched to Wes. "I'm Owen. Big fan."

Wes clasped his hand and pulled him into a bro hug, complete with twin thumps on each other's backs. "Good to meet you, man. Brooke's told me a lot about you."

It was true. I'd been accidentally hyping up Owen to Wes since my second lesson.

Wes stepped aside. "This is my fiancée, Claudia."

"Fiancée? Wow." Owen gave an approving nod as they shook hands. "Congratulations, that's great."

He finally glanced at me, and our eyes snagged.

"Hey."

I could pull so much context from the single syllable. He said it softly, like he was offering a truce while my family was present. There'd be no bottled-up drama between us today, just good old-fashioned competition.

"Hey," I said back with a smile and little nod to signify I understood.

"So how are we doing this?" Wes asked, interrupting the moment. "Guys against girls? Siblings versus . . ." He trailed off, because "fiancée and coach" sounded clunky.

Owen glanced at me. "Considering I've been working with this one for ages and we've never actually played a real game together, I'd like to be on her team for at least the first game if that's okay."

My heart warmed at the thought of us finally on the same side of the court.

"Makes sense." Wes bobbed his head. "Oh, before I forget, I brought you something. A little hooty-hoot for you." He knelt to dig into his bag and pulled out a white-and-navy Barnham Owls shirt. "Wear it proudly."

Owen looked awestruck as he took the thing. "Are you *kidding*? Thank you!"

His grin was as wide as the little boy's at Penn Station.

"Just don't wear it tonight; otherwise, he'll look like a plonker with his fan club," Claudia cautioned.

"Tonight?" Owen frowned as his eyes shifted to me.

"Oh, uh," I stammered at the accidental invitation. "We're going out tonight, to dinner and stuff—"

"You're coming with us, right?" Wes demanded. "Losers buy the first round of drinks. Not that I'm implying anything, but maybe I *am*?"

Owen's jaw worked as he glanced between us.

"You should come," I said softly.

He let out a little sigh as he weighed his options.

"Unless you already have plans," I added.

I held my breath, because the buffer Wes and Claudia would provide could help patch things up between us even more.

"Yeah, that sounds great," he said, fixing his gaze on me. "Thanks."

THERE WAS NO reason to be nervous, seeing as I had a ringer on my team, but I felt like I was about to perform for Owen *and* my brother. It was more than a game; it was my sporty debut.

I hadn't even factored Claudia into the equation, but after her white-hot game-starting serve, I shifted my focus. It wasn't just a test of my performance. We needed to *win*.

Claudia's serve bounced on my side of the court.

"All you," Owen coached softly as I ran for it, even though I already knew it was mine.

I didn't want to begin the game by getting overexcited and hitting it out-of-bounds, so I chanted "soft, soft, soft" as I readied my paddle.

I returned it cleanly, and we were off.

Wes came in hot with bangers; Owen and I worked on owning the kitchen. Wes was playing like a show-off, smacking back every ball *hard*. It was impressive, sure, but it wasn't a sound long-term strategy. He'd eventually get sloppy or wear out. At least that's what I hoped, although given his life was fitness, I wasn't sure it was possible.

The soft-play defensive strategy on our side of the court worked for a while, but I could sense Owen getting antsy to smack a few balls back at Wes. I knew he had just as much power and better form, but he was letting Wes get overconfident.

Owen was playing chess.

At one of our early lessons, he'd told me that as the game skewed more bro-y, it was starting to resemble tennis, with more hard shots as opposed to long dink rallies that were easier for newbies and older players. I could definitely see it happening as we played. Wes had an occasional player's approach—smack the shit out of the ball every time it came near—not a real strategy.

Owen had taught me more than just the mechanics of the game. He'd shown me how to pick up on my opponent's tells and go-to shots and how to best counter them. Neither one of us got stressed as Wes and Claudia pulled ahead.

After they scored another point, Owen walked over to me, spinning his paddle in his hand, his tell for venting frustration. "Your returns are great, but let his big shots go out. Remember to watch his swing; that'll tell you what's coming. Don't be a hero and jump to try to steal them out of the air. Just let them sail by, okay? I know that goes against every instinct, but trust me."

I nodded and palmed the damp tendrils off my forehead. "He's got no finesse," I muttered.

"Exactly," Owen agreed. "And that's how we win."

After all our time working together, it felt like our game was psychic. A simple nod or grunt from Owen and I knew what I was supposed to do. And he gave me the space to make choices on my own rather than doubting me and cutting me off.

I watched Owen start returning shots that required Wes to either use his dicey backhand, or run around the ball awkwardly to try to hit it forehand, or miss it completely. I followed suit and frustrated the hell out of my brother.

Claudia did her best to emulate Wes, probably because he'd taught her to play. Her shots didn't have the same zippiness, which allowed me to counter with the drop shots Owen had taught me. I loved Wes's groans of frustration as he raced to the kitchen to try to return my balls, only to watch it bounce, bounce, bounce before he could reach it.

"What the hell, Brooke?" Wes complained as I fired my own banger down the middle after a series of dinks. "You're on fire."

I shrugged a shoulder, trying to play it off like it was no big deal, and turned to Owen for confirmation.

He winked at me and held his paddle out to tap mine. "Nice."

No surprise, we won the first three games. By the last one, Wes finally put his analytical skills to work and abandoned his strategy of "all bangers all the time." He and Claudia opted to hang out at the kitchen line, and we started having long dink rallies, which, given we'd been at it over an hour and a half, was a welcome break.

It was as if Owen and I had wordlessly agreed to take it easy on them, to end on a high note. It was a squeaker—we technically could've crushed them—but Wes and Claudia won the final game.

The four of us met at the net to touch paddles.

"Who *are* you?" Wes asked me in amazement as he wiped sweat from his forehead with the hem of his T-shirt. "You're so goddamned good!" He turned to Owen. "What did you do to her?"

We all paused to glance at Owen, and I felt a little itchy about how he might answer the question. Owen had definitely done something to me; I just couldn't figure out what.

Our eyes met, and suddenly it was just the two of us.

"I didn't *do* anything," he answered, still locked on me. "I just helped Brooke see what was always there."

Chapter Thirty-Three

Claudia joined me at the mirror in the locker room as I put away my hair dryer, already looking flawless despite being barefaced and with her hair still wrapped up in a towel.

"I like him. Owen," she said as she dabbed moisturizer on her perfect face. "Are you guys a thing or . . . ?"

I tried to keep my expression neutral despite her picking up on something I still couldn't wrap my brain around. "Did it seem like we're a thing?"

I glanced around the locker room and was relieved to see that we were now alone, since everyone at CPA knew Owen.

Claudia paused with her finger hovering in front of her cheek, meeting my eyes in the mirror's reflection. "I couldn't tell exactly, but I sensed something . . ." She flickered her fingertips as she searched for the word. "*Unresolved*, I guess."

To me, nothing that had happened during the games was out of the ordinary, other than me kicking so much ass. Owen and I had interacted the way we always did on the court. No outward flirting, just sincere appreciation and respect for each other.

Okay, maybe I was a little uptight about keeping things civil between us, but you'd think that would make our relationship seem strained. What was it that Claudia picked up on that was quiet enough for us to be oblivious, but loud enough for her to notice?

"Honestly, I don't know what we are," I finally admitted softly.

When I looked at my reflection, I was frowning.

I trusted Claudia, and since my brother loved her, I already did as well. But I didn't want to dive into the near misses Owen and I had lived through before a long night out together.

"Okay." Claudia nodded as she leaned closer to the mirror and resumed lotioning. "So I wasn't wrong. Is it awkward for you that he's coming tonight? I take the blame for inviting him."

"Not at all," I said quickly as I pulled out my small makeup kit. "We could use a . . . a reset."

"Right," Claudia said with a nod. "Understood. Just catch my eye if you need to escape to the loo for a gossip or cry, got it?"

I couldn't have written Claudia to be more perfect for Wes or me. I'd always wanted a sister, and it seemed like I was finally getting my wish.

"Thank you."

I was preemptively sad that they were leaving the next day.

"Don't worry, Wes and I will keep it light." Claudia pulled the towel off her head, and she could've tucked her wet hair behind her ears and looked perfect. "I guarantee the two of them will cozy up to discuss Barnham stats. We'll be football widows in the corner, nursing our pints."

I didn't correct her that I couldn't be a widow without first being at least wife-adjacent.

Thirty minutes later we were both glossy and ready to go. Claudia left to meet Wes in the lobby while I finished packing my things and shoving them into the locker. We planned to swing by and pick up our bags either at the end of the night, thanks to Owen and his all-access status, or if things got sloppy, the next morning.

I'd opted to straighten my hair and wear a flowy white skirt and black tank top that I realized too late dipped a little too low. I channeled Meredith and threw my shoulders back.

I might not have achieved off-duty model status like Claudia, but I looked *good*.

I'd forgotten to pack any sort of purse for the night, so I tucked my lip gloss, ID, and credit card in my bra and headed for the lobby. I was so busy adjusting my boobs to make sure their purse status wasn't obvious through my thin tank that I wasn't looking where I was going until it was too late.

"There she is!"

I looked up and froze with my hand cupped on my underboob.

It was breathtaking, smiling Kai, staring at me like he'd been waiting to see me.

"Ohmygosh, you scared me," I breathed, moving my hand quickly. *"Hi."*

My central nervous system had taken a beating during the game, so I felt like my body responded to seeing him with a "for fuck's sake, what *now*?" despite the fact that he was the sole reason I was in the club to begin with.

"Hey, yourself." He moved a step closer, scanning me so quickly that I nearly missed it. "You never texted me back the other day."

"Huh?" I frowned at him. "But I did. At least I think I did."

No, I was sure I did, since I'd waited for him to respond.

Funny that I hadn't obsessed about him blowing me off, but then again, I'd had plenty on my plate over the past few days.

"That's weird. I didn't get it." He leaned against the wall. "You look gorgeous. Where are you off to?"

"Thanks." I smiled reflexively. The compliment wiped away his white lie about my text. "My brother and his fiancée are visiting from England so we're going out tonight. Dinner, drinks, the usual."

"Nice. I'm heading out after I play; maybe we can link up later?" He smiled, and for the first time, I noticed the dimples I'd somehow missed.

My stomach plummeted. Of course, part of me wanted to jump at the opportunity, but not now. Not tonight. Our little foursome had the perfect equilibrium, and adding Kai would throw it off for a bunch of different reasons.

"That would be fun," I said convincingly. "I'm not sure exactly where we're heading, but why don't you text me later and we can figure it out then?"

It was a little test. If he really wanted to meet up, he could reach out, but I wasn't about to text him first.

"Done." He cocked his eyebrow and pointed a finger at me. "We're making this happen. Right?"

I manufactured a smile to prove that us meeting up was exactly what I wanted even as my gut warned me that it was a terrible idea.

"Right. See you later."

Kai smiled softly at me, holding my gaze for a beat longer than necessary. "I really hope so."

That *look*. Weaponized swooniness and thoroughly convincing.

I couldn't tell if the off-kilter sensation rolling through me was anticipation or worry that I might be forced to navigate Kai and Owen at the same time.

The text came through right after Meredith finished her round of hugs. We were in VIP seats at the bar, ready for the surprise drinks she was mixing up for us.

Meredith's bar was the perfect spot to wind down our night, because I could tell that Wes and Claudia were barely holding on thanks to the jet lag. We'd enjoyed amazing food and easy conversation. Ending up in the bar's soft-focus mood lighting felt right.

My phone danced across the tile surface. It was late enough in the evening that it *had* to be Kai. My hands went sweaty as I glanced over at Owen. His eyes flicked to me quickly like he could feel it too, then refocused on Claudia as she described her meet-cute with Wes.

I grabbed my phone and flipped it over. Would Wes and Kai get along? Would Owen leave the moment he heard Kai was coming? What would Claudia think about me once I introduced a guy who was definitely not a part of a love triangle?

I shook my head. No. Inviting Kai to join our perfect little foursome felt wrong on so many levels. Even though it was what I'd wanted, it wasn't what I wanted in *this* moment.

I was so busy trying to pre-navigate how I was going to respond without burning bridges that it took me a few seconds to see that the message was from building management, not Kai.

Hold on. There'd been a *fire*?

A window air-conditioning unit had malfunctioned and sparked into a fire on the floor below us. More specifically, the *apartment* below us, the complainers, and thanks to them and "an abundance of caution," we weren't allowed back in our apartment until they tested the structural integrity of their ceiling and our floor.

"Mere, *fuck*!" I frowned at her, holding up my phone. "There was a fire at our place! Check your phone; they said we can't go back to the building tonight."

Wes and Owen stopped talking abruptly, and Meredith fished her phone out of her back pocket.

"No," she moaned. "Not *now*. I don't want to have to move right as I'm about to sign a lease for my studio."

She wasn't quite at that stage yet, but she was speaking it into existence.

"How bad is it?" Owen asked, sounding worried.

I reread the text. "There's not much detail. It sounds like they evacuated the building in time and no one was hurt. Let me jump on the building message board for the real story."

Meredith was called away to serve a group of girls dressed as Guy Fieri, something that would normally crack her up, but she barely managed a smile.

I navigated to the world's most passive-aggressive message board, where people with too much time on their hands complained about everything from the mail delivery to tenants who had the nerve to fry food in the privacy of their apartment.

"So?" Wes asked, his brow furrowed.

"Someone posted photos. It's not incinerated or anything, but I'm sure it reeks of smoke."

The blurry picture was taken from the hallway and showed the blackened wall and ceiling across from the open front door.

I handed Wes my phone, and after he frowned at the image, he handed it to Owen, who then passed it to Claudia.

"This absolutely fucking *sucks*," Meredith said as she came back to our end of the bar. "It better not be major damage."

My phone chimed again.

This time it was Kai.

> Hey, where are you? We just finished dinner.

It was after ten, and thanks to the fire, I was in no mind to even think about trying to meet.

"I can stay at Colton's, but what about you guys?" Meredith asked.

I tried catching her eye, to let her know that fate had the worst timing ever, but she was rightfully caught up trying to figure out how to deal with being temporarily homeless.

I placed my phone face down on the bar. He'd waited until late to reach out; he could wait a few more minutes as we figured out what the hell we were going to do.

Suddenly, connecting with Kai didn't matter.

"I guess we can get a hotel?" I offered.

"Right, I'm on it," Claudia said, staring into the glow of her phone.

Meredith scurried back to us after serving a group of white-haired men in suits. "Turns out there's a *major* medical convention at Javits. I'm guessing the close-by hotels are full."

The situation had officially become a nightmare.

"Guys, just stay at my place," Owen said.

We all turned to stare at him.

"I'm serious," he continued. "I have a guest room and a fold-out couch in the basement. Plenty of space. It's late—it's easier this way."

First of all, a *basement*? Did Owen live in Narnia?

"Mate, no, you don't have to do that," Wes said. "We can grab a couple of rooms. We don't want to put you out."

"Um, actually, no, we can't, babe," Claudia said. "I just did a quick search and there's nothing."

Once again, I was faced with the burden of Owen's never-ending generosity. Although now I had the promise of payback when I read his chapter summaries.

Which he still hadn't emailed.

Everyone turned to me as if I had a real decision to make when there was only one possibility open to us. I glanced at Owen to try to gauge just how put out he was by the idea of surprise hosting three randos.

He nodded, a little encouragement to convince me that he was indeed offering to open his house to us. Despite all the bullshit we'd been through, he was still willing to be there for me.

This time felt like the biggest offer yet. Owen wasn't just giving me his time; he was inviting me—*us*—into his private world. I was going to get to see where he relaxed at the end of the day. Where Marti liked to hang out.

Where he slept.

Maybe. He could very well keep that space closed off from me. Probably in his best interest to keep me far away from his bedroom.

"Are you sure everything's booked?" I glanced around at the three of them.

"I triple-checked," Claudia said.

"Brooke, it's *fine*," Owen assured me.

I think we both sensed how "not fine" it could turn out for us. A bunch of drinks in, inhibitions lowered thanks to the camaraderie of the evening. We very well could run into each other in a narrow hallway in the middle of the night, half dressed, and then further complicate . . . *everything*.

Because now that I'd seen his thighs, I was curious to see what else he was hiding.

Worry clawed at me. I knew how *I'd* react if I happened upon him in the moonlight; it was his response that had me stressed.

But we didn't have much of a choice.

"Okay, then," I said softly, crossing my arms over my chest. "Guess we're having a sleepover at Owen's."

Chapter Thirty-Four

We stopped by CPA on the way to Owen's to grab our gym bags, which meant we wouldn't be completely dependent on his hospitality. We all had toothbrushes at least.

As he'd mentioned, Owen's townhouse was just a quick walk from the club, which was great, considering the rain hadn't stopped all day. We wound up in a beautiful neighborhood, sharing umbrellas on a street with brownstones that had impressive *Sex and the City* staircases out front. It was the land of giant windows, flower-filled planters, and climbing ivy.

Not at all where I'd envisioned him living.

"This is me," he said as he jogged up a set of stairs to a shiny black front door.

I shot a look at Wes and he widened his eyes.

Marti greeted us at the door, spinning with delight when she realized that she had three additional admirers to charm.

"Oh, I *love* your dog," Claudia cooed, dropping to her knees to pet her.

"Thanks," Owen said as he collected our umbrellas and placed them in the tile anteroom. "I need to warn you that she might end up sleeping with you. Hope that's okay."

"Our bed is open to all animals," Wes said as he squatted

next to Claudia. "We're hoping to adopt a pup soon. A little Barnham mascot."

I followed Owen in, and when he flicked on the light in the foyer, I had to stifle a gasp, because the space to the right of the door featured a room-length, floor-to-ceiling bookshelf.

With a *ladder*. A sliding ladder that was the stuff of every bookworm's dreams.

"Wow, you're quite a reader," Wes said as he walked into the dim space.

"Oh, I haven't read all of these yet," Owen replied quickly. "But I have a lifetime to get through them."

So his to-be-read list was house-sized. Got it.

Owen tossed his keys on the hall table beneath a big black-and-white abstract artwork that actually was a painting and not a print.

"What can I get you to drink?" Owen asked. "Wine? Something harder?"

He flipped on more lights as he made his way through the place, and I followed behind him in silent awe, because his home was nothing like I expected. Not that I thought he lived in a one-bedroom with a mattress on the floor or anything, but given the way he dressed, I never imagined that he'd be living in a home that could feasibly show up in a YouTube *Architectural Digest* tour.

It was airy but masculine, with high ceilings and dark walls and an orderly but not off-puttingly tidy aesthetic. There were a few dirty dishes stacked on the black counter by the sink and a grouping of healthy plants sitting in the deep windowsill, including an orchid, a plant I'd never managed to keep alive. I could see French doors on the far wall that no doubt led to an equally delightful outdoor space in back.

"Mate, I'm sorry to ruin the party, but we're on fumes," Wes said, glancing at a barely awake Claudia. "Would you mind if we turned in for the night?"

"Of course, I get it," Owen said. "Let me show you where you'll be."

We all followed him down a narrow flight of stairs to a basement that didn't feel subterranean thanks to windows and a door leading to his backyard. I wasn't sure about the mechanics of how the underground-but-not scenario was possible; all I knew was that it was just as comfortable and well designed as the rest of his home.

Owen walked to a narrow closet and opened it to reveal stacks of perfectly folded linens. "That couch pulls out to a bed. Sheets and pillows are in here. Towels too. Powder room is right over there." He pointed across the space.

I forced myself not to let my jaw drop. A basement *bathroom*? Owen had hit the housing jackpot and I wanted to know how.

Marti hopped onto the couch, clearly waiting for her bedmates to hurry up so they could snuggle.

Owen turned to me. "You're on the second floor with me."

I gulped and followed behind him, up the basement stairs and the floating staircase in the main hallway to a small bedroom with chocolate-brown walls and white bedding that looked sumptuous even from a distance.

But I wasn't ready for bed.

"Hey, can I take you up on that wine?" I asked him. "I'm all stressed from the fire stuff. I just need to unplug a little before I go to sleep."

"Yeah, I'm not tired yet either, but one more glass of red wine should do the trick."

I dropped my gym bag in the bedroom, kicked off my shoes, and followed him back to the first floor.

"I wish it wasn't raining; we could sit out back," he said as he pulled gigantic goblets and a bottle of wine from a kitchen cabinet.

"Here is fine," I said, pulling out one of the modern sling-leather barstools.

"No, don't sit there!" Owen held his hand out and I froze. "They are *so* uncomfortable. I've been meaning to replace them, but I like how they look, so I only sit in them when I'm going to be quick."

I smiled to myself. So this glass of wine was going to be slow?

"Here." Owen handed me an overfull goblet.

"Can we hang out in your library?"

He chuckled. "I wouldn't call it that, but okay."

The couch in the front room was dark gray and velvety, the exact sort of spot perfect for sinking in and napping a Sunday away, especially with rain streaming down the front windows. As much as I wanted to run over and examine Owen's book stash, the couch was calling my name after a very long day.

I situated myself in the corner of it. Owen flipped on a small brass lamp behind the couch and opted to sit on the opposite end rather than the chair a distance away. I took a long gulp of wine.

I forced myself not to ask about his beautiful living space, even though housing was a safe topic of conversation in the city. There was simply no elegant way to ask how he could afford it on a pickleball instructor's salary. But then again, living with Meredith had been a crash course in quiet familial wealth. She didn't have to come out and tell me that a distant Waxman had made a killing in real estate; the second home in Aspen and first-class vacations provided plenty of context.

But then again, he'd told me that his father was a mechanic and his mom was a hairdresser.

"What?" Owen asked me, wearing a bemused smile.

With Owen, nothing went unseen, even something as fleeting as a frown of confusion. I'm sure it was somehow related to his gift for coaching—the ability to notice something as seemingly unimportant as pointer finger placement on a paddle—but it meant that I needed to stay on top of my poker face. He probably knew exactly what I was thinking about, but I wasn't going to give him the satisfaction of admitting it.

"Nothing. Just feeling very mellow." I drew my legs up and crossed them under my skirt. "Although I think I was back to hypergripping today. My forearm is killing me."

He nodded. "Yeah, it happens when it's an important game. We forget our basics. Try this."

Owen set his wineglass on the marble table in front of the couch and pressed his thumb against the middle of his arm up near his elbow, rubbing in slow circles.

I mimicked what he was doing on my own arm.

"Good, right?" he asked.

"Eh." I frowned. "I don't feel anything."

He tsked disapprovingly and moved down the couch to me, abruptly taking my wrist in one hand and pressing his thumb against my skin with the other before I could even comprehend what he was doing.

His knee wound up just a couple of inches from mine.

"Can you feel *this*?"

He smoothed a firm circle against me, and I melted from the unexpected mix of sensations. My arm was sore enough to feel bruised from the abuse of the game, but the way he was massaging it made it hurt in a good way.

"Oh my *god*." I sighed. I had to fight to keep from letting my eyes roll back in my head. "That's it, right there."

It was such a tiny, forgotten junction of muscles, but the way Owen was working it made me understand just how crucial it was. He pushed his thumb against the skin in the center of my forearm up by my elbow, then moved it an inch outward, unleashing a completely different painfully delicious sensation.

His hands were dangerous, even on my freaking arm.

"Are you *kidding* me?" I let my body sag as he continued massaging. "That is . . ."

He moved his thumb a quarter inch down and I shivered.

"Let me guess; you also did an intensive massage apprenticeship in Sweden?" I asked.

He let out an appreciative laugh. "Not quite. But I did plenty of time on the rehab and massage table back in my tennis days. I picked up some pointers."

"Do tell," I gently encouraged, hoping he'd open up but not stop touching me.

"Can't. I need to focus on your fucked-up flexor carpi radialis."

"That's your official diagnosis, Dr. Miller?" I laughed softly. "Fucked-up?"

"Unfortunately, yes. That's what happens when you don't listen to my advice. But I'll get you all fixed up."

As usual.

We both went quiet in the dim stillness, the rain on the window providing a gloomy soundtrack as his fingertips punished my aching muscles.

Owen and I were back in that hazy, undefinable space where the pull to be close, touching if possible, was hard to resist. Being near Owen felt natural now. *Necessary.* I knew he thought getting close was a mistake—I was holding my breath, waiting for him to angrily retreat from me like always—but I couldn't write off the way I felt in the moment as being touch starved or horny.

No, I wanted *him*.

I wanted Owen. Not Kai.

Owen.

It was as if he could read my thoughts, because he slid his hand from my arm as I admitted it to myself.

"You might feel a little bruised tomorrow, but it should fade quickly," he said as he grabbed his glass and retreated to his corner of the couch.

He downed the wine quickly, like he was ready to be done with me. I didn't want to say good night yet. I reclined so that I was facing him, my back against the arm of the couch.

"Hey." I stretched my leg out and poked him with my big toe. Owen jumped, startled out of whatever had him now frowning. "You still haven't sent me your chapters."

"Right, I keep forgetting," he said, leaning forward so he could pull his phone from his back pocket. "I'll do it now."

I watched his profile in the glow from his phone. I felt like I knew every inch of it.

"Sent," he said. "Please be honest."

"Of course," I agreed. "But I have a good feeling. I know how you teach; now all you have to do is translate it to the page."

"Yeah, easier said than done." He let out a hoarse laugh.

"That's why I'm here."

A beat while he seemed to consider what sending his pages to me meant. I understood the naked feeling of taking a precious idea and sending it out into the world.

"Thank you."

I now knew better than to suggest that it was a payback for his generosity and instead just gave him a soft smile.

Something was happening and we both felt it. The stilled air, dim light, and memory of his hands on my skin were guideposts on the way to the inevitable.

His eyes found mine in the darkness, and we watched each other wordlessly. My leg was still stretched across the couch, dangerously close to his thigh. I willed him to shift his hand a few inches, so I could feel his palm on my skin again.

My heart thumped so forcefully that I wondered if he could hear it. I crossed my arms, hoping to muffle the sound, only to have my breasts nearly spill over the edge of my tank top.

Owen's eyes slid down my torso slowly to take me in, then back up to meet my gaze. He didn't hide his appreciation, and his expression seemed to suggest what he was thinking.

Mine.

I tried not to visibly tremble at how obvious he was being, even without words.

But this time, it wasn't Owen fighting off what was to come. He was *enjoying* the wait.

Everything in our surroundings seemed to be conspiring to push us closer . . . the rain, the wine, the cloudlike couch, the dim lamplight . . . but I wasn't about to test my theory.

I didn't want to get rejected yet again.

Owen cleared his throat softly and shifted so that he was fully facing me in a way that suggested a lion about to pounce.

"I'm going to kiss you now, Brooke."

Chapter Thirty-Five

It wasn't much of a warning, because the moment he said the words, Owen's mouth was claiming mine.

I let out a little surprised squeak, which quickly shifted to a low moan of pleasure. He knelt above me on the couch, one knee between my thighs and his other leg bracing himself on the ground. Owen's hand snaked behind my neck and rested there, like he was holding me in place.

The sweet relief of finally kissing him felt like coming up from under water and taking that first gasping breath of air.

How I *needed* this.

Owen's tongue brushed along my lips right as he pressed his knee fully between my legs, and I shivered as a shock of pleasure ran through my body.

I felt him smile against my mouth as his other hand gathered up the hem of my skirt. His touch was urgent as his palm covered the top of my thigh.

"We can't stop this time," I murmured against his mouth, sounding just as desperate as I felt. "Please don't stop."

He pulled away to gaze down at me, looking wilder than I'd ever seen. "Oh, there's not a chance we're stopping," he breathed. He lowered himself again to whisper in my ear. "I've been waiting too long for this."

The growl in his voice was an unexpected jolt. This was impatient Owen, the one who expected me to fall in line and do whatever he said.

As always, I was willing.

He shifted his weight again, this time smoothly moving his leg over mine so that he could lower his hips on top of me. I rose up greedily to meet him, desperate to feel more of him pressed against me.

We settled that way as we kissed, the length of his body on mine, and I wrapped my legs around his thighs so that I could move even closer to him.

I was blazing with heat now, the cool air-conditioned comfort of his home no competition for the fire he was stoking inside of me. We were moving at a frenzied pace, mouths hungry, hands exploring, but it still wasn't fast enough for me.

He pushed his hand between us and his fingertips found the edge of my underwear.

"Take these off." Owen's voice was raspy in my ear, his warm breath an unexpected caress. "I want to touch you."

It was his way of ensuring that I wanted this as much as he did. He wasn't going to tease me into submission. After all our stops and starts, he was confirming that I wanted *him*.

I wrenched them off awkwardly with one hand while still trying to kiss him, wiggling beneath him to slide my underwear down my legs and onto the floor beside us.

"*Thank* you," he whispered as he slid his hand to my heat.

My breathing shifted to shallow gasps as he gently explored me, expertly circling and stroking between my legs, slipping deep inside, then shifting to focus on my clit.

I arched against him as our mouths crashed together again. My heart was pounding dangerously fast, and it felt too big for my chest. I was gradually becoming unhinged, but Owen seemed fully in control and loving every second of his power over me.

He paused to pull back and scan my face. "Do you feel good?"

I bit my lip and nodded.

He bowed closer to my ear. "Tell me. What do you like?"

I took in a shaky breath.

"I like . . . your hands . . . touching me." It came out as a strangled whisper.

He ran his teeth along the side of my neck, alternating between kisses and bites.

"And what should I do next?"

His fingertips skimmed between my legs then stopped, and I nearly cried out with need.

"Take your clothes off?" I offered meekly, because what I really wanted was for him to keep touching me.

He shook his head slowly and shifted to his knees, his eyes burning into mine. "Let me clarify . . . What should I do *to you* next?"

I shivered.

"Take my clothes off?" I managed.

"Oh, fuck yes," he murmured as he got to work.

First, he gathered my skirt, fisting the fabric in both hands and gently pulling it down, like he was unwrapping a gift. He let out a sigh of appreciation as he tossed the crumpled thing on the ground.

"You are fucking *stunning*," he said as he ran his hand from my lower stomach and down my thighs. "Absolutely perfect."

It was a featherlight caress, but it was enough to get a shaky breath out of me.

"And now this," he said, leaning forward to gentle my tank off, leaving me in just my bra.

Owen gazed down at me hungrily and my stomach tightened in response. I wasn't used to being so openly admired. So appreciated. My skin heated as his eyes traced over me, followed by his hand. He cupped my breasts over the lace of my bra and brushed his thumb over each nipple. I arched my back to try to get closer to his hand as it traveled down my torso.

I reached up to clasp his shoulder, to try to pull him down to me again.

He grasped my wrist tightly and shook his head. "No . . . I need to look at you."

When he released me, I slid my hand under his sleeve, hoping that my touch would be enough to refocus him on something more than just looking. His arm was a brick of muscle, and I couldn't wait to feel it wrapped around me.

He finally finished his inch-by-inch inventory of my nearly naked body and leaned down to kiss me again. We crashed together, as if the few seconds of not touching and kissing was a reset and had tripled our hunger for each other.

We somehow ended up on our knees on the couch, wrapped around each other and holding on for dear life.

I wanted every inch of him. In the frenzy of Owen focusing on the mechanics of unfastening my bra, I managed to slip his shirt over his head to reveal his chest. The broad expanse was yet another secret he'd been hiding from me. I traced it with my fingertips, gentling through the scattering of hair along his pecs, then flattened my palms against his skin and slid them around to his back.

How was he so *soft*?

Owen rumbled against my mouth as I slid my hand down to cup his ass through his jeans.

It was hard to focus on anything other than the way he was working me into a frenzy, slipping inside of me, teasing my tender nub until I had to bite down on his shoulder to keep from crying out. I felt like I could come within seconds.

I finally managed to reach between us to pull at the button on his jeans, clumsy with need. I shoved them down enough that I could grasp his hard length through his boxers while he kept touching me, edging me closer.

I wasn't shocked to discover that he was packing yet another surprise for me. I had no clue how he hid it in the loose basketball shorts he wore, but his cock was a monster.

"*Condom*," he rasped. "Damn it."

He clutched his half-down jeans and speed-waddled to what I assumed was a powder room. I giggled when I heard him muttering expletives as cabinet doors and drawers opened and closed.

"Victory," he said as he stumbled back to me, holding his jeans up with one hand and the condom in the other. He raised it to his mouth to rip it open.

"Now wait a second," I scolded softly. "My turn."

I pushed him back a little so that I could peel his jeans and boxers farther down his thighs. Owen watched me, his stomach concave and his breath husky as I gripped him. I leaned down and kissed the glistening tip, and he let his head drop back with a groan. He threaded his fingers in my hair and wrapped it around his hand, gripping tightly.

I opened my lips to take his length in my mouth, and I was barely halfway down his thick shaft when he pulled away abruptly, making a wounded noise like it took every ounce of his strength to stop me.

I ignored him and continued working his cock with my tongue, taking him all the way in my mouth.

"*Fuck...*" Owen whispered as he hit the back of my throat.

My gag reflex was nonexistent.

"I'm stopping you now," he whispered unconvincingly.

He gave my hair a little tug, but I gripped onto his hips tighter.

I wasn't sure how he managed it, but Owen somehow flipped me so I was flat on my back on the couch with my feet on the ground. He knelt in front of me, placed his hands on my inner thighs and pushed between my legs, sealing his mouth against my slick seam and getting an instant moan out of me.

"My turn," he murmured before he plunged his tongue inside of me again.

I couldn't catch my breath, and I found myself going up on my toes and rocking closer to him, tangling my fingers in his hair as he worked his magic on me. If his fingers were expert level, his tongue was a maestro. I felt almost crazed as he inched me closer to the edge.

And then I was caught off guard, flying and falling all at once, my whole world expanding in this single moment of release. I cried out, hoping that the walls and floors in his place were thick.

Finally, there was no breath left in my lungs. I went quiet.

I'd barely recovered, still half on and half off the couch, panting with my eyes shut. I heard the crinkle of a wrapper, and suddenly I could feel Owen's heat near me again.

"C'mere," he murmured as he pulled me to standing.

My legs were liquefied but I wasn't standing for long. Owen dropped onto the couch, then pulled me onto his lap so that I was straddling his thighs.

Owen locked onto me, his eyes stormy. "Yes?"

His thumb stroked my cheek gently. I leaned into his hand, and he cupped my face, smiling at me in the dim light.

I nodded, raised up onto my knees, and then lowered myself onto him one aching inch at a time. When our bodies were flush again, we both sighed, like we'd arrived at a destination we'd taken too long to reach.

And then a mix of urgency and languor, as if we didn't want to rush but we couldn't help ourselves.

Owen's hands rested on my hips, helping me, guiding me, urging me on.

"You're killing me, Brooke," he whispered as we moved together. "I've wanted this for so long."

He flipped me over in a single swift move so that I was beneath him on the couch. Owen leaned down to kiss me as he thrust deep. I couldn't imagine it feeling any sweeter, but then his fingers were back between my legs, urging me closer, faster, like he wanted me to come again before he did for the first time.

I tried to fight it off as every part of my body tensed and got ready to unfurl once again. I wanted to savor our moment, but Owen was rolling his hips against me so perfectly, his fingertips so right, that I couldn't stop myself. I arched up as I cried out with pleasure and relief.

Owen increased his tempo, and a few seconds later he collapsed on top of me, panting. I wrapped my arms around him and welcomed his full weight as he recovered.

"We just fit together," he finally whispered in my ear.

I hugged him closer and nodded.

I think I'd always known it.

Chapter Thirty-Six

I woke up to find Owen snoring softly beside me, his arm thrown over his eyes.

We'd stumbled up to his room in the darkness at who knows what time and fallen asleep the moment we pulled the sheet up over us. With Wes and Claudia two floors below us, I knew they wouldn't catch me sneaking out of his room, although there was a slim chance they'd heard some of the prior night's festivities and already had some idea of what was up.

Owen must've felt me watching him sleep because he rubbed his forehead and opened his eyes slowly, immediately focusing on me.

"Good morning," he said sleepily.

I had to hold myself back from cuddling up against him despite the fact that he'd spent plenty of time nestled between my legs the night before. We were in an unknown middle place, undefined after what we'd shared and where we'd come from.

"Good morning."

When Owen reached out to grasp my arm and pull me across the bed to him, I figured out that we weren't quite as undefined as I'd assumed. I snuggled up against his bare chest and nuzzled my nose against his neck. His soapy scent had faded into pleasant, familiar Owen-ness. He planted a kiss on the top of my head as he wrapped his arms around me.

"I need to be a good host and get the coffee started," he said softly against my hair. "As much as I want to stay here."

He slid his hand down my back to cup my ass, and it was enough to make me have to squeeze my legs together from my instant need for him. I raised up on my elbow and cocked an eyebrow at him.

"They're probably still asleep. Wes sleeps like the dead."

I slid my leg over the top of his to sell my point, and he groaned a little.

"Doubtful," Owen answered as he moved closer to me. "They had a canine alarm in their bed. Marti is part rooster."

And then, as if to prove how well he knew his dog, a single sharp bark echoed through his house.

"She needs to go out." He sighed. "They're definitely up now."

We kissed quickly, too quickly, and scrambled to get dressed. I made the pretense of going into the room where I was supposed to sleep to brush my hair and teeth and try to *not* look like I'd been well fucked the night before.

Owen was already acting like a barista at his complex coffee machine by the time I walked down to the empty kitchen. He was in a T-shirt and shorts that actually fit him, looking adorably disheveled with his hair standing up in some patches and flattened in others. I was proud that I was the reason.

"I was half wrong and you were right," he said as Marti ran over to greet me. "She managed to pry the basement door open, but they're still asleep. I already took her out."

Marti twisted back and forth in between my hands like she

couldn't figure out which side of her body needed the most petting.

"I've got to wake them soon," I said as I stood up. "They have to catch a train to make it back for the rest of Murphy activities before they head to the airport tomorrow. I think he said something about a nature hike with my parents? They like to keep every minute scheduled."

He paused with his hand on a lever. "Are you sure you're not adopted?"

"Hey." I tried to play-kick him, but he grabbed my ankle and held on to it.

"Hey, yourself," he murmured, making me hop on one foot as he pulled me closer to him.

Owen grasped the underside of my thigh and pulled me close for a kiss that I never wanted to end.

Our confusing middle place was shifting into a defined one.

I was about to jump on the counter, pull up my skirt, and suggest a quickie, but Owen's phone pealed with a series of chimes.

"Damn," he said as he reluctantly pulled away from me. "Someone needs to talk to me *now*. Four texts in a row."

I watched him with a full heart as he reached behind me to grab his phone and scroll to the messages. His eyebrows went up, then slowly furrowed. He turned to me with an expression that set off alarm bells in my head.

"What's wrong?" I asked quickly. "What's happened?"

"It's Kai," he said flatly.

I squinted at Owen, searching his face for the laugh I was hoping would come. Was he *that* good of an actor?

"Asking about you," Owen continued in a wary voice. "He said you made plans to meet up last night and you flaked. You didn't answer his text. He wants me to tell him what I think of you, since you train with me and I probably have a sense of what you're like."

Owen's face went blank in a way I'd never seen. Like he was looking at a stranger. Cold eyes, granite jaw.

My stomach turned inside out as I tried to find a way to explain.

"No, hold on. We didn't make plans," I said quickly, taking a step closer to him. "It was nothing."

Owen moved away so smoothly that I almost didn't notice, because I was so focused on the hurt in his expression.

"I passed him outside the locker room at CPA, and he asked what I was doing later." My words mashed together. "I was vague, because I didn't want him to meet up with us, but I guess he assumed I was serious about it? It wasn't planned or anything."

Owen stared at the ground.

"Hey," I said softly. "I didn't want to be with him. I wanted to be with *you*. That's why I didn't text him back."

He nodded, still refusing to look at me.

"What are you thinking?" I asked, gently grasping his arm.

Owen continued nodding while staring down, like he was having a conversation with himself, sorting things out in his head before he opened his mouth.

"This is feeling *way* too familiar," he began. He pulled away from me to refocus on the coffee machine.

An unexpected wave of seasickness rolled through me. "Owen, no. Oh my god, it's not like that."

I just wanted him to look at me, so he could see how desperate I was to convince him that he was wrong.

He flipped handles on the machine with increasing ferocity.

"Yeah, I've heard that line before."

My mouth went dry, because from his perspective, it probably did mirror what he'd been through before. But this was different. *I* was different. All the muse bullshit didn't matter, because I was falling for someone real, and wonderful, and even more inspirational than some stranger I'd decided to fixate on.

"Owen, come on. Let's talk. Please."

He whirled to me, his eyes flashing and his expression grim. He started to say something right as the basement door crashed open.

"Good morning, party people," Claudia sang as she walked into the kitchen. "Who wants brunch?"

She froze when she saw our expressions, and Wes collided into her from behind.

"What's up?" Wes asked, glancing between us. "Is everything okay?"

There was no way I wanted to get into it with them, or worse, fake our way through a meal while Owen glowered at me.

"Yeah, we were just . . . figuring some stuff out," I said, flicking my eyes to a very barista-minded Owen.

"Morning, folks. Coffee?" he asked without looking over at them.

"We, uh, should probably get going," I said nervously, because the last thing I wanted to do was leave the conversation without resolution. "We need to get your stuff from my place and see how bad the fire damage is."

"Right," Claudia said slowly. She was intuitive. She knew something was up. "Of course. We'll strip the bed."

"Hey, Marti was a phenomenal bedmate," Wes added, oblivious.

"Yeah, she's a good girl," Owen agreed. "Very loyal."

He was already checked out, but he'd managed to get a little dig in at me.

Wes and Claudia retreated to the basement, and I took advantage of being alone to get right in Owen's face.

"We'll talk more once they leave, okay? Please." I was practically begging him. "Let's figure this out. Just trust me."

I reached out to try to take his hand, but he slipped away under the pretense of getting mugs.

"Same damn script." He chuckled mirthlessly as he opened cabinet after cabinet, like he was a guest and not the owner of the home. "For fuck's sake, why didn't I listen to my gut?"

I tried to come up with something convincing enough to at least get him to listen to me, but Marti barked and scratched at the back door, and Wes came up clutching a ball of sheets and towels.

The morning was moving on, but I was stuck staring at the mess I'd accidentally made. I needed to fake that everything was normal so I didn't hijack what was left of Wes and Claudia's visit.

OUR APARTMENT WAS habitable but slightly smoky, which felt fitting given my state of mind. Meredith was spending Sunday with Colton, and before everything went to shit, I'd planned to camp out at our kitchen table and get back to writing.

There was no way I could focus on HEA vibes now, deadline or not.

I hated saying goodbye to Wes and Claudia. There wasn't enough time to explain everything that had blown up in the past twelve hours, so I faked happiness until I dropped them off at Penn. Claudia had given me an extra-long hug, and when she pulled away, she'd murmured, "I'm here if you need me."

I had to bite the inside of my cheek to keep from tearing up.

A text buzzed in and I grabbed at my phone like it was a lifeline. It was from Claudia, not Owen responding to my three increasingly desperate messages.

> Forgot to send this to you. Very cute!

It was a slightly off-center photo taken out on the street on our way to the restaurant, an unguarded moment between me and Owen in the misty darkness. The rain forced us to share an umbrella so we were huddled close, and based on the way our bodies were aligned and our strides were matched, it looked like we were dance partners heading out to wow the judges. Owen was talking and smiling, and I was looking up at him with a slightly awestruck expression, like he was revealing the secrets of the universe, or at least how to improve my backspin. We were illuminated from behind by a passing car's headlights, making the falling rain sparkle like a million diamonds all around us.

I stared at the photo for a long time, scrutinizing every detail. Whatever we'd shared was something worth fighting for.

> Thanks for sending. Safe travels. XO

I padded across the room to leave my phone on the kitchen counter, because I needed zero distractions for what I already knew was going to be a crappy writing session. Lately, I'd been excited to tease out the details of Austin and Abby's shifting relationship, but today I felt zero pull to open the document. Even Einar and Zandria couldn't get me into the right headspace.

I propped my elbows up on the kitchen table and stared at my laptop, willing myself to say off Reddit so I could focus.

Then I remembered that I had the perfect diversion that actually needed my attention and could be a way back to Owen: his chapter outline.

He hadn't told me the direction he was taking for his book, but I assumed it would be a universal sporty angle, so he could tweak the content to fit any audience. I could already see him on a stage, delivering keynotes to various corporate sales teams across the country. If he packaged it right, he could make a killing, not only in speaker fees but also in back-of-the-room book sales.

I opened the document expecting some sort of vague, punny title, but his book was called *Athlete-Centered Coaching: The Importance of Balance and Empathy in Sports Mentorship*.

I cocked my head like a dog hearing a siren. This most certainly was *not* a universal, broad-appeal topic. I kept reading.

What Owen wanted to write was sports psychology for coaches working with everyone from student athletes up through adult trainers, not a pithy pop-psych book for corporate managers. The chapters included topics like intrinsic and external athlete motivation, resilience, emotional awareness and stress management, the myth of the obedient athlete, and the importance of observation and intuition.

He'd included a two-page reference section as well, citing various studies he planned to incorporate.

I stared into space as I considered his approach. Owen didn't care about writing a bestseller. He was pitching a heavy, niche topic that might not find a home with a major publisher.

But it was *important*. And if he could strike the right tone, he could transcend the psychology speak and write from the heart about his own experiences as a young athlete with a tough coach, as well as incorporate vignettes from other athletes. I couldn't call myself a true athlete, but even I had insights on how a long-ago throwaway comment from a coach figure had altered my self-perception.

Owen's book needed to happen, with or without me.

Chapter Thirty-Seven

Monday morning. Still no word from Owen. I was back at Jimmie McDaniel, paddle in hand, on a mission.

I was desperate for an endorphin release, but I also needed to keep practicing since the tournament was on the horizon. Part of me wanted to withdraw, but an equal part wanted to see it through. I was signed up. I had a goal. I wanted to see what real competition felt like.

I also had an ulterior motive for showing up.

I crossed my fingers as I approached the fence, and luck was on my side, because Howard was literally holding court with three other white-haired men.

"Well, good morning." Howard waved to me as I approached. "You look like you're ready to make my kind of trouble."

"Hi." I waved back. "I'll sub in whenever."

"We're nearly done with this game," one of the other men called to me. "I have to leave."

"Sounds good," I answered.

It wasn't a leisurely wrap-up to the game, which was surprising given the average age on the court was probably seventyish. Their strategy was sound enough that the majority of the action was up near the kitchen, and when it was time to slap a ball out of the air as it zipped up the middle, they freaking *sprinted*.

I couldn't believe the intensity I was witnessing.

They finished up and tapped paddles over the net, trash-talking the whole time.

"Get in here, Brooke," Howard called to me. "Come meet these reprobates."

He introduced me to Walter, the man who had to leave, as well as Danny in a visor and Bruce wearing wrist sweatbands that he actually used.

"So how long you been playing?" Danny asked.

"Not long enough to be as good as all of you," I marveled.

"Just wait until you hit eighty-five like me," Bruce said. "*Then* you'll be a master."

I shook my head in disbelief. Not only did he look twinkly-eyed and spry, he moved like someone twenty years younger. "Hold on . . . you're eighty-five?"

"Don't be so impressed," Danny said as he stepped in front of Bruce. He pointed at his chest. "Eighty-*seven*."

"And I'm the baby of the group," Walter added as he packed his bag on the sideline. "Seventy-seven."

"Okay, wow. I guess motion is the lotion." I was awestruck as I glanced between them.

"That's it," Howard agreed after polishing off half a water bottle. "Never stop moving. Never stop challenging yourself. It won't be as easy when your bones get old like ours, but you'll have a great foundation, and you'll be way ahead of all of your creaky, old friends."

I'd never considered how my anti-sport sentiment could have had negative long-term health implications.

"I'm off, fellas," Walter said with a salute. He turned to me. "Give 'em hell, Brooke."

If only. Bruce and I got our asses handed to us in the first game, and as we kept switching up the teams with each consecutive game, I discovered that my hunch had been right; Howard was the ringer of the group.

We finished up as the sun started creeping onto our court, then congregated by the fence to rehash and trash-talk.

"Did you ever play tennis?" Danny asked me.

I shook my head. "I've never been an athlete. This is all new to me."

"Now that's surprising," Bruce said with an approving nod. "You said you haven't been playing long but you're a natural. Killer backhand."

I grinned at the compliment.

"She has a *coach*," Howard said, leaning closer to the group. "I certainly don't want to take away from your natural abilities, but consistent coaching makes a difference."

My heart dropped a little at the reference to Owen.

"And speaking of your coach," Howard continued. "Now I know why he looked so familiar when I met him. Dimoveo."

I frowned at him. "Not sure what that is?"

"It's a money transfer thingy, a . . . uh . . ." Bruce waved his hands as he tried to come up with the missing word. "What do you call them?"

"Apps," Howard said knowingly.

"Right, it's an app. Started by two guys in college. One of them was from India and the money transfer fees were killing him, so he and his roommate came up with the idea. They developed it and got bought out. *Very* lucrative deal."

It was unexpected intel.

I locked onto Howard. "So did Owen work for that company?"

He laughed good-naturedly. "Work for? No, he's one of the *founders*. I'm surprised he didn't tell you."

I tried not to go bug-eyed at the reveal.

I wasn't surprised Owen hadn't told me, because getting backstory out of him was all but impossible. Suddenly his beautiful home and worldwide hobby-testing made sense.

And his job as a pickleball instructor.

Owen didn't *have* to work.

There was no need for me to know anything about his bank account, but the reveal opened up new insights about him: Why he was guarded and kept people at an arm's length. Why he didn't like talking about his background. And why he opted to be über-schlub at CPA. He was surrounded by finance bros who probably recognized him from the press around Dimoveo, so the disguise was a way to keep from getting cornered to talk about investment opportunities.

The news actually made me uncomfortable. I hadn't gone out looking for information about Owen—I'd never so much as googled him—and now I knew way more than I should. After all, he'd never mentioned it to me, for a good reason.

My heart hurt in new and surprising ways.

A phone went off.

"That's wifey." Bruce grinned as he pulled his phone out of his bag. "Making sure I didn't have a heart attack."

"Maybe we'll get lucky next time." Danny laughed and smacked him on the back.

We all gathered our things and got ready to leave, but I hung back, waiting for Howard.

"Can I talk to you for a second?" I asked him as he headed out.

"Of course." He lifted his hat and swept his hair across his head, then placed it back on, jauntily tipped and precariously high. "How can I be of service?"

My stomach dipped, which was a stupid reaction given that what I was about to do wasn't a big deal.

"So I'm signed up for the New York Parks Pickleball Summer Tournament—"

"Good for you." He nodded approvingly. "You're going to do great!"

"Thank you." I pushed on. "Right now I'm signed up as 'needs a partner,' which is fine, but I thought that it might be fun if you—I mean the timing's not great because it's coming up on the twenty-fifth—but if you have the time, maybe you'd want to sign up as my partner? I know it's weird for me to ask, but I thought—"

"You want to play with *me*?" Howard's eyes lit up as he broke into a wide smile. "Of all of the crackerjack players you know, you want this old man by your side?"

He pointed at himself, delighted and a little dubious.

"I do." I smiled back at him. "I think we make a great team. It's my first competition, so going into it with someone I know would take away some of the stress."

"And we're the same level, correct? Three-plus-ish?"

"I feel like a fraud, but yes, that's what Owen says I am."

"Well, okay then! I'm retired so I can do what I want when I want. And I want to kick some butt with you."

I beamed at him. "Fantastic, thank you! I'm not sure about switching up my reservation to 'has a partner,' though."

"I'll take care of it. I know people," he said with a wink. "One of my former students is in the public programs department."

We walked out of the court together, making plans to play a couple times before the tournament. Even though so much in my life was going wrong at the moment, it finally felt like I had a little spot of sunshine in the form of an octogenarian pickleball ace.

Chapter Thirty-Eight

I woke up Tuesday morning half tempted to just show up at CPA for my lesson despite the fact that I still hadn't heard from Owen. Then I considered how sad and desperate I'd look standing outside the locked door, begging to be let in.

I curled up in bed and remained miserable.

My texts and calls to Owen did nothing. I was starting to feel like a stalker, relentless and blind to the fact that the object of my affection wanted nothing to do with me.

But deep down, I knew that he did. I just needed to prove it to him.

Which was exactly what every stalker thought.

I finally dragged myself out of bed, ignoring my scratchy throat, which I hoped was nothing more than being overtired. I needed to muster up some enthusiasm, because I was tagging along with Meredith later in the day to check out the space she was considering for her studio. She'd been so busy and excited that I hadn't gotten into the Owen details.

It was better that way. I didn't want to think about him.

I navigated to check my email. Howard had made good on his promise to edit my registration, and he was now showing up as my partner in the tournament roster. It was some much-needed cheer in my miserable timeline. I'd even texted Owen about the change, hoping it would be neutral territory and happy news, but he'd ignored that message as well.

I *had* to connect with Owen eventually, even if it meant barging into CPA and causing a scene at the front desk. Not my ideal way to get his attention, but desperation could push me to do crazy shit.

Like learning how to play pickleball to try to impress a guy.

I heaved a sigh and squeezed my eyes shut. I was an idiot who made idiotic choices.

A new message popped into my email from Piper, with the subject line "Are we still chatting today?"

Fuck. We'd set the meeting at the end of last week, but I'd been so busy with Wes's visit and the resulting mess with Owen that I'd completely forgotten about it. Plus, Piper never seemed to remember that I was on EDT not BST, so her casual pre-lunch Zoom meeting was during pajama time in my world.

But still. Normally I wouldn't let something like a status call with my editor slip my mind.

I was officially a mess.

I found the meeting link, shoved my hair on top of my head, pulled on a clean T-shirt, and logged on.

"I thought you'd forgotten about me." Piper fake-smiled at me when the video started.

"Sorry, I had guests over the weekend and it threw me off," I said apologetically. "How are you?"

Her expression went tighter, but the smile somehow remained. "I'm well and eager to discuss a new direction with you."

Yes. Finally some good news.

"Really? Okay, I'm all ears."

She cleared her throat and adjusted her glasses. "We're moving to a new payout model, which means that our authors will now reap the fruits of their labors when their books do well. So instead of a second payment upon receipt of the finished manuscript, we're moving to paying royalties based on sales. A more traditional scenario, if you will."

"Huh." I tried not to frown, because I hated the sound of no second payment. "How will that work exactly?"

"You'll still receive a small advance when you turn in your first ten thousand words, and then you'll be paid a percentage of sales six months after each book launches, and then every eight months thereafter. For as long as the book is available."

It most certainly was *not* good news. My gut simmered as I considered just how bad it was.

"Um . . . when will this be put into practice? And do you have royalty projections based on my past book sales?"

"We're beginning with your Montana cowboy series."

She said it so smoothly that I almost forgot about the contract I'd signed, just like for every book I wrote with them. A contract that stipulated *two* payments, the second one of which was due to me very soon.

If I ever finished the damn book.

"We signed a contract, though," I said gently, hoping that there was still room for negotiation. "I'm getting ready to turn in the completed manuscript, and I was counting on that payment."

"I know." The corners of her mouth turned down like she was apologetic. "Unfortunately, you voided the contract when you didn't turn in the agreed-to word count for the first section. But, Brooke, trust me, this scenario is going to work out beautifully for you!"

Tell that to my credit card payments. I tried not to grind my teeth.

"We did run numbers, to give you some peace of mind. Let me share my screen to show you."

Her face disappeared, replaced by a graph with numbers that made my blood run cold.

"What's the royalty percentage?" I asked, feeling sick to my stomach as I studied the thing.

"Two percent across the board," she said in a stupidly upbeat tone. "Ebooks, audio, paperbacks—"

"But you don't always publish paperbacks," I interrupted. "You haven't for my last two books."

"Oh, that could change; don't worry," she cooed at me.

"I *am* worried," I exclaimed, since she was making it sound like it was a done deal. "That's a tiny advance and a long time between payments. And two percent is nothing."

"Not if you sell a lot of books." Piper grinned like she was delivering a punch line and not a death knell.

"*I* can't do anything to sell books," I reminded her. "It's not like I can jump on social media and promote them. No one knows I'm Dakota. Once the book is out of my hands, I'm powerless to do anything to move it."

"Right, right," she said quickly. "Rest assured that we do everything in our power to promote. And won't it be lovely knowing that you'll get a nice royalty payment as time passes? Like Christmas!"

Christmas as celebrated by Scrooge. Based on their projections, all that the new model would do is take my primary paycheck, reduce it by a third, and then spit out a little tiny payment at best once a year.

I was fucked.

"We have new paperwork you should look over," Piper continued. "And a revised contract for the book you'll be turning in . . . when exactly?"

I sighed as I gathered the courage to say what had to come next.

"Actually, if you force me to accept the new payout structure, I *won't* be turning it in."

My response shocked both of us.

"I'm sorry?" Piper's faux-chipper expression fell.

A scene played out in my head: Austin and Abby rushing out of the horse barn, desperate and scared, then their bodies dissolving and slowly disappearing into vapor.

I felt terrible to see them go, but I knew what I had to do.

"These changes don't work for me," I said firmly. "It's basically a demotion. Is there any chance we can keep our current payout for this series, then discuss a different model for future books?"

I already knew the answer.

"Brooke, I'm still processing what you just said about the first book in this series. You're *refusing* to submit it?"

I shook my head and leaned closer to my laptop. "Not if you're not going to pay me as we agreed."

"But . . . I explained to you that . . . Brooke, we have a *contract*."

"You said I voided it."

Her eyes flashed. "You *cannot* publish that book under your own name. Those characters belong to Liaison. Our legal team will come after—"

"Piper." I sighed. "I'm not going to do that. That would be fraud, but apparently you're not familiar with the concept."

"We already have a rollout underway," she sputtered. "We've announced the series. Brooke, please."

I shrugged and hoped I didn't look as stressed-out as I felt. "You've mentioned that Janet Li wants to get into this genre; I'm sure she'd be thrilled to take over."

Piper's expression softened. "But we love your writing."

"Not enough to pay me," I fired back.

My heart was thundering in my chest, because I was basically talking myself out of the only steady income I had at the moment. I was going to wind up writing every shitty press release and instruction manual possible to make ends meet.

Although . . . maybe this was my sign to give up on writing completely and go back to copywriting full-time? Because it sure as hell wasn't working out for me.

"I have to admit that I'm shocked by your reaction." Piper shuffled through papers just off-screen. "I think you should take some time to consider everything before you make a rash decision."

"Is there any way we can keep things the way they are?" I asked.

"This is a company-wide decision that we took a great deal of time considering."

"So that's a no." I paused to take a deep breath. "I'm sorry. I'm stretched thin as it is. This change means that Liaison isn't viable for me."

Her mouth went tight. "Then we'll need to involve legal in this conversation."

"That's fine," I said, sounding lighter than I felt. "Happy to chat about the voided contract with them."

"Perfect," she sniped. "We'll be in touch."

She disconnected before I could reply.

I stared across the room in a daze and tried not to cry as reality seeped past my anger. I had no job, no Owen, and no reason to even *need* a muse. Austin and Abby were officially out of my life. As much trouble as they'd given me, I already missed them.

I'd planned to spend the day in Montana, getting them closer to their happily ever after. I sniffled and wiped my nose.

I still had Verdantia. And Einar and Zandria. I hadn't heard back from Celeste about the pages I'd sent her, but now that I had absolutely *nothing* to focus on except for the dumpster fire that was my life, at the very least I could distract myself with their story.

I navigated to where I'd left off. Einar injured by an invader's sword, Zandria tending to his wounds, trying to be strong for him and hiding her worried tears.

Three hours later, I finally looked up and took a breath.

Chapter Thirty-Nine

"How hard is it to make a mocha?" I asked Meredith as I glanced over my shoulder to the counter where one barista was working and two were watching him. "Not trying to be a Karen, but let's *go*, my dudes."

I circled my hands impatiently.

"You do realize that you're probably the only person in the city drinking a hot beverage during a heat wave?"

"I like what I like," I grumbled softly.

"Did I tell you that this shelving unit in the storage area stays?" Meredith asked me, gazing at a photo of a standard-issue metal IKEA shelf on her phone like it was a picture of Colton.

We'd just come from touring the space she was hoping to rent and decided to grab some coffee to swoon over the details. Or Meredith was swooning; I was manufacturing enough enthusiasm that she didn't suspect how crappy I was feeling.

"It's perfect," I agreed. "Meant to be."

I longed for some of that kismet in my own life, though not specifically real estate–centric.

"*Brooke*," the barista called out.

"Finally." I jumped up with a sigh.

I normally wasn't so impatient, but I felt like I was living in a constant state of PMS. The night before, I'd gotten pissed off at the water dripping down my arms as I washed my face. Of course, the coffee stirrers were out, because even the little things were conspiring to shit on my life.

I felt a presence hovering behind me.

"Well, there you are."

My pulse kicked up, but only because I was in no mood to plaster on a smile for the person who'd accidentally derailed the only good thing in my life.

"Oh, hey!" I said as I turned around to face Kai.

I wasn't surprised to see him given we were close to the building where he worked. This time, there was no golden hour light on his face, no bluebirds swooping in the air above him. He was just a good-looking guy, smiling at me like I owed him something.

"You went dark on me last weekend."

He said it as if it was shocking, but I guess given the way I was usually a deer in the headlights in his presence, he probably assumed that I was a sure thing.

I fidgeted as the cup started to scald my fingertips. "Oh yeah, I'm sorry about that. It turns out there was a fire in the apartment below mine, and everything was a mess on Saturday night."

"No *way*." He widened his eyes. "You good?"

I opted to embellish a little. "It was dicey for a while, but yeah, we're fine now."

I glanced over at Meredith to see if she was watching, but she was still glued to her phone.

"Maybe you and I can get a make good on the books?" Kai asked. "Dinner?"

In any other version of my story, this would be the climax. The moment I'd flipped my life upside down to reach. Instead, it felt hollow.

I finally put the hot cup down on the counter. "You know what? I have to be honest with you. I'm not in a great headspace for social stuff right now, because I'm going through some professional changes that are sort of terrifying. I really need to focus on my work for the next few months."

I was expecting some sort of bro-tantrum, but Kai was nodding good-naturedly before I even finished speaking.

"I feel you," he said. "Been there. Hey, no foul. I'll see you around CPA, and if you ever want to play, I'm in. Grip literally told me *yesterday* that you're incredible."

My heart dropped to my feet. Despite everything that had happened between us, Owen was still talking me up to Kai.

"He's a phenomenal coach," I replied, working hard to keep my expression neutral.

"Like I told you, he only coaches the best of the best, so don't give him all the credit."

It was the second time he'd mentioned it, so either it was a humblebrag about his own skills or there was a grain of truth to whom Owen opted to work with.

Which obviously made zero sense given where I'd started out.

"Anyway, good luck getting your shit done," Kai said. He pumped a fist. "I believe in you, Brooke!"

Yeah, he was still a golden retriever.

"Thanks." I laughed despite myself. "That makes one of us."

I grabbed my coffee and walked back to my chair, mulling over the brief conversation. Kai was dangerously hot, and lighthearted, and probably fun as hell, but I finally realized that he didn't fill my cup. I'd wasted so much time chasing after an *idea* of a person, instead of investing in the one who actually mattered to me, in so many ways.

The one who'd been right in front of me the whole time.

Meredith looked at me with wide eyes as I sat down across from her, dealing with her own existential crisis. "Am I making a mistake? Be honest."

"Mere, *no*. You've wanted this forever."

"But it's really expensive," she whispered.

"This is Manhattan," I whispered back.

"What if no one comes?"

"That'll never happen, but worst case, you'll be out of the lease in two years."

"Hold on, hold on—pause for a sec." Meredith squinted at me like she was seeing me for the first time. "What's going on with you? Are you okay?"

I knew she'd eventually figure out that I was in a bad place. I hadn't wanted to get into it with her, especially because she was in her own big life-defining moment. Add to it the fact that she'd been quietly pro-Owen since day one, and I knew the conversation was about to get uncomfortable.

"I've been better."

I reluctantly spilled the whole story, from the Owen-trauma to leaving Liaison and finishing with the Kai run-in, which she somehow managed to miss.

"Oh, Brooke . . ." she said once I finished. "I'm sorry I wasn't there for you. I've been so wrapped up in my—"

"*Stop*," I interrupted. "Life is crazy right now; it's okay."

She leaned over to squeeze my hand. "Do you want to dissect, digest, or distract?"

"Distract. I've already dissected everything down to the marrow. Owen still thinks I'm into Kai, end of story."

"So he's not responding at all?"

I shook my head.

"I mean, I get it," I added. "He got hurt really badly with that horse girl. But he won't even hear me out."

"Can you blame him? You were pretty relentless about Kai."

"The idea of Kai," I corrected.

"Yeah, well, he didn't know that. All he could see was someone he was pining for, pining for someone else."

"You think he was *pining* for me?"

Her expression shifted to "are you fucking kidding me." "Brooke, the guy has been giving you free pickleball lessons for weeks now. You had a horse date in New Jersey. C'mon. And have you forgotten about the Hamptons gropefest? He's been into you since the day I fractured my foot."

"It's all my fault," I said mournfully. "I'm an asshole."

"Maybe a little . . ." She wrinkled her nose at me.

I didn't laugh.

"So what happens next?" Meredith asked.

"Before everything blew up, I told him I'd get back to him about his chapter summaries for the book he's writing. I'm not sure he wants my feedback at this point, but I have ideas that could really help him. And he's done so much for me, so . . ."

"Everything is going to work out. I have a good feeling," Meredith said sagely as she leaned back in her chair.

"Not if he won't talk to me," I said mournfully.

"You'll find a way to get through to him."

"Carrier pigeon?"

"Why not?" She chuckled. "We're both in an uncomfortable

transition stage, but this is where the growth happens. You're done with Liaison for a reason. Now you can focus on—"

"Not being able to afford rent," I finished for her.

She harrumphed at me. "You can focus on your *real* book."

"While I go broke."

"Not gonna happen," she said over her mug. "Better days are coming."

Her phone rang. "Yup, it's Colton, looking for the update."

I decided to check my email, to see if the dire legal stuff from Liaison had ended up in my inbox yet.

My vision went hazy for a few seconds, because the only new message was from Celeste, and the subject line was "Archer—OMFG!!!!!!!"

Chapter Forty

With the way things had been going between us, or *not* going, I figured the email I sent would be my final communication with Owen, so I'd made it thorough.

After he ignored my half-dozen texts and stuttering voicemail message, it felt like the only acceptable way to reach out. Plus, I attached his outline with my revisions and suggestions included.

I spent way too long working on the body of the email, because it was yet another chance to get in front of his eyeballs so I could try to sell myself, like I was a marketer aiming for those seven to twenty exposures to *me*. I kept it short:

Owen,

This book is important and you *have* to see it through. You have a gift that I was lucky enough to experience firsthand. You changed me, and I'm better for it, in so many ways. Now it's time to share what you know with the rest of the world. Make it happen, Owen.

Truly,
B

I hoped the insights I'd added to his outline would help him, even if it was just the cheerleading I put in the margins. I knew firsthand how ruthless the industry could be. I wanted Owen to feel armed with positivity before the inevitable rejections started coming.

Although thanks to the email from Celeste, I was a writer with hope on my side for the first time in ages. She'd absolutely loved the *Archer* pages I'd sent and had basically demanded that I finish it yesterday.

On it. But first? Pickleball.

I was at Jimmie McDaniel waiting for my final practice session with Howard before the tournament, trying not to think about the Owen-sized hole in my life. I almost felt like my skills were devolving without his consistent insights, even though Howard and I won every game we played.

Most of the tournament pressure was off a little after doing some research about past New York Parks pickleball events. I'd envisioned a TV-worthy production, with rows and rows of seats for spectators and sponsor banners ringing the courts, like what I'd seen in YouTube pickleball tournament videos. Instead, it looked like normal public play with the added benefit of a referee, and small crowds of people standing around watching, who were probably just other players waiting for their own games to begin.

Very low-key, which was exactly what I needed.

I settled onto the already hot metal bench outside the court and refreshed my inbox a few times. No reply from Owen, but I wasn't surprised. This was our new, depressing normal, me desperately trying to reestablish contact and Owen freezing me out.

In Romancelandia, the solution to our problem would be an

extended grovel, to convince Owen that I'd made a mistake thinking that I was falling for the wrong guy. The fact that *I* needed to be the groveler went against the trope of the guy trying to win the girl back after fucking up royally, but real-life love stories weren't always as predictable as fiction.

I'd gotten to the courts early to observe other players, which was yet another Owen suggestion. The four women were playing the world's slowest round, pausing to chat and laugh after each bad shot. What I was watching was perfect despite their less than stellar effort. It was a big part of what the sport had to offer: community, camaraderie, and intervals of intense exercise—in this case, in between the gossip.

I'd gotten hooked on pickleball, and it sucked because absolutely every element associated with it was haunted by Owen. I'd almost been tempted to go back to my pink-and-yellow paddle, because every time I wrapped my hand around the one Owen gave me, I was reminded of him.

But of *course*, I played better using the paddle he'd carefully selected for me.

The women gathered at the net to chat, so I pulled up my notes app and went back to plotting *Archer* while I waited for Howard to arrive. In the days since Celeste's email, I'd managed to write a few thousand words that I felt really good about. I was now at a moment in the book that suited my current depressed state of mind; Zandria was lost in the woods after trying to chase down what she thought was an orphaned alicorn foal, but was in fact an illusion designed to weaken her for capture. Einar was determined to find her despite his wounds, both the physical ones and those from his fight with Zandria.

"Good morning! You look *very* serious."

I jumped. Howard had materialized beside me without me even realizing it.

"Oh, hi." I laughed at my skittishness. "Just doing some plotting for my next book. I tend to go into the zone."

"In all things," Howard agreed with a nod. "I've seen how you get out there." He gestured to where the ladies were finally back to playing, then sat down beside me. "So when will I see said book on the shelf at the Strand?"

I was used to dodging the question. "Not sure. There are no guarantees in publishing, so there's a chance you won't."

He frowned at the thought. "Quite a gamble for you, yes? Dedicating all of your time and effort to something that might not come to pass."

A brilliant summary of my chosen profession that I was of no mind to process.

"Yup. But the sad fact is, I can't stop myself. Sometimes an idea takes hold of me and I'm off."

"How many books have you written?"

I paused to consider it. "I haven't counted, but let's just say I'm a prolific ghostwriter. Or I *was*, but I'd prefer to not talk about that mess at eight o'clock in the morning. Too complicated."

"Understood." Howard's gaze shifted from me to the gameplay. "They're not very good, are they?"

"But they're enjoying themselves," I offered.

"Indeed." He nodded. "I'm guessing that we'll be playing against two of them once they finish? Won't be much of a practice session. None of my guys could make it this morning. Worst case, if they can't stay and play, we'll just work on drills. I think we're in good shape for the big day."

I glanced down at Howard's knee brace. "How are you feeling?"

"About as creaky as an old barn door, but that's life. You?"

Brokenhearted. Foolish. Miserable. Worried.

"Fine." I smiled despite the dull ache in my chest. I jutted my chin toward the court. "Looks like they're finishing up."

"Good." Howard got up slowly. "Let's go ruin their day."

Turns out, the only day ruined was ours, thanks to me. I played like I'd never set foot on a court. All of my shots were too hard. A dink? Never heard of her. I served into the net. And my accidental pop-ups were ridiculous, to the point where I was basically setting up our formerly sweet old lady opponents to smash the ball in my face. Sure, they'd been holding back during their gossipy play, but on a regular day, Howard and I could've buried them.

I got so frustrated that I nearly threw my precious paddle during our final game. I mustered up a tight grin as we tapped paddles over the net once it was over, furious at myself for a million different reasons.

Howard and I walked toward the door side by side and silent. He finally spoke up, like he couldn't hold back any longer.

"What's going on with you today?" he asked softly.

His voice was almost grandfatherly with concern, and it was enough to open the floodgates I'd been keeping locked up tight.

"I'm . . . I'm dealing with a lot right now." I sniffled as tears sprang to my eyes. "*Life*. It's too much."

"Yes, but it's better than the alternative," he mused, watching me out of the corner of his eye as we walked out to the street. He turned to me. "Are you sure you want to play in the tournament? It's perfectly fine to back out, you know. We can try for the next one, in the fall."

Not playing in the tournament would derail my only concrete goal. Even *Archer* didn't have a due date; it was all up to me. I'd realized that I craved a deadline, a point where timing and effort merged and I was forced to deliver something.

"No, we're *doing* this. I'm not backing out."

"Wonderful," he said with a nod. "Then we'll consider today our dress rehearsal. I've done my fair share of community theater—I was recently Buffalo Bill Cody in *Annie Get Your Gun*—and a bad dress rehearsal is an omen for a good show."

He reached out to give my shoulder a squeeze, and my eyes flooded again.

"You're going to be okay, Brooke."

I felt my chin tremble. "I'm really trying to believe that."

Chapter Forty-One

"You look like a winner," Meredith said to me as I twisted to scan my reflection in the mirror. "Scary strong."

I'd opted to wear an old standard for the tournament, my black sleeveless shirt and skort, because I didn't want to worry about surprise scratchy tags or too-small arm holes as Howard and I kicked ass.

But of course, the tournament was no big deal, which meant there was no need for a spiffy new outfit. I was just playing a slightly more regulated game than usual. We wouldn't have to worry if a ball was in or out; the ref would tell us. I wasn't even a little nervous, or at least that's what I kept telling myself. Meredith and Colton were coming to watch, and Nia told me she was with me in spirit while she was off signing books on the West Coast.

The one person I *needed* to be there still hadn't responded to me.

I couldn't dedicate any headspace to worrying about Owen even though my regrets were constant low-level background noise in my head. I didn't have to be consciously thinking about him; Owen was always with me. I knew exactly how he'd respond after every shot I made on the court, either offering a correction or celebrating my progress. Whenever I heard a perfectly placed ball bounce off my paddle with the telltale thwack, Owen was there. He'd taught me how to differentiate between a ball bouncing off the edge of the paddle and one hitting the sweet spot, and now I couldn't unhear it.

"Colt is meeting us there," Meredith said as she grabbed her things. "We should probably head over. Registration and all that."

Meredith seemed bossier than usual, like she was nervous for me, which sent an unwelcome kink to my gut. I had to keep reminding myself that the tournament was nothing more than achieving a goal. I didn't have to win; I just had to play. To prove to myself that I could.

"Yup," I said. I grabbed my bag. "I'm ready."

I walked outside half expecting the street to be crowded with people in court gear carrying paddles, like it was the Thanksgiving Day parade but make it pickleball.

I clearly hadn't fully convinced myself that the tournament wasn't big deal.

When we arrived at Wollman Rink, I reversed my perception yet again. It was the first year holding the tournament on the beautiful pop-up courts, and it seemed to have made a difference in the level of excitement. The low-key vibe of past years I'd clocked in photos had leveled up, big-time.

"*Damn*," Meredith said, widening her eyes at the long registration line. "Glad we're early."

I shivered despite the hot sun. This was supposed to be an unsanctioned, easy-peasy, fun tournament, but the gathering crowd suggested otherwise.

Owen had mentioned the seasonal courts at Central Park when we first started training together, but I'd opted out when I looked up photos of them. Initially, I wasn't in the headspace to try to navigate the fourteen very busy, by-reservation courts. I was happier hiding out at CPA off-hours or at crappy, old Jimmie McDaniel, playing with whoever showed up that day.

Now I was about to make my competitive debut on the fancy periwinkle-and-turquoise courts. There were already spectators ringing them, leaning over the barrier and sitting on top of it. I spotted a guy handing out sports drink samples. Someone else selling pickleball T-shirts and hats.

And a local news van.

Fuck. It *was* a big deal.

"I don't see Howard," I said as I scanned the crowd. "Maybe he changed his mind?"

Meredith laughed at me. "I know what you're doing. Stop. He'll be here, you'll play your best, and we'll be so proud of you no matter what happens."

An arm slid around my shoulders. "Meredith's right. We're already proud of you."

I turned abruptly. *"Dad?"* I spotted my mom right behind him. "Oh my god, what are you guys doing here?"

He was beaming at me proudly, his eyes squinting up behind his round glasses.

"How could we miss it?" my mom asked as she swooped in for a tight hug. She was in her usual Athleta gear, looking fit enough to jump on a court and dominate. "Wes told us how good you are, and he mentioned the tournament, which you neglected to tell us about, so we coordinated with Meredith to be here."

"You did this?" I asked Meredith as I hugged my dad.

She gave me a mischievous grin. "I helped."

"But it's just a stupid match," I sputtered as I glanced between them. "You shouldn't have come; it's nothing."

My dad took my hand and squeezed it. "We watch your brother play, and now we're going to watch you. We're *very* excited to be here. This is a big deal, Brookie."

Seeing them was a balm on my soul given everything going wrong in my life, but it also put an extra layer of pressure on the day. They were about to witness a version of me they'd never experienced.

"Seriously, you guys, it's nothing. I'm sorry you're wasting your Saturday. It won't take too long; we can grab lunch after and try to salvage—"

"*Stop*," my mom scolded gently. She reached over to smooth a loose strand of hair off my forehead. "We brought chairs; we're ready to camp out for as long as it takes to see you win."

Of course they brought chairs, because they were well-versed in organized sports spectatorship.

My phone buzzed and I clawed at it nervously. "It's Howard. I need to meet him at registration. His wife is with him too." I stared at the three of them, still gape-mouthed with shock. "I guess I should go . . . but I don't know which court we're going to be on so do you want me to—"

"Go," my dad said with a laugh and hand flap. "We'll find you. Don't worry about us."

"We're grown-ups; we'll be fine," Meredith added. "Get your head in the game, woman!"

I watched them for a beat longer, gave them all quick hugs, then jogged off to find Howard.

Hours later, when the sun was finally sliding off the courts, Howard and I were sweaty, tired, and semi-victorious.

He'd been right about the dress rehearsal aspect of our last game together, because we couldn't have played better. I'd worried that the spectators just outside of my field of vision would throw me off, especially knowing that my parents were among them for my sporty debut, but every gasp and cheer from the crowd made me play harder.

In the end, we wound up in a very respectable third place in our bracket.

Howard couldn't stop smiling at me. He'd worn all black as well, even switching to a black visor instead of wearing his blue "Professor Pickleball" cap so we'd look like a united front. The age difference between us probably threw off our competitors, which we used to our advantage to finesse our way to third place.

We waited for our bracket's turn on the podium, cheering on the rest of the players as they collected their prizes.

"What's in the envelopes?" I nodded to one of the sponsors handing out green Parks T-shirts and small gift envelopes to the winners. "I didn't realize that we'd actually get something other than bragging rights."

"I think some free court time here? Quite an improvement over poor old Jimmie, yes?"

I glanced around the manicured arena. "It's an upgrade for sure, but I'm partial to Jim. Great times with great people."

Although moving my game to courts without any Owen memories made sense. I could start fresh in a place where we'd never spent time together.

We watched another group pose for photos on the podium.

"I'm surprised that we did so well but also not," Howard said. "There was some real talent out there."

I gave him a soft punch to the shoulder. "No one expected Hurricane Howard."

He chuckled. "Likewise, you surprised everyone with Brooke's bodacious backhand."

"My secret weapon," I agreed.

That Owen had taught me.

"Let's have the winners from group six," a guy with a mic said, pacing near the podium. "Group six, please."

"That's us." Howard nudged me.

We walked toward the podium, and a shout went up, including my dad's two-fingered whistle, which I'd heard a million times at Wes's soccer games. I laughed and waved at my cheering section, which also included Howard's lovely wife, Susan.

We shook hands with the two other teams that beat us and took our spot on the riser.

Third place felt fucking *amazing*.

"Okay, folks, presenting our group six awards, we've got our newest sponsor, the Chelsea Pickleball Academy," the organizer said. "Big round of applause for this gold-level sponsor."

I was so busy making faces at Meredith and Colton while they snapped pictures that the words didn't register at first, until I saw a familiar form emerge from the cabana clutching a stack of T-shirts.

"*Owen?*" I whispered as he loped closer, dressed for a country club.

"Hey, that's your coach!" Howard cheered. "Would you look at that? Serendipity!"

But I knew it wasn't.

Owen was here for a reason, and I fucking hoped that it was me.

Chapter Forty-Two

My heart felt like it was about to explode out of my chest and land at Owen's feet.

My entire body was infused with equal amounts of joy and fear, because I wanted to believe that he'd *made* this moment happen, fully anticipating that he'd be handing his former student some sort of award, but at the same time, I was terrified it was a cosmic joke on me.

Howard was oblivious, of course, so I went up on my toes to try to find Meredith in the crowd, to share the holy shit–ness of Owen showing up. No surprise, she was locked on to what was unfolding. Her eyes went wide as she pushed her fingertips to her mouth in shock, watching Owen sort through the stack of T-shirts and envelopes.

I swallowed the lump in my throat, because it would look weird to cry on the podium.

There was no hint that Owen was uncomfortable with me standing on a dumb wooden riser just a few feet away from him, to the point where I wondered if he even *realized* that I was his third-place recipient. But then he glanced up from the stack of envelopes and directly at me with a look that said, "I'm coming for you."

With what, I couldn't decipher.

The mic guy announced the first- and second-place winners, and Owen handed over their swag with a smile. Then he was *right there*, just inches away as mic guy called out our names.

Owen handed the shirt and envelope to Howard first and gave him a firm handshake. I swallowed hard as he took a half step and ended up in front of me.

"Congratulations," he said, poker-faced. "I knew you could do it, B."

I held my breath, waiting for him to pivot away abruptly. I was so focused on the fact that he was really right in front of me and not in my dreams that I didn't notice the shirt and envelope he was offering to me.

"These are for you," he said softly, giving my prizes a shake so I'd see them.

"Thank you," I finally managed as I took them.

"Hold for a quick photo," mic guy said as a woman with a real camera appeared in front of us.

I couldn't do anything *but* hold, which meant that I'd be immortalized in an official tournament photo on the Parks website wide-eyed and awkward, stiff-arming the shirt out in front of me and clutching the envelope so hard that it nearly bent in half despite the gift card inside.

"Okay, thanks, folks! Next group," mic guy said. "Group seven, report to the winner's circle, please."

Howard, Owen, and I moved away from the crowd. I was happy to have my octogenarian buffer, because how could Owen walk away from my cheery partner? He'd have to at least chat for a little while, so he wouldn't come across as rude.

I'd just lap up those precious minutes like a hungry kitten, drinking in every nuance of Owen's responses so I could decipher what was going on behind his placid expression.

"Did you see this one today?" Howard asked Owen proudly, clasping my shoulder. "What a star!"

Owen's face was softer than I'd seen it look in a while. I'd gotten too used to the cutting eyes and clenched jaw, so I allowed myself to feel a little bit of hope as I waited for him to respond.

"I *did* see her. I watched every second of your matches."

His eyes met mine, and I had to look away quickly, because I didn't want to cry. I still didn't know the chicken or the egg scenario with the CPA sponsorship of the event, so I didn't allow myself to get too excited. Maybe the club marketing person had signed on to do it, and Owen was forced into showing up?

"You two are quite a team," Owen continued. "I was just as impressed with you, Howard."

"Why, thank you." He bowed his head at Owen. "I certainly gave it my all. Now, if you'll excuse me, I need to find my Susan in this mess," Howard said as he peered around the crowd. "Brooke, I'm not sure if we'll be playing here or at Jimmie next, but let's get back out there soon."

We hugged each other, and he disappeared into the crowd. I was about to manufacture questions about the tournament so Owen would stay and talk when Meredith and Colton crashed into me.

"Hey, you, *congrats*!" She shot me a look heavy with subtext.

My parents were right behind her, which meant the awkwardness with Owen would now be incalculable.

"Oh, honey, you were so good!" my mom cheered as she pulled me to her. "I had no idea."

"I did," my dad said. "She's *my* daughter."

He joined the hug.

"Guys, this is Owen," I said when I finally untangled myself from my parents. "My coach. *Former* coach," I added quickly. "These are my parents, David and Kay."

I was positive that Owen wasn't expecting to meet my parents, and I held my breath to see how put out he'd be by the onslaught of cheerful Murphys.

"Hello! Wes told us all about you." My mom beamed at him as she shook his hand in both of hers. "He said he wants to be your best friend."

Owen coughed out a surprised laugh. "Seriously? The feeling's mutual."

His eyes darted to me.

"So what did you think about Brooke's performance?" my dad asked him. "Professionally speaking. Because I was just *awestruck* by her athleticism. Did she tell you that she used to hate sports?"

"Dad." I groaned like I'd reverted to my easily mortified thirteen-year-old self. "Let's not."

"Brooke did share that with me." Owen ignored my protest. "Turns out she's a natural."

I felt my face go hot when his eyes found mine and remained a beat longer than necessary.

"We're taking Brooke out to dinner before we head home tonight," my mom said. "Who's in?"

"Oh, wish we could," Meredith said. "Colton made dinner reservations for us at Bungalow to celebrate me signing the lease on my new space."

"Lots to celebrate between these two," Colton added.

"That's *right*. Brooke's been keeping us posted," my dad said. "Good for you, Meredith."

"Owen? You'll join us for dinner?" my mom asked him in the tone that she used when she expected agreement.

I distracted myself with the T-shirt in my hands, so I wouldn't have to watch his face as he told the most persuasive woman in the world no.

Owen cleared his throat and gave my mom his full attention. "I wish I could. Sorry to miss it."

My chest hollowed out, but I shouldn't have been surprised that he didn't want to subject himself to parental inquisition.

"Welp." My dad slapped his stomach and looked around at us. "I'm ready for a predinner snack. Let's go get coffee or something. Then I'm guessing you'll want to go home and change before dinner?"

I plucked at my damp shirt. "And a shower. Third place was still a battle."

Everyone started exchanging hugs and handshakes for our slow farewells. I tried to focus on the pleasantries, watching Owen out of the corner of my eye. He edged away from the group, possibly working on an Irish goodbye.

We moved toward the exit as a unit, with everyone still talking and laughing while Owen and I trudged along behind them. The vibe in the air was celebratory, with everyone around us enjoying a day of good sport, but all I felt was worried.

I finally found the courage to steal the moment before it was gone.

"Thanks for being here," I said quietly as we walked side by side. "I know it was a work thing, but still. It's great seeing you."

He stared straight ahead as we navigated the crowds. "It wasn't a work thing."

A shot of hope spiked through me. We both slowed in tandem while I waited for him to keep talking.

"I wanted to be here. For *you*."

I let out a little undecipherable noise, half shock and half happiness, and Owen swiveled abruptly to look at me.

"It's what we were working toward, right?" Owen explained. "Well, one of our goals . . ."

"Owen, *don't*," I cautioned, my voice thick. There was no way I wanted to dredge up the Kai stuff on what had been a pretty amazing day.

"About that," he pressed on.

Silence stretched between us. I held my breath.

"I was hoping that we could talk."

I sagged with relief. At the very least, we weren't going to have an awkward "goodbye forever" on a busy sidewalk with my parents looking on.

"Okay." My voice wobbled on the two syllables. "Do you want to call me later or . . . ?"

"Can you come over? After your parents leave?"

Hope took flight inside of me.

"Yeah, of course," I answered too quickly. "I'm not sure what time it'll be, though. Is it okay if it's late?"

The rest of my group was now absorbed into the crowd, so far ahead of us that I couldn't even see them. Owen and I came to a stop, two rocks in a stream as people passed by us.

"It's fine," Owen said. His jaw flexed as he worked up to the next part. "I'll wait for you as long as it takes."

Chapter Forty-Three

I somehow managed to stay present during dinner with my parents as we covered everything from my *Archer* writing process to their latest aches and pains to Wes and Claudia's wedding planning. It was a perfect celebration and catch-up, and while I loved spending the evening with them, it was almost impossible to focus.

"I'll wait for you as long as it takes."

Owen's final words to me were seared into my brain.

After we'd spooned up the last of our crème brûlée—so cliché but so delicious—they hopped in a cab for Penn Station for the three-hour train ride back to Chevy Chase.

I was free to find out what "waiting for me" meant.

I texted Owen, because I was too nervous to call.

> Still good to talk tonight?

> Yes. Can you come over or should I meet you somewhere?

His house somehow already felt familiar and comfortable, despite the negative energy I'd brought to it. Plus, I wanted us to be alone for the conversation to come.

> Yup OMW

He was sitting on his front step with Marti when I arrived a short time later. My heart sped up at the sight of him, hanging out with the world's cutest dog in his lap. She barked a hello as I climbed the steps.

"Hey there. Sit," he said. He scanned me quickly. "You look nice."

"Thanks." I glanced down at the navy T-shirt dress I'd thrown on before dinner with my parents. "Liar."

The lights flanking his front door were lantern scones that looked like they had real candles inside, casting an atmospheric glow on us. It was the perfect night to sit outside since the heat wave had broken, and every so often, a breeze flitted past to remind us that cooler days were coming.

I scanned Owen as I sat down a safe distance away from him, but his face didn't betray what was going on inside. As usual.

Marti jumped off his lap and wiggled her way over to me.

"Careful, friend." I laughed as she nearly rolled herself down the steps trying to get me to pet her belly.

"Your parents get off okay?" Owen asked.

"They did. I can't believe they came all this way for the day."

"I guess everyone agrees that today was a big deal," he said softly.

A goal achieved, thanks to him, but also to me. I could've pulled out when everything went to shit, but I pushed myself all the way to third place.

"Thanks again for being there," I replied, my heart warming again at the memory of him appearing on the courts.

"Hey, it makes sense from a business perspective, right? Lots of exposure for the club." Owen paused. "But like I told you, it wasn't the only reason I was there."

I felt like I couldn't get a full inhale as I waited for him to keep talking. The silence between us stretched on while we watched cars glide past on the street below.

"I read your suggestions for my book," he finally said, the last topic I expected to cover during what was basically a peace summit. "Thank you. They were perfect."

I was relieved that after everything I'd put him through, at the very least I'd provided some helpful feedback.

"Obviously, I know nothing about coaching," I replied. "I was coming at it from an editing perspective, and I tried to think about how to make it sellable, but I wasn't sure—"

"Brooke," he interrupted gently. "*Stop.* Everything you suggested was dead-on. Stuff I hadn't even considered." He paused a beat, focused on petting Marti. "Maybe I could use your help after all?"

Owen said it tentatively, like he wasn't sure if my offer was still good.

And while I was happy that he was open to my support, I suddenly felt like I needed to recalibrate exactly what was going on between us. My stomach dropped, because maybe all he wanted was for us to find our way back to a semblance of friendship? To be writing buddies?

"Yeah." I managed to sound upbeat, like the possibility of it wasn't incinerating me from the inside out. "Of course, anytime."

Marti inched closer to me, dragging her belly on the stair. I scratched behind her ears absentmindedly, because all I could focus on was a single thought:

I don't want to be your friend.

He'd said as much to me, and now I understood the sentiment. I couldn't tamp down the feelings that had taken over me. Friendship would be too painful, too impossible after knowing what *was* possible.

There were moments in the city when everything seemed to pause at the same time, when all the traffic and airplanes and pedestrians went silent in unison for a single millisecond, and then resumed the cacophony quickly enough to make you wonder if it actually happened. Now, waiting for Owen to keep talking, it felt like that millisecond wouldn't end.

He leaned forward and balanced his elbows on his knees. "Do you remember what you asked me at our first lesson?"

I hunched, preemptively embarrassed. "I'm sure I asked you a lot of stupid questions, so take your pick."

Owen cleared his throat. "You asked me if I'd ever had an immediate reaction to a person. A 'bam' connection, I think you called it."

Apparently, the specter of Kai would never leave us.

"Owen, please don't go there now," I begged in a thin voice. "Okay? I don't know how many ways I can tell you that—"

"Brooke . . ." he interrupted. "I need you to know that I had that reaction when I saw *you*."

I felt like my heart stopped beating while Owen's eyes searched my face.

"You were playing with Meredith, Colton, and that finance douche," he continued. "Or should I say, you were *attempting* to play. But I couldn't take my eyes off of you." He paused to glance down at his laced fingers. "You were holding the paddle like a goddamn flyswatter and doing that skip-run thing, but to me, you were . . . flawless."

He breathed out the final word, sounding almost awestruck.

"Owen..."

"Hold on, let me keep going." He shook his head, his expression pained. "When I heard that you wanted to learn to play, I figured *that* was how I could connect with you. Give you a couple of lessons, impress you with my pickleball prowess, then cut to the good stuff. But when you told me about Kai..."

"I'm such a fuckup," I whispered as I hugged my knees and bowed my head. "Why did you keep me on as a client?"

"How childish would I look if I voided your lesson package because you had a crush on someone else? I had a job to do; I did it."

"But you *kept* helping me."

He let out a short bark of a laugh, like he was embarrassed.

"True. That was me basically powerless to stop hanging out with you. I talked myself into believing that training with you was professional development for me. I haven't worked with a newbie in a long time. Turns out, I liked the challenge you presented. And..." He let out a long, pained sigh. "I liked *you*."

Hope sparked inside of me once again, wild and bright, but I forced myself to remain calm until I'd heard him out. There was a chance he'd come to his senses and was breaking it to me gently that he'd moved past whatever he'd once felt for me.

"I told you how badly the Sophie era fucked with my head. There was absolutely no way I was going to put myself in that position again. Of wanting someone who didn't really want me."

It took all my strength to keep from reaching for his hand so I could squeeze it tightly while I told him how wrong he was, but I still didn't know how his side of the story was going to end.

"You know that's not the case," I said in a quiet voice. "Or at least I hope you do."

Marti perked up as a guy strode past with a gray French bulldog that was stopping to pee on every vertical surface. She let out a warning rumble, then launched into a full-throated freak-out.

"Hey, hey," Owen tutted as he picked her up. "What the hell is *that*?"

Marti tried to parkour herself out of his arms after the dog.

"I'm not sure what that dude did to her, but she's clearly got a grudge. Let's go inside," he said over the barking.

I followed him in, trying not to fixate on where he'd left off. Him wanting me.

Owen placed a still-agitated Marti on the floor in the foyer. She immediately trotted upstairs. "Neighborhood watch, reporting for duty," he said as he watched her run up. "Want to go sit out back?"

I glanced into the world's most perfect room wistfully. "Can we hang out in your library?"

On the couch where we made love?

"You make it sound so fancy." He chuckled as he walked in and switched on a lamp. "It's a room with books."

I followed him and felt the tense bands in the back of my neck loosen.

"It's an endless wall of books with a *sliding ladder*," I added. "So library."

We settled on opposite ends of the couch facing each other. There was static between us, just like last time, only now it was tinged with worry, not heat. I realized that I was staring at him, trying to analyze every eyebrow flick and frown as he settled on what he was going to say next.

Meanwhile, my heart was careening around in my chest, waiting for my turn to plead my case again.

Owen scrubbed his hand over his face. "Where were we?"

A moment of quiet while I gathered my courage.

"You said you liked me. Past tense."

The corner of his mouth kicked up as he nodded. "That's right."

"I need you to know that I like you too," I said tentatively. "Present tense. A lot."

His face softened into a full smile. "You've been trying to tell me that for a while, huh?"

"I have." I grinned back at him as tiny blossoms of happiness started to burst open inside of me.

"I'm sorry I made it so hard on you. It's just . . ." Owen gestured in front of himself, then sighed. "There's no point for me to keep repeating myself. I'm sort of a broken record." He went quiet, and his expression turned a little sheepish. "You'll never guess who finally convinced me."

I shook my head and shrugged a shoulder.

"The man himself. Said he asked you out to dinner and you said no. That, plus the millions of texts from you made me realize that I was being . . ."

"Obstinate?"

He raised an eyebrow. "Fancy word."

I tapped my temple. "Writer."

"I was thinking 'asshole,' but we can go with 'obstinate.'"

Owen leaned over to take my hand, and when he slid his palm against mine and closed me in his grip, I felt like I could finally exhale.

"My turn," I said.

I'd already told him much of what I was about to say, but not in person, so that I could watch his expressions as I confessed how much I'd grown to care for him.

To *need* him.

"You make me really happy, Owen. Being with you was the best part of my week, even if I had to wake up so early it made my eyes bleed. You pushed me, and at first I hated you for it. But look at me now. Third place, baby!"

I sat up straighter and gestured to myself like I was a gold medal winner.

His eyes crinkled as he laughed, and my body filled with warmth at the sound.

"But it's more than that." I pushed on before the weight of the moment got away from me. "You helped me discover a part of me that I didn't think existed."

He shrugged. "Any coach would've done the same. You find barriers in your athletes and knock 'em down."

I shook my head. "No, that was *you*. And that's why your book is so important."

"You're relentless." He sighed as he dropped his head back against the couch, our joined hands a bridge between us.

"And *right*."

He rolled his head to look at me, and when our gazes snagged, I felt the back of my nose prickle.

Because the answers were all there in the depth of his dark eyes.

Still, I needed to hear it from him. To find out what was going to come next in our story.

I felt lightheaded, like I hadn't eaten all day. Shaky. Desperate for some sort of resolution.

"You have my heart, Brooke," Owen finally said as he ran his thumb over the back of my hand. "It's been yours since the very first moment I saw you. My very own *bam*. But it went deeper than that. It wasn't just physical attraction. I liked everything about you."

Heat rushed to my face at him accidentally shining a light on the shallowness of my own *bam* moment. I didn't even know Kai. He was nothing more than a character I'd created.

"I tried to fight it," Owen continued. "Hell, I tried to help you get the guy, because I just wanted you to be happy." His brow pinched at the memory. "Even if it hurt me."

I sniffled back my welling tears.

"I loved working with you," he said, his tense expression breaking into a smile. "How *fierce* you were when it came to mastering a skill. Your determination to get it right. Your ability to laugh at yourself when you couldn't. I thought I could learn to be okay with just being your coach and friend. That watching you grow as a player was enough, because that was all you needed from me. All you wanted from me."

His voice went a little hoarse at the admission, and a tiny fissure splintered through my heart at the thought of causing him so much pain.

"But I felt a shift happen," he continued, his gaze finding mine again. "And I started to believe that we could actually . . . *be*. That you felt the same way about me. Then I got that text, the morning after. All of the old worries flooded back. The mistrust and second-guessing every conversation. I guess I snapped."

He brought our joined hands to his lips and pressed a kiss to the inside of my wrist. "I'm sorry. I'm sorry that I let my history get in the way of our future."

He moved my hand to press it to his chest, covering it with his protectively. I could feel the heavy thump of his heart, which nearly matched my own.

"And what *is* our future?" I asked tentatively.

Owen leaned over and pulled me onto his lap in one smooth movement so that I was straddling him, and gripped his hands on my thighs. Heat pooled between us, and despite the relationship-defining conversation we were in the middle of, all I could think about was ripping off his clothes so I could feel his skin against mine.

"Our future is however we decide to fill the pages," he whispered, looking up at me with tenderness that made me catch my breath. "Together."

Owen reached up to thread his fingers into my hair. He slid his hand to the nape of my neck and drew me closer to him, pausing when our lips were just inches apart, our eyes locked. My breath went shallow as his gaze skimmed my face, a small smile playing on his mouth. I was desperate for him but mesmerized by the tension of the right now.

He gently tucked a strand behind my ear.

"There's more," he murmured. "I need you to understand that it's the beginning of a love story."

There were no more words necessary. Tears pooled in my eyes as our mouths finally crashed together in a kiss that confirmed what we both felt in our hearts.

It was more than a crush, or an obsession, or a *bam*.

It was love.

And I couldn't wait to write our next chapter.

One Year-ish-Plus Later

It didn't feel like real life.

Or at least *my* life.

I was used to going to book signings for my friends, and authors I fangirled over and *wished* were my friends, but to be sitting in front of a crowd of people in between the tall bookshelves at the Strand, who were all there for me?

I was fizzy with nerves but I couldn't stop smiling.

And then there were the familiar faces in the crowd smiling back at me. Owen. My parents. Meredith and Colton. Howard and Susan. Celeste. And two rows' worth of students from the Introduction to Pickleball classes I'd started teaching at CPA.

I still couldn't quite believe that the rest of the people I didn't recognize were here for me. I glanced over at Nia, my conversation partner for my launch event. The full house was probably due to her added star power, but I couldn't complain. By the end of the event, I hoped they'd all be walking out carrying signed copies of *The Archer's Paradox* thanks to her endorsement.

Nia had been through dozens of author events, so she'd been a stabilizing presence beside me during my inaugural book chat, leading the discussion with insightful commentary that allowed *Archer* to shine. We'd just opened the floor for questions, so I was now at the mercy of the audience.

My dad's hand shot up before anyone else had a chance.

"Mr. Murphy?" Nia said with faux formality. "What's your question?"

Of course he stood up and projected like he was using a megaphone. "Do you think the new HBO fantasy series about fairies and unicorns impacted your path to publication?"

I smiled at him because he already knew the answer and he was teeing me up to draw the parallels between my book and the wildly popular new show. "Great question! So *Archer* went out on submission right as the publicity for *Light from Darkness* started gearing up, and while there are no fairies in my book, there's hearty alicorn representation, as you can tell from the cover"—I held up the gorgeous thing—"along with some unicorn cameos. I guess the buzz for the show helped drum up interest in my manuscript. The world is taking a breather from dragons and refocusing on hooved creatures, and I happened to be in the right place at the right time. *Archer* went to auction and had a speed run to publication, to capitalize on the craze." I paused. "It usually doesn't happen this quickly."

Nia nodded. "Yeah, it moved *fast*. That's not normal."

We both laughed, because when it came to publishing, nothing was predictable.

Another hand went up and my stomach twisted. Someone I didn't know.

"Yes?" Nia pointed toward the woman.

"Hi, Brooke, I can't wait to read your book. I'm an aspiring writer and I was hoping that you'd talk about your process. I'd love to get your advice."

I chuckled. My process was still an unpredictable mess, with one major change.

I no longer believed that I needed a muse.

The final laps to completing *Archer* had been the most satisfying of my writing career. There was no writer's block or blank-page stress, just a smooth highway of words and words and words. Not all of them were *good*, but that's where editing came in. Once I wholeheartedly committed to Einar and Zandria, I was able to hammer out the rest of the book in record time. Writing their story was nothing but joyful for me.

"You definitely don't want to follow my lead as a writer," I cautioned. "I've gotten in trouble because of my process." My eyes flicked to Owen and he winked at me. "I guess my best advice is to commit to a word count every day and hold yourself accountable. *How* you get there is up to you. Should you write an outline? If you think it'll help, definitely, but if it trips you up, move on. Is it better to use Word, or should you invest in a writing app? Totally up to you." I saw the woman start to frown at me since I wasn't providing much direction. "What I'm trying to say is, your process is just that—*yours*. Sure, there's a ton of advice out there for how to write a book, and definitely audit it and steal what you can use, but above all, get the damn words on the page."

A few people applauded.

My mom raised her hand. "What are you reading and loving right now?"

Another tee-up question.

"Well, I'm lucky enough to be a beta reader for this one." I hitched my thumb toward Nia, and she shimmied her shoulders. "She's currently scaring the crap out of me with her work in progress that I'm not allowed to talk about. It's *so* good." I paused and waited for Owen to look at me. When he did, we shared a secret smile. "I'm also reading the final draft of another debut author's book that I'm so excited about." I took a beat before mentioning the title that his publisher wanted and he wasn't in love with. "It's called *Unlocking Potential: Mindful Coaching* by Owen Miller. Owen, say hi."

He shook his head like he was pissed at me, which I knew was an act, then half stood and gave the crowd a wave. My heart swelled with pride.

"When most of us think 'coach,' we think sports, right? But all of us are coaches, whether we know it or not." I refocused on the woman who'd asked about my writing process. "I just coached you. Not *well*, but I did offer you some guidance. At least I hope I did."

My dad laughed loudly.

"Parents coach their kids. Managers coach their employees. Coaching is just unlocking a person's potential to maximize their growth, whether it's on the pickleball court, in a dog-training class, or in the boardroom. This book is going to help all of us learn to be better coaches in every aspect of our life. I've been on the receiving end of Owen's coaching, and let's just say he brought out a side of me that I didn't know existed."

Heads craned to look at Owen, and I noticed a few women's glances lingering on him. But how could they not? He'd opted for literary smolder tonight, in a black button-down and glasses that he'd finally admitted he needed since he'd been doing so much screen staring.

Another hand went up.

"What are you working on next?" a man in the back row shouted.

"Thanks for asking!" I exclaimed, since both Nia and I had

forgotten to talk about it. "I'm deep in book two of the series, holed up in my writing cave."

The writing cave that Owen had created for me in his basement, which was bright enough to not qualify as subterranean. It was a cozy spot with an antique desk we'd found in London and bookshelves of my own filled with my color-sorted collection.

Merging our lives hadn't been a discussion until Meredith forced the issue when she'd come home wearing an engagement ring right as our lease was up. Owen and I had only been a few months into dating, but we agreed that fate was pushing us together. Once I was settled in, it felt like I'd always been there. Marti gracefully accepted me as a new bedmate, opting to snuggle against me instead of Owen, to his dismay.

"Okay, folks, I'm seeing the 'wrap up' signal from our host," Nia said. "Everyone, grab your books and get in line for the signing portion of the night. Thanks for being here; now go buy a bunch of copies of this wonderful book!"

I fought off a new swarm of butterflies as the applause died down, and I made my way to the table that had a massive bouquet of peach roses and ranunculus, courtesy of Wes and Claudia.

Holy shit, I was about to sign *my* book.

Nia gave me a quick hug before I sat down.

"I'm so sorry I can't stay," she whispered, clasping my arms. "But you've got this. You were fantastic."

"Thank you for making it so fun," I replied. "And for believing in me."

She left to go to a family function before she could get cornered into a conversation, leaving me to face the hordes on my own.

Celeste slipped in to give me a quick hug and hand over a bottle of Veuve Clicquot. It turned out that my book was her biggest sale yet.

"Onward," she said excitedly. "It's just the beginning!"

As I signed, I blanked on old friends' names, wrote "Bryan" instead of "Brian" inside a book and had to scrap it, spent far too long talking about pickleball bags with one of my students, and never stopped grinning.

Because it was real. The hardcover book with bold typeface over the top of a darkly romantic illustration had my name at the bottom.

When Meredith and Colton wound up in front of me, I paused to pull something out of the pocket of my pretty new dress.

"What's this?" Meredith frowned as she took the slip of paper from me.

"I had an outstanding debt at the Bank of Waxman," I replied. "I'd like to close my account now."

"Oh my god, you dork." She swatted at me. "I totally forgot! Sign the book and we'll figure it out later."

"*Books*," Colton said as he hoisted a stack of a half dozen on the table in front of me.

"You don't have to do that," I gasped.

He pulled a receipt out of the top copy. "It's done. And they're gifts. Sign, please."

They moved on quickly since Meredith knew the drill, and I continued signing, pausing to stop for photos and hugs.

My parents edged up to the table.

"I can't wait to read *The Archer's Paradox*! I hear it's *amazing*," my mom sang out overly loud so the people just happening upon my table might be convinced to pick up a copy.

"Mom, you've read it three times already." I laughed. "You were one of my first readers."

I'd dedicated the book to them, which had made my mom weep when she saw it.

"They don't know that," she said out of the corner of her mouth. "Still good for dinner after? Owen said he picked a really nice spot."

"Yeah, I'm dying of hunger," I whispered.

"Hey, don't complain," my dad said as he gestured to the line behind them. "This is a good problem. We never doubted you, sweetheart. We knew this day would come."

My eyes welled up, and I bit the inside of my cheek to keep the tears from spilling over.

The rep from the bookshop did a great job gently moving people along, until there was just one person left waiting, hugging my book to his chest.

The person who'd helped make the words happen.

Not a mystical source of inspiration, but a very real, very loving, very supportive person who'd helped me find my way to myself and, with that, my book.

Every time I looked at Owen, my heart did a little stutter step. He felt like home and an adventure at the same time, two impossible extremes that somehow both existed within him.

"What are you doing?" I asked him as he placed the book in front of me like it was an offering to a queen. "You know I have a boxful at home."

He glanced around, then leaned across the table to kiss me.

"*Numbers*, B, numbers," he scolded softly, cupping my cheek. "Every sale counts. Now, sign please."

He opened it to the title page and flattened it before sliding the book to me.

The love on his face, the *pride*, was the perfect end to a whirlwind evening.

During the event, I'd struggled with every signature, not sure how to encapsulate my deep appreciation for the person on the other side of the table. But this time, I knew exactly what I wanted to write.

For Owen,

Thank you for being my favorite plot twist, and my very own happily ever after.

Love forever,
B

Acknowledgments

I live close enough to a pickleball club that I can hear gameplay when I sit outside on my porch, so it made sense that I eventually found my way over to the courts and joined the growing ranks of pickleball newbies. I immediately loved the game, as well as my fellow players, who were patient with me as I found my footing.

My pickleball journey began at Doylestown Pickleball with founder Jeremiah Thomas, who gave me my first lesson and fielded my millions of odd questions afterward. Major thanks to Jeremiah and the rest of the "DP" crew for being so supportive of this book!

I was also lucky enough to tour a one-of-a-kind private pickleball club in New York before it opened. Thanks to Hell's Kitchen Pickleball founders Stephen Richter and Rich Maczuga for rolling out the red carpet for me as I dug into my research for *Pick Me*. (I still need to get my hands on some HKP merch!)

I wanted to understand more about coaching and the mindset of college athletes, and a former Princeton basketball player and the current head coach of the Caltech women's basketball program, Annie Tarakchian, provided me with tons of incredible insights. Thank you for helping me identify the common denominator of a good coach, and the heart of this story: care for the player, on *and* off the court.

If you've read any of my other books, you know that I welcome the chance to include animals on the page (usually dogs, but also cats, sheep, and goats), and this time around the cowboy ghostwriting angle gave me an excuse to be a horse girl for an afternoon. I owe a big thank-you to Red Rox Farm owner Marika Jones, who walked me through my first-ever horseback riding lesson on a horse named Pickles, which felt like serendipity.

And as always, forever thanks to family, friends, author buddies, my agent, Kevan Lyon, editor Tessa Woodward and the rest of the publishing team at Avon, booksellers, readers, book bloggers . . . your support means *everything* to me!